# Where the
# Lost Aprils Are

# Where the Lost Aprils Are

## by Elisabeth Ogilvie

*Dead memory that revives on doubtful ways,*
*Half hearkening what the buried season says*
*Out of the world of the unapparent dead*
*Where the lost Aprils are, and the lost Mays.*

*From "Relics" by A. C. Swinburne*

McGraw-Hill Book Company

New York    St. Louis    San Francisco
Toronto    Düsseldorf    Mexico

Book design by Marcy J. Katz.

23456789BPBP798765

Library of Congress Cataloging in Publication Data

Ogilvie, Elisabeth, date
    Where the lost Aprils are.

    I.  Title.
PZ3.0348Wh  [PS3529.G39]       813'.5'2       75-4563
ISBN 0-07-047606-3

A condensation of this book appeared in *Good Housekeeping*.

*To Mollie McNeill, who gave me the idea, and in memory of Jamie McNeill, who always believed it was a good one.*

## WHERE THE LOST APRILS ARE

*Dead memory that revives on doubtful ways,*
*Half hearkening what the buried season says*
*Out of the world of the unapparent dead*
*Where the lost Aprils are, and the lost Mays.*

# chapter 1

Sometimes Miriam Guild awoke with the physical ache to be twenty-three again, and she would not be able to throw off her depression for hours, sometimes for days. Since she was only twenty-seven, this passion to erase time was unreasonable, so she had never confided it. She managed it quite well, and almost always could get through her work and social life at these times without anyone's knowing the difference.

When she wanted to be twenty-three again, she wanted to go back before *that* April and see if she could make it all come out differently. Yet she could not force herself to face that April; consciousness censored itself so well that even in sleep the recurrent nightmares never touched on fact.

Worse than waking with that hopeless longing was to wake up crying. She would go to bed pleased with an evening out, healthily tired, and sleep well, to wake up in a storm of tears that left her so exhausted she couldn't possibly hide it.

At the office on those days she was no good. She was a liability when it came to being objective about manuscripts, and dealing with authors. Everyone commented on how ill she looked, which made her feel worse. So when these mornings occurred she called up and said she was sick. Somehow, perhaps with her own help, the idea spread around that she had migraine, and she let it go at that.

From May to December the attacks tapered off. But, once the year was around the corner and sliding blizzard by blizzard toward spring, they would start again. One here, another ten days later, then a week later, then two in one week, and so on. Her boss was an old migraine veteran and wanted to send her to his specialist. She resisted by saying she had her own specialist and he was trying something new.

*She* was. Three years of it was too long, and Mike Andric wanted to marry her.

"We will move into the country," he said, "and have children. By instinct you're an earth-girl, and you're forced into an artificial environment. You need real forests, not a stone wilderness."

His words evoked, between her and his mountain bandit's face, a stand of monumental old pines with their needles all glistening and seething in a west wind. *I have a forest*, she almost said to him then, but something locked her throat against the forbidden and blotted out the vision.

Yet she loved to hear him go on, and when she was with him there was a solid comfort about all of life. She felt that she could sit forever with his arm about her, and nothing bad could ever happen. It did happen, of course. Always, the very next morning after one of these easy evenings. She wondered if she should send him away for good, yet she craved the aura of safety that he brought with him. She didn't know if this was love or not. He deserved more from her than to be treated like a security blanket.

If only she could decide. And meanwhile March was here and April was coming. *April is the cruellest month*, T. S. Eliot had written, and she wondered how he knew.

On a Saturday morning when she could have slept late, she woke herself early with her gulping, wrenching sobs. She rushed from her bed as if from a forest fire, and into the bathroom, and under a cold shower. She kept crying just the same, so she stood there until she was shaking with cold and the crying fit had exhausted itself. Then, bundled into a terry robe and with her hair wrapped up in a towel, she left the bathroom, and heard someone at her apartment door.

It was only a little after six, so she couldn't imagine who it might be and she didn't care. She tried to ignore it, but the bell kept ringing, and finally she went to the door and said in her tear-thickened voice, "Who is it?"

"Your beloved. At least I hope I am. We're going out into the country and look for spring."

She sagged against the door. "Mike, I'm sick this morning. It must be a virus. You can't come in, you'll catch the bug."

"I'm bug-resistant. You sound god-awful, and if you don't let me in I'll go for Joe."

The super had a special feeling for Mike because their fathers came from the same region in what is now Yugoslavia. Feeling like a condemned felon on the way to Tyburn Tree, Miriam opened the door.

Mike said graciously, "You look as god-awful as you sound."

"If you start the coffee I'll get dressed," she said, and turned away, but he took hold of her and made her face him.

"No virus did that to your face. You've been crying. Why?"

"It's none of your business."

"It is if you're going to be my wife." He could look either kindly ferocious or ferociously kind, with his black eyes and broad cheekbones.

"I don't know if I'm going to be your wife," she said, sodden and sullen. "I never said. I'm not fit to be anybody's wife. Mike, will you please *go*?"

"Miroslav Andric never retreats," he said. He pushed her down on the sofa and sat beside her, pinning her with a granite arm around her. "Tell me why you're not fit. Were you a teen-age call girl? Have you done time? Been a junkie? Are you a lush?"

She shook her head to everything. Then, very quietly, he asked, "Have you had a child? *Do* you have a child?"

She shook her head to that too.

"Perhaps you can't have kids, then." He took both her hands in his free one. "That's nothing to cry about. We can adopt. There are kids waiting for us, no matter how we get them. We'll find them, and they'll be ours."

"As far as I know, I'm perfectly sound that way," she said seriously. Then she tried to wrench her hands free. "Listen, Mike, you're too good! You deserve something better than me. I have this business, this crying—well, it happens and I

3

have no control over it. Mike, that's my migraine. It's easier to let people believe in that than to let them know I wake up in this state every so often, bawling my head off 'til I'm sick."

They looked each other in the eye until her nerve broke, and she tried for a grin. "Makes you think, doesn't it?"

"You must have a recurrent dream that's very frightening."

"Not frightening. I'm never afraid. It's just a terrible feeling that I'm always sure I'll never get over. Let's face it, Mike, I'm probably psychotic."

He was still gazing at her as if he'd never seen her before, and of course he hadn't. Not like this. "Is it grief?" he asked. "Pity? Betrayal? Longing? Loneliness?"

It was all of them and more, but she couldn't say so. The wonder was that she'd been able to say this much. "Please make some coffee, Mike," she said. "I'll get dressed."

She went quickly and shut her door. Shivering in the well-heated room she dressed, and brushed the snarls out of her damp hair. She wore it short, and it was already curling around her head. She rubbed color into her face with a rough towel, and did a fairly convincing imitation of a Healthy Young Woman Bounding into the Kitchen in Search of Breakfast. It did not convince Mike. He would not let her escape into the day as if into a bottle.

"It has to be a dream."

"Sometimes there are dreams, but never on the crying nights. At least I don't remember any. And the sounder I sleep the more likely it is to happen."

"Then you plunge to depths that you're usually able to stay out of. But something has to happen to trigger the tears. Listen, next time try to write down the first thing you think of when you wake up——"

"I told you—it's not thought, it's a *feeling*——"

He took her into his arms. "My darling, I've known you for a year, and I can't believe that with your intelligence you've completely blocked out whatever this terrible experience was." He was very kind, very gentle, and his chest was broad and solid. She resisted a desire to nestle.

4

"Maybe it's a tendency to melancholia," she said lightly. "What was that about a day in the country?"

He showed one of his surprisingly subtle aspects that day by never mentioning the early-morning scene. When they came back to the city that night she was almost convinced that all she had to do to make everything right for herself was to marry him. She didn't want him to go away from her that night. The question, or entreaty, kept fluttering behind her lips all the while they cooked a late dinner, and she was over-joyed because it must have meant that she loved him.

Or was it just wanting a security blanket or a teddy bear? Something to go to sleep with and wake up with, so that she could be convinced that everything was all right?

It was this doubt that kept her from saying, "Don't go," though she knew that he was waiting for it. She kissed him goodnight with extra fervor and he said softly, "Well, now . . . I'll call you first thing tomorrow morning."

"Not too early, I'm going to be sleeping hard. I just know it."

"If whatever it is wakes you up," he said grimly, "you call me at once. We're going to tear that thing to shreds, Miriam."

It woke her. It had to. Always, after she'd been with Mike. This time, staring through streaming tears at the rain stream-ing down the windows, she knew her euphoria of the night before had been illusion. Marry Mike, and wake every morn-ing to *this*?

"Oh, no, no, *no!*" she moaned aloud, and somewhere through the winding tunnel of woe she heard herself wailing the same triple protest a long time before.

# chapter 2

When Mike called her at a respectable hour for Sunday, she hoped her languor sounded merely lazy. "It's all that fresh air and walking, and now the rain. Guaranteed to stupefy."

"You sure?" he asked suspiciously.

"I'm sure." She faked a yawn and said, "Excuse me."

"Hey, do you want to go see Theda Bara and Rudolph Valentino at the Museum of Modern Art?" he asked. "Perfect escape on a rainy Sunday afternoon. Right back into your grandmother's time."

"I'd love to, but——"

"Which means you wouldn't love to in the least. What are you doing besides yawning?"

"Going through my junk. It's an atavistic impulse toward spring cleaning. I've got boxes I haven't looked at since back in the Harding administration.... See, *I* watched Rudolph Valentino personally."

He laughed. "All right. I'll be over this afternoon and bring the makings of a good Montenegrin meal."

She couldn't say, *Don't come because afterward the hangover nearly kills me.* That wouldn't have held him back anyway. "All right," she said.

Then, honorably, she went to work on her closets. She worked slowly, her hands were both heavy and weak, and her brain felt that way too. All she could think was that she should get away from Mike, give up the job she loved, turn this cleaning bit into packing, and get away from New York as far as she could, as fast as she could.

But where? With the whole wide country to think about

she couldn't choose. Trembling with a sort of claustrophobia, she knew only that there was one spot where she *couldn't* go, and yet, with it blotting out everything else, spreading over the map of the country like a lethal fungus, she couldn't name it or in any way admit its existence except by the wordless denial.

She didn't have to go to a psychiatrist to find out what troubled her. She knew, and it couldn't be cured. —Now her cleaning and sorting took on a purpose. She went ruthlessly through her clothing and laid aside a pile of good things to go to the Salvation Army. When Mike came in late afternoon, she had dragged the cartons from the hall closet into the living room, onto the rug before the minute Victorian fireplace, and she was burning old postcards, letters, snapshots, Christmas cards, clippings.

"A compulsive collector, hey?" Mike settled down on the other side of the hearth rug. He looked into the nearest carton, as yet untouched. "Boy, what riches. Brings out the glutton in me. Can I go through this one? Maybe I'll find out what makes you tick."

"Be my guest." She laughed. "All you'll find out is that I'm a born miser. I save wrappings, I collect string, and elastic bands. And here's the *worst* thing." She dropped her voice. "I used to save cat and dog pictures. But by perseverance and prayer I cured myself."

"That's my brave girl," he said solemnly. "You sure there's nothing in this box you'd rather I wouldn't touch?"

"I think there's a double-negative somewhere in that question, but I won't try to track it down." Facing the final solution had given her a reckless poise. "No, I'm positive there's nothing incriminating in there. I destroy all secret information at once, the way I was taught by the C.I.A."

He dipped out a handful of papers, "Well, I won't open any letters, but I warn you I'll read all the postcards." He discovered one at once. " 'Dear Mir— It's true, Roman men are *marvellous*. Shan't ever come home.' Signed *D*. Did she come home?"

8

"Yes, and married a lawyer from Larchmont."

"And dreams of the Spanish Steps and the Trevi Fountain, no doubt."

"No," Miriam said. "She told me once that now whenever she thinks of Rome she worries about all the stray cats. She's essentially a mother, you see, rather than someone who wants to be pinched in buses."

They both laughed and settled back to their boxes. After a few moments he said, without looking up from the ballet program in his hand, "What are *you* essentially, Miriam? And don't tell me you're an editor and that's that. You're something else that surfaces out of a deep sleep——"

"The Loch Ness Monster."

"And mourns," he went on, flicking over the pages of the program. " 'Kubla Khan'," he read aloud. "That must have been a spectacle. 'In Xanadu did Kubla Khan/A stately pleasure-dome decree.' And what was that line about a woman wailing for her demon-lover?"

"There's something about milk and honey-dew too," she said lazily, holding up old negatives to the lamp. "Sounds delicious. Why do people save things like these? I don't even know who the people are." She flipped the negatives into the fire. Mike went on rummaging.

"Ah, here's something you must have saved with a purpose in mind," he said with pleasure.

"What?" She looked up from her sixth-grade autograph album.

"A tape," he said, and simultaneously she saw the small red plastic box in his big hand. "No label on it. We'll have to play it to find out, and it will probably bring out the downfall of the Presidency."

She had to hold herself from making a lunge for it. The sight of it in his hand drove nails through her temples. *I didn't know it was there. I didn't know it was there.*

"It's just foolishness. It should have been thrown out long ago."

"Aha!" He began to laugh, black eyes going into slits be-

9

tween peaked eyebrows and high cheekbones. "You're singing dirty songs on it, is that it?"

It gave her an inspiration. "Nothing so good. I was doing Czerny exercises—that's on the piano, in case you're ignorant, and I hadn't touched a piano for so long, I taped myself to hear just how bad I was."

He said mildly, "That's right, your mother was a pianist."

"Yes. And I am, or was, a fair one."

"With no piano."

"There's no room here." She held out her hand, careful to control the gesture. "I'll take that, and maybe play it over for myself sometime as a form of self-torture." She even smiled into his eyes, and he, unsmiling, put the box in her hand. With exquisite control she did not instantly close her fingers in a tight lock over the box; she brought it back to her in slow motion; she did not hurl it at once into the fire, but laid it on a shelf of the coffee table as if it were of only minor interest and curiosity. They went back to sorting. Her head felt at once empty and ringing, as if with echoes. Later, she managed most casually to lay some old sheet music over the box to remove it further from the moment. Across from her Mike sprawled full length, his shoulders resting against the sofa, reading in a looseleaf notebook.

"How about some coffee?" he asked without looking up from it.

"That must be pretty interesting reading," she said, getting to her feet.

"Your biweekly themes from tenth through twelfth grade," he said. "I can't tear myself away from them."

Under cover of laughter she tried to plot how to pick up the red plastic box. But by dropping something on top of it she'd foiled herself. She'd have to make some little flutter and fluster of papers. No, trust that he'd taken her word for it and had put it out of his mind as of no consequence. . . . *Don't even look in its direction.* . . . She got into the kitchen safely before a violent shudder overtook her.

"Do you want coffee or a drink?" she called loudly.

"Coffee. When I want a drink I'll fix it myself, I don't approve of women bartenders." He sounded preoccupied.

"Male chauvinist! What have you found now? My poetry? Do me a favor and burn it without reading it."

There was no answer. She reached for the coffee canister, and in the other room a piano began a simple, quiet introduction. But she had no piano, so it had to be the FM radio. No, not that; she had only an instant to recognize it, no time to prepare herself before *he* was there, summoned alive and singing out of a flimsy strip of tape.

> " 'My love is like a red red rose
>     That's newly sprung in June:
> My love is like the melodie
>     That's sweetly play'd in tune.
>
> As fair art thou, my bonnie lass,
>     So deep in love am I:
> And I will love thee still, my dear,
>     Till a' the seas gang dry.' "

She tried to protest, but she could only gag silently, and listen.

> " 'Till a' the seas gang dry, my dear,
>     And the rocks melt wi' the sun,
> And I will love thee still, my dear,
>     While the sands o' life still run.' "

She bent over to the counter with her eyes squeezed shut, recognizing the tearing grief that came to her in her deep sleep and woke her; yet she couldn't make a sound in protest, because she had to listen all the way to the end.

> " 'And fare thee weel, my only love,
>     And fare thee weel a while!
> And I will come again, my love,
>     Tho' it were ten thousand mile.' "

It was perfect to the end, to the last whisper of the *s*. The agony was perfect too. It couldn't have been improved upon. When the last note was irretrievably gone, the tape was stopped. In the silence she still crouched over the countertop with her fingers frozen around the canister.

Someone locked an arm around her and with brutal fingers loosened her cramped grip.

"Get out!" she shouted. "Get away!" Mike was trying to take her into his arms, saying something, but she wouldn't let him. "You had no *right!*" she accused him. "You don't know what you've done!"

"No, I don't know," he was saying quietly. "But then we don't know what you've been doing to yourself for so long, do we? And it's my right to find out."

"What right?" she challenged him.

"I love you, and you're suffering. My God, do you think I can stand that, any more than you can stand whatever's going on with you?"

She cried out in inarticulate, indefinable emotion, and in a kind of fury he grabbed her shoulders and shook her, and she had the choice between sliding on into something she couldn't stop, or fighting as hard as she'd ever fought in her life to hold on to herself.

"All *right!*" she said finally. She found herself sitting by the table with Mike standing over her. "You can stop bullying me."

"Here." He held a glass to her lips. She jerked her head back and took the glass from him, swallowed. One sip seared its way straight down to her stomach and spread its fire there. He had brought plum brandy. When she'd finished coughing she looked at him with watery eyes and said, "When do you start on that Yugoslavian supper?"

"I said Montenegrin, but the hell with that." He pulled a chair up close to hers. "So it was Czerny exercises, was it?"

"That's what I thought—" But it was a poor lie. "I won't talk about it, Mike. I'm warning you. I can't talk about it."

"I can see that," he said gently. "But you can write about it,

Miriam. Look, my darling, Do you *want* to go on like this, only half a person, haunted, wincing, afraid to take a chance on life? I love you, but I'm trying to heal you for your own sake. I couldn't pass by a hurt animal, and——"

"Can you recommend a good vet?" she asked in a shaky voice.

He smiled slightly. "I recommend *me*, if you can start thinking about me not just as the man who wants to marry you, but as a friend. After all, a couple of people who get married should be friends, anyway." He squeezed her hands. "So will you try to write it down?"

"I'll try." She'd say anything to shut him up. "Now shall we get supper?"

When he was ready to leave he said soberly, "Look, I don't want to badger you. I never wanted anything so much in my life as to help you out of this, but I don't intend to call up every half-hour and ask if you're working on it. So I'm not going to call you at all until you're ready."

"I have a job," she protested. "I haven't the time——"

"You'll write a little every day. Maybe an hour in the morning and an hour at night. But something every day without fail." He kissed her. "If you want me, you call me and I'll come. But I won't come without a call from you."

"Mike, you're too good for me," she began, painfully, but he stopped that with a harder, rougher kiss.

"None of that now. No breast-beating *mea culpa* stuff so you can weasel out of facing facts."

When he had gone she thought that if she had had the strength she would have run away then, but she was worn out. In the living room everything was scattered around on the hearth rug as they had left it, and the fire was dying. Apprehensively she looked for the little red plastic container, but it wasn't in sight, and there was no tape on the machine. Mike had either taken it or tucked it away somewhere where she couldn't find it.

For the moment she was glad of that, because she might

have experienced an irresistible temptation to play it again. Now that she'd achieved a kind of calm she felt as if she were walking a freeway with a fragile glass balanced on her head, and even a draft from a passing car could shatter it.

She went to bed in the dark and sank instantly into sleep. When she woke up it was still dark. Twenty past one, and she was wide awake. She had been dreaming, and she could remember the dream, so pleasant that she resented being forced out of it.

She had been in the backyard of the lower-middle-class Connecticut suburb where she had grown up. Her mother had worked unceasingly on that yard, and had turned it into a flowering and sheltering glade. Miriam had cut out paper dolls with her friends on hot summer days there, had a swing from a stout limb of the big cherry tree, which she later climbed; here she read through Sunday afternoons, lying on the grass with the dog beside her, and her mother reading in a canvas deck chair. Often someone came through the gate under the white lilacs for tea or cold drinks. The adult talk would run on like a pleasant obbligato to her own preoccupations.

And all through Saturday afternoons, and weekdays after school when she did her homework out there or played, there were the stumbling or dancing notes of the piano as her mother gave lessons in the living room. Miriam ignored *The Bluebird Waltz* or *To a Wild Rose* or *Für Elise*, but, whenever her mother took over to show a more advanced pupil how something should sound when he had finally learned it, Miriam would stop whatever she was doing to listen.

Miriam was Helen's pupil too, because her mother felt she should learn music as she had learned to read. Miriam took the piano as a part of normal life; her mother was a church organist and choir director besides being a pianist. Miriam wanted to be a nurse, a teacher, a deep-sea diver, a rancher, a movie star, a rich wife, a rich mother (English nanny and enormous perambulator), a model, a writer. This ambition lasted the longest, and her first real job was in a publishing house.

She had a walk-up apartment in New York, chosen for its sunny kitchen and toy Victorian fireplace, but the green glade was there whenever she went home, or a white winter-bound yard where birds came to feed. The lessons went on. She had no piano in her flat, but she played when she was home. After her mother's death she put the piano in storage, and had refused to think of it again, until the April of her twenty-fourth year.

After that April she sold the piano, resolutely shutting the doors on any qualms of guilt or disloyalty. Now, three years later, lying in the dark, she felt her fingers striking phantom keys in the *Black Key Etude*, and she thought with something like pride that if she could get up now and play it she would astonish herself.

It was slightly like being delirious with a high fever, because the evening's woe was still with her. It had stopped bleeding while she was quiet, but what would happen if she moved?

She got up and washed her face in cold water, brushed her hair, put on her robe, and went out into the kitchen to eat cornflakes and milk as if the childhood spell of the dream were still upon her. She kept a shorthand pad on the table where she wrote shopping lists and notes to herself, and now she picked up the pen and began to describe the dream, thinking, *If Mike wants something written, he'll get something.*

Of course Mike knew all about the yard, the music lessons, and the neighbors, just as she knew about where he had grown up. But he didn't know everything. In the quiet kitchen with the circle of light over the table holding back the dark, she wrote the first important thing about herself that he didn't know.

# chapter 3

My mother had always been Mrs. Guild to the neighbors, but when I was twelve she told me that she had never been married.

"You mean I had no father?" I asked in shock. "All that about him being killed in the war is a *lie?*"

"Of course you had a father," she said. "And he loved you very much. And he did die in the war."

"So that's why you won't let me see those movies."

"On principle I don't think you need to see war movies." She said it calmly, keeping her eyes on her sewing.

"But why didn't you get married before——"

"It wasn't possible. You don't need the details, Miriam. You wouldn't understand. When you're older, you will. For now it's enough for you to know that you've nothing to be ashamed of."

Shame never entered into it as a personal consideration, though I began to understand why we didn't have any relatives, and why we never went to Maine to visit the small town where my mother was born. I used to tease her to tell me the name of it, so I could find it on a map—it was important to me, like an anchor—but she would not; again she said, "You don't need to know."

But she had always told me things about her country childhood, the grandparents who had raised her on their farm, her friends, her teachers, her pets, so I had all that, and the freedom of two thick albums of snapshots. So, in a sort of anonymous way, I had her history and a tantalizingly chopped-up version of my own.

Eventually I decided that the only difference between myself and my friends was that my parents hadn't been married in church by a minister. They were still my parents, they had loved each other and me. If my father hadn't been killed, he would surely have returned to marry my mother, and by now we would have been a complete family, and I'd have younger brothers and sisters.

As I advanced deeper into the teen years, and a girl had to leave school because she was pregnant, I began to see my mother with both pity and awe; I imagined her as a young girl, though she had been past twenty when I was born. I was obsessed by a curiosity that made me feel alternately guilty and excited. Reading and the movies had filled my head with romantic ideas, and I was convinced that I was the product of one of the great love affairs of the century.

What was my father like? Had he been handsome, rich, and aristocratic? The last part was unlikely; she had at least told me he came from the same town. Had he been married to a demanding invalid wife whom he could not divorce and who would not divorce him?

But after that brief conversation when I was twelve my mother never brought it up again, and I couldn't do it. Secretly I used to study this slim, busy woman, seeking for traces of the girl who had been so passionately in love.

And I would study myself in the mirror, trying to find my father. I didn't look like my mother. She was a very thin, lithe, fast-moving woman with red-blond hair that kept flying out of place and the pale skin to go with it. She freckled in summer, and her eyes were the color of aquamarines.

I had thinness but extra height, dark hair at once heavy and springy, and blue-gray eyes, a stronger jaw than I liked; it used to worry me, but if it came from my father it was all right.

I'd see a man who appealed to me, and wonder if my father had looked like *him*. Gary Cooper was the one for a long time, succeeded by Cary Grant and then by Gregory Peck. Once there was a math teacher at high school who, I'm sure, thought he was the object of a particularly intense and embarrassing, though silent, adolescent crush.

None of that matters now. I wasn't a tragic child, and I felt myself deprived only at the times when other girls' fathers were so useful and so much fun. We didn't even have male relatives around. I realized in later years that sometimes men were interested in my mother, nice eligible ones too, but she never returned their interest.

She died when I was twenty-two, of internal injuries following a bus accident. She was still a young woman; attractive, sensitive, talented, and true to one man whose name I didn't know, whose picture I had never seen.

God knows what her nights must have been. I remember her light burning as she read through midnight into the morning hours, and in winter, when the windows were closed and the neighbors wouldn't be disturbed, I slept on billows of soft melody from the piano downstairs.

Suddenly she was gone, and there would never be a chance to say, "Mother, what was his name? I have to know now, I'm grown up. What was he like? What did he do? Do I look like him?"

I'd had only a small portion of her. The rest belonged to him, and I would feel this furious compulsion to shout at them, "It's two against one! No fair! No fair!" But they were beyond my rage. Alone in the world I rebelled against and rejected my loneliness. I had to know who I was.

At the time of my mother's unexpected death I hadn't been able to go through her things. I'd just piled small stuff into a trunk and sent it to my flat. After a time I took the books and Navajo blanket off it, and opened it.

Not that there was much besides some books, a little jewelry, and her music. She had little to connect her to her life before me except the albums. These were what had given me whatever sense of identity I had. The grandparents snapped in various activities around the farm, with the camera they'd given her one birthday. Herself, skinny and pigtailed astride a big plow horse, or bottle-feeding a lamb. Other youngsters, up through high-school age; I used to stare at the smiling faces squinting into the sun and wonder which of the crew-cut boys was my father.

Her parents were there. They had died young when their flivver skidded off an icy bridge on a country road at midnight. They were laughing in almost all their pictures, ignorant of what lay ahead, always to remain young, younger than I was as I studied their features with a magnifying glass. My widow's peak came from my girl grandmother, I admitted, grudgingly pleased to have made some connection with my own history; I'd have been happier to have discovered it beyond question on one of the boys.

My mother had identified almost everyone by a first name, long ago when green ink was considered jazzy, along with little circles for dots over the I's, and humorous captions. Knowing all the faces and matching names by heart, I now labored over the background, trying to pick out fine details. But much of it was universal in any of a hundred New England villages. All I knew for a fact was that it was somewhere in Maine, where there were hills.

When my eyes were tired, and I felt cross and lightheaded with frustration, I went through her jewelry. She had a few old pieces that had been handed down to her, and there was her graduation watch, things like that. Then there was all the costume jewelry I had given her when I went through the stage of trying to make her over into something more exotic. She wore the stuff to please me, but I'm sure she would never have bothered otherwise.

I shook my head at some of my more juvenile choices, and dumped them into a box for the super's young daughters. I picked out the heirloom pieces to clean and wear, and saved the watch. In all my life I'd never before pawed around in her jewelry box, though it used to tempt me mightily when I was small. So I never knew until this day that it had a false bottom. I picked up a ribbon tab, and the moiré floor came up, and there were the letters.

Something like a cartoonist's version of lightning shot through my head. *Those are from my father,* I thought. My hand stopped in midplunge as if another hand, invisible, had gripped it around the wrist.

"But I have a right to know!" I nearly shouted, and took the letters.

They weren't from a man, however, which was almost a relief to my heaving stomach. They were from someone called Fern, and I remembered Fern in the albums, wearing a clown suit with a ruff and making a terrible face; on a toboggan, and in a sedate group of dressed-up little girls snapped outside a country church on Easter, 1928. She'd been a high-school cheerleader too, and a 4-H girl exhibiting a huge fat lamb.

There were only three letters, but long ones, and I read them greedily at first, devouring without chewing. Then I went back over them, not missing a detail. I gathered that she and my mother had corresponded faithfully over the years, so my mother mustn't have kept all the letters, only these, the last ones she received. The final date was about six months before my mother's death, so I wondered if something had happened to Fern first. Most of the letters were taken up with news of Fern's own family. Her children had spread out over the country, and my mother had evidently kept her informed about *me*; she was impressed by my job.

In the last letter she said, "I don't feel a bit older than eighteen, in spite of the grandchildren, 'til I look in the mirror!"

But she had not written after that, and my mother had kept these last letters out of sentiment, or from a human hunger to hang onto the last shreds of something dear for as long as possible.

The letters were postmarked *Parmenter.*

# chapter 4

*I*t was a grim Sunday afternoon in early March when I first read that name, and I thought I'd go out of my mind with suspense if I couldn't locate Parmenter at once. Two girls who worked with me were coming for supper, and I called their flat and asked them to stop at a service station and try to get a Maine road map.

When they arrived, full of jovial quips about my taking off to go hippie in the Maine woods, I told them I was trying to make vacation plans as an antidote for the particularly nasty March weather we were having, and that sidetracked the conversation into safe territory. We talked about the obvious spots in Maine, and I never once let my eyes or thoughts stray in search of Parmenter.

At last they went. I held off as long as I could, cleaning up the kitchen, showering, laying out my clothes for the next day. I was apprehensive to the point of nausea. Parmenter might be too small to be mentioned in the list of towns and cities on the map.

It was listed, but there was an anguished and endless moment when my finger hovered over the right spot but found nothing. And then I saw it, set in an area blue with ponds and streams. My shaking forefinger came down on it hard and for an instant it was as if all of me were there. Not only my finger was shaky; I was trembling with chills.

I could fly to Augusta and hire a car on the next long weekend, but I knew in my bones that a weekend would be no good, it would be worse than nothing. I hardly slept that night, and at two in the morning I was ready to quit the job that had been such joy and pride and challenge for me. I felt that if I didn't get to Parmenter soon I would lose what little identity I had.

But these were two-in-the-morning thoughts, and by daylight I was wanly sane, trying to brace myself for the ordeal of waiting for my vacation.

Then one of the things happened that makes you believe in the Fates, either benign or malignant, depending on what they hand you at the psychological moment. I was given the project of editing a manuscript by our most exciting discovery in years. We were Books for Younger Readers, but this man wrote for teenagers, or "young adults" as we preferred to call them, with such power and authority, rich color, and drama, that the firm had hopes of eventually removing him from any limiting category.

*Eventually*. He was still learning, still undisciplined. He had done two books for us, or rather had submitted great dazzling outpourings about three times the length they should have been for reasonably priced books. Viewed objectively, the work was not only brilliant with fire and action but was also a shapeless mess.

He would not, or could not, cut, and left it to us; he had never once put in an appearance at the office to discuss revisions, being too busy looking up his Montenegrin kinfolk and picking their brains for his stories, or hunting for a farm to buy cheap; or he was working night and day on the next book.

Another editor had handled the first two, and had begged off the third, saying he'd lost ten pounds with each book. I thought Andric was marvelous, but never expected I'd be trusted with the new book. One glance at a carton containing roughly about a thousand pages and I could see why my predecessor said he'd felt like a novice diamond cutter ordered to split the Kohinoor.

"You're not to change one word of it," Mr. MacKenzie said. "You're to preserve the essential texture, and see that the action is sustained . . . and get it down to where people can afford to buy the book. There may be two books in there.

You'll see. You can work at home; in fact you'd better. Take all the time you need, and let's pray we can locate him somewhere when the job's done so he can approve it. We'd like to bring it out for the Christmas trade."

"Can I take it to Maine and work on it?"

He was as surprised to hear it as I was to have asked it. "Maine? Why Maine, for God's sake?"

"You don't know what my flat's like in the daytime. The building, I mean. Frantic," I lied glibly. "This little town I know—I can really dig in there. You've got to live *in* a book like Andric's—be his second self, as much as you can. . . . It's in the hills, it's farm country. Not like the Balkan setting, of course, but nearer to it than New York City. I'll be away from everything, I can lose myself in the work."

He kept pulling at his lower lip. I knew he still saw me at twenty-three as a motherless child. If any male seemed disposed to linger at my desk, Mr. MacKenzie always had something to ask me, or for me to do, as if I were too naïve to take care of myself. As a matter of fact, I'd been too obsessed by my unknown father to be able to concentrate on any other men, even though I went out with them often enough, and had even tried to convince myself a few times that I was in love.

"Are you going *alone?*" he asked finally.

In relief I laughed out loud, and that must have convinced him. "Alone except for Miroslav Andric."

He grinned. "I just didn't want anything to distract you from the work, that's all."

"I'm leaving the distractions in New York."

He patted my shoulder. "I'm glad you've got the sense not to rush into anything. Take your time, and you'll have a good chance of being as happy as my wife and I have been. . . . All right, go to Maine."

I was able to say, quite calmly, "I'll finish up what I've got on hand first. Deirdre Drummond's final draft just came in. I'd like to see it to the printer."

That night I wrote a letter to the Town Clerk of Parmenter. I didn't tell him what personal significance his town had for me, but that I'd heard of the village as a lovely and quiet spot, and I would like to spend the month of April in such an atmosphere, to complete some work away from the strain of the city. Was there a cottage I could rent? Failing that, would someone take me as a boarder?

I didn't want to be a boarder, but if that was the only way I could stay in Parmenter, that was how it would have to be.

After a long five days the answer came. The town clerk was a woman, Selma Hitchcock, and her letter was neatly typed and very friendly. Yes, it was a lovely spot, and unspoiled. Too quiet for most people; probably that was the reason it was still unspoiled. It was a good place for artistic people like myself. (I was flattered by the assumption.) They often had writers and painters around there in the summer and autumn.

A Mrs. Katherine Barstow had a nice little cottage on her farm, and it had heat and modern plumbing, so that even in a cold April anyone could be comfortable. I could get all the fresh milk and eggs I needed for next to nothing. Only thing was, Kitty wanted references, but that was understandable, when you considered some of the characters drifting around these days.

*Kitty*. There'd been a Kitty in some of the snapshots. I went for them, shaky again. It doesn't have to be the same Kitty, I scoffed, but still I stared at the tiny faded face of a thin girl in jeans posing proudly with a horse, her long hair and the horse's mane both blowing in a sudden gust of wind. I found her again in a group of youngsters posed smiling by a bus, all dressed up. "Washington trip," my mother had written underneath. "Class of 1938."

I wrote to Mrs. Barstow as soon as I could collect my references. One was from Mr. MacKenzie, written imposingly on the firm's stationery; one from the minister of the church where my mother had been organist and choir director; the third was from the vice-president of the bank where I still had an account.

For all the minister and the banker knew, I could be living a life of unprecedented wickedness in New York, but they'd known me as a nice little girl and so gave me enthusiastic references as a fine young woman. It sounded very dull, but I wasn't going to Parmenter as a *femme fatale*.

I received shortly a communication written in very black script on good bond paper with an attractive letterhead of a fourleaf clover design, and the name "Fourleaf Farm." The references were acceptable. The rent was a hundred dollars a month because it was off-season. There was no television but, just in case I happened to be musical, there was a very good piano. Mrs. Barstow mentioned this because it seemed to be an important point for some people; she'd had singers and other musicians take the cottage just because of the piano. However, she understood that I was an editor. Meeting an editor would be a new experience for her, she added graciously, and signed, "Katherine Barstow (Mrs. Cleveland A. Barstow.)"

The mention of the piano was like a radio signal beamed to earth from a lost star. When I'd sent my mother's Baldwin to storage, I'd thought that I'd never want to touch a piano again. But now, if I'd been the type to look for occult influences and mysteriously coded messages from Beyond, I'd have seen the mere word *piano* as a sign, symbol, blessing, summons—what have you.

Besides, I would have to do something when I wasn't working on the manuscript or out on my search, and I was ashamed to have even wanted to throw away what my mother had intended to be both comfort and pleasure to me, as her music must have been to her.

I packed an assortment of her music along with the photograph albums, the manuscript, plenty of paper, and my typewriter. To prove to myself my good musical intentions I even bought a very good little tape recorder so I could check my progress.

Looking through her books on one of those last nights before I left, when I was too overwrought to sleep and worrying about a freak snowstorm canceling my flight, I came across a lightly marked verse in an anthology of poetry. I must have seen the marks before, but they had never meant anything in particular, because my mother always marked things she liked. But now, at the end of March and with my search ahead of me, they leaped out at me.

> *Dead memory that revives on doubtful ways,*
> *Half hearkening what the buried season says*
> *Out of the world of the unapparent dead*
> *Where the lost Aprils are, and the lost Mays.*

The last line haunted me through a night when I kept coming awake with the words speaking themselves in my head. My birthday was in early January, so I must have been conceived in April.

This search wasn't only for what *I* wanted, the identification of the all-important *me*. No, I was going back to find her lost Aprils.

# chapter 5

By the time I left for Maine I was lightheaded from lack of sleep and food. I'd been too nervous to eat properly for the past week, and I'd worked overtime so as not to leave anything for somebody else to finish. I dozed uneasily between New York and Boston, but from Boston to Augusta I was so excited I thought cynically that I'd be lucky if I didn't collapse from emotional exhaustion the instant I arrived.

The first of April in Maine can look like the middle of winter, but this was a spring day and no doubt of it. When I left the plane at Augusta the combination of cool air and warm sunshine revived me absolutely, and it was as if I had never been tired in my life and never would be again.

Mrs. Barstow had said a car would meet me, and the driver picked me easily out of the eleven passengers. There were only two other young women, glamorously got up in skin-tight ski clothes and wraparound tinted glasses; they were instantly snapped up by a couple of matching male types and swept off in one of those miniature sports cars that roar like jets.

"You're Miriam Guild," the driver informed me jovially, thrusting out a large freckled hand. "I'm Ed Dunton. Where's your gear?" He was a big man, overweight, his clothes straining where they weren't rumpled. His cap's earlaps were turned up as a sign of spring, and his pants were tucked into high-laced larrigans; I heard my mother's nostalgic comment, *April is mud-time in Maine.*

He invited me to ride in front, and talked all the way from Augusta to Parmenter. I had the feeling I didn't really have to say much back, though he was hoping to glean a few grains of information. If he didn't get it, he would be philosophical. I was briefly disappointed that he hadn't said at once, "Guild, huh? That's a Parmenter name." Or that he hadn't seen a striking resemblance to someone in town. But I could explain that away by admitting I wasn't looking like anything or anybody today except a disheveled character with an urban pallor and eyes like two burnt holes in a blanket. Probably he thought I was suffering from a hangover and lived a wild, ulcer-producing, if not licentious, life in New York City.

In a pleasant stupor I half-listened to his commentary, gazing out at stone walls crossing yellow-brown pastures spangled with cattle or sheep, or rising empty to a gauzy blue and white sky. I saw ponds still dull silver with ice, but brooks came roaring down rocky gorges to the road. Barns were open to the sun, everything seemed to consciously bask in the windless warmth. Everywhere along the sides of the road and in the fields there were more birds than I had seen for a long time.

There were the orderly rows of bare apple trees, and the hills in graduating shades of blue to the horizons. There was very little traffic except for the short distance we traveled behind a school bus delivering subprimary pupils to classic farmhouses or bright-colored little ranch types, or to trailers still banked heavily with spruce boughs.

Then, too soon, a finger sign at a fork pointed to Parmenter, and I swallowed with a very dry throat.

"Won't be long now," said Ed Dunton. " 'Course you know what you're getting into, I hope. You must have picked the place because it's quiet, because that's all you can say about it."

"I want to be in a place where I can concentrate on my work."

"Well, you can concentrate here all right, unless the silence drives you batty. Most excitement they ever have in Parmenter, since the big fight about us joining up in a school district with Fremont, is when Kitty Barstow's prize bull gets loose, or the woodchoppers on the back road get drunk on Saturday night and throw axes at each other."

"I hope the bull doesn't get loose too often," I said. "I'm nervous enough about plain cows."

"Oh, well, he'd never head down to the cottage," he assured me. "Not that one. Right out onto the road, that's for him. In summertime I've seen traffic lined up clear back to Cobb's Brook on one side, and Quimby's Corner on the other. Great big Holstein, and he can hold the bridge like Horatius, now I'll tell ye."

I laughed. "But how do they get him back in?"

"So far, he's clever as a kitten. Hand-raised, that one. But you can't tell how long it'll last, so nobody takes any chances. Kitty's boy can manage him."

The road dipped to a sheet of water like pale blue glass, climbed a hill, and abruptly entered a village. There was the common of the snapshots, beginning to green, and at the far end, like the North Star, a white New England meeting house raised its steeple among bare elms. I knew that church too. We slowed down to let a pick-up back out from the opposite curb, and there facing me was a white-framed, eagle-crested Honor Roll. The names were lettered in black, and some had gold stars after them. They'd put up the first honor roll after the Civil War, I knew that much. A new one came after the First World War, and then this one in World War II, using smaller print to take in all the names from 1860 on.

My father's name was on it. I didn't know what the name was, but I had to read them anyway. "Can you let me out a minute?" I asked.

"Sure. Something you want to pick up?" He swung in where the truck had been, and called, "Hi, Levi!" to a man sweeping the pavement in front of a hardware store.

"Where's the post office?" I asked.

"Across the common." He pointed.

I slid out, saying, "I won't be long."

"Take your time. Hurrying's a national disease, I always say. I'm trying to keep it out of my home town."

So I walked for the first time in Parmenter, and for me it was the moonwalk. I crossed the street and stepped onto the path that led past the Honor Roll. There were birds on the grass and in the bare elms a pair of gray squirrels chasing each other, and a sense of quiet human activity all around the common.

The flag, on a pole as tall as the elms, suddenly snapped out in a surprise gust. I felt a tightening at the back of my neck and thought, *Don't be a nut.*

I read only the names for the second World War. Korea followed, and they'd lost one man in Vietnam. They'd lost five in World War II. Already I recognized two names, Dunton and Parmenter. It was upon the other three that I concentrated, so I'd remember them: Jonas Moore, Toivo Laaka, and Robert Rollins.

Then I hurried over to the post office, modern red brick like post offices in most small towns nowadays, and bought a supply of stamps and postal cards. The girl clerk was friendly but not curious.

When I got back to the car I had to say something, or else be caught with my feelings on my face. "There was a Richard Dunton on the list," I said.

"A cousin of mine. Good boy. Went through the University of Maine, studied forestry, and then got himself killed on the Rhine." His voice turned raspy as if after all these years he still resented the death.

Richard Dunton. Was he the one? I said impulsively, "My father was killed too."

"That so? Well, Dick didn't leave anybody but us older ones. I dunno whether that's good or bad. A man's old enough to fight and be killed, seems he should have had a chance to leave something of himself behind him. To kind of carry him along."

"Yes," I said. What if it was me he left behind? There'd

been a Dick in the albums. All at once I wondered how I could stand this. Already, it was much more of an emotional strain than I'd endured already. And supposing I didn't find out, and had to go away a failure. Would it be a lot worse than if I'd shut it all off from me in the beginning, the way my mother wanted me to do? She'd had her reasons, and here I was plunging like a fool into forbidden territory that could be the darkest Africa of the soul, as far as I knew, or a drifting ice floe in the Antarctic.

Ed Dunton said in his normally amiable tone, "We've got Fourleaf Farm on both sides of us now."

The landscape was essentially the same as what I had already seen, but because I would be staying on the farm everything became subtly different. It was a collage of more pastures, stone walls, and tight modern fencing; a stand of firs cresting a hill, broad gentle slopes contour-plowed, warm shades of brown forever changing under shifting cloud shadows. In the pure particular light of this place animals became imbued with an almost sacred significance, as if they and the earth were all that mattered here.

By this time I felt as if I'd lost a layer of skin, and the prospect of meeting strangers was overwhelming. Cheer up, you nut, I braced myself. In an hour or even less you should be in your own place, and you can lock the doors on the world, and get some sleep, and tomorrow morning you'll be fine.

I was a great believer in this, and sometimes it worked.

"Do they call it Fourleaf Farm because there are a lot of fourleaf clovers there?" I asked brightly.

"I guess it might have been so once, back when the Barstows first had it. It's been Barstow land since, oh—early 1800s. I know that for a fact. My grandfather used to tell about one Barstow boy, George Washington Barstow he was called, hated the farm and his old man and run away from home, and went to sea, and made a fortune in the West India trade. . . . 'Course, it wasn't near as big a place as it is now," he mused. "Used to be small farms around here, but I doubt if you could find even a cellar hole left. And it's grown even more since Cleve died. My Lord, how it's grown. He was a damn—darn smart farmer and he married a woman that was just as smart in her own way, and mebbe more so. Some claim she's too smart with a dollar," he added dryly. "But you can't blame her none, she's had the boy to think of. Cleve, he dropped dead in the field one day. Well, she's one of the biggest landowners around here. Some folks would be land-poor, taking on that much, the way taxes are these days. But not Kitty. She don't miss a trick."

We descended to and crossed a low bridge over a rushing stream that bubbled like boiling tea between its banks, took a curve where peepers sang from silveryalder swamp on both sides of the road, and climbed. The taut tidy fencing began again, running along inside stone walls, and ahead appeared a sign hanging from a post: It showed a fourleaf clover in green and gold, and the name "Fourleaf Farm." Below it hung the triangular Tree Farm emblem I'd seen at some other driveways. There was a large mailbox with the name Barstow lettered on it; we turned in between that and the signpost, and followed a gentle diagonal ascent toward the house. On both sides the old stone walls and the modern fencing continued. Maples bordered the drive, still bare but beginning to flush against the sky. Birds were everywhere. My mother would have known what they were, I thought. This isn't *terra incognita*; it's my land, where I first became a spark of life.

The house was big and square behind a row of maples. Before we reached it I caught a glimpse of the complex of farm buildings a little distance behind it, set off by what seemed like miles of white fencing; then we had swung in behind the maples and stopped before a front door with a fanlight, and crocuses on either side of a brick walk.

The first sound I heard when the engine stopped was the bleating of lambs.

"Cottage is down that way," Ed Dunton said, pointing off to the west where a dirt road disappeared into woods. "I can't drive you down there, it'll be a mess of mud. They'll take you down in the jeep. Where in time is everybody?" He blew the horn.

Nobody's home, I thought hopefully. I can find the place myself. But no key, so that was out. —The front door was energetically thrown open and a woman declaimed, "Well, for heaven's sake! I *thought* I heard something!"

She came sailing down the walk, large, smiling, wearing an apron over her dress and flour smudges on strong bare arms. Mrs. Barstow, I hoped.

"We weren't looking for you 'til later, plane must have been on time for once," she told me. She had ravishing dimples in her flushed round cheeks, and I realized she was too young to be Katherine Barstow. "Kitty's had to go to tend to some business. Over to Harkins'," she said to the driver.

He twisted up one side of his face. "Figgers."

"Well, at least she'll make the land pay for itself, and that's more than Tack could ever do." She turned back to me and put out her hand. "I'm Faye Moore. Faye with an e. I guess you'd call me the hired girl."

"You don't grow any littler, do you?" Ed asked. "A man'll never have to shake the sheets to find *you*. When are you getting married?"

"You want to be careful how you hint, Ed, you might find yourself accepted."

"I better get out of here fast." He ducked as if dodging a blow, whinnying with laughter, and slid into the car.

"Wait a minute, how much do I owe you?" I asked.

"Oh, he's not in that much of a hurry," said Faye. "He'd wait for the devil himself if he could make a dollar out of it."

"Eight dollars," said Ed, "and don't heed her. Working for the rich has stretched her moral fiber something wicked."

I gave him two more dollars for his conversation. He drove off, jauntily blowing his horn in a jazzy measure, and Faye shook her head. "Never grew up, that one. Well now. I guess you could use some lunch."

"I never thought about stopping for groceries. All I could

think of was getting here. This last week has been a tough one."

"Oh, you can get a ride into town this afternoon and stock up, and after that you can hitch a ride whenever you need to. There's enough of us running back and forth. Come on in." She led the way. "Your stuff's all right out there 'til the jeep comes back. Kitty took it so she could get down Harkins Lane."

In the big square entrance hall, shadowy after the brightness outside, a white staircase rose in a curve that must have been the builder's challenge and masterpiece. At the back of the hall we went into a roomy kitchen completely modernized, many-windowed, and scented with the incense rising from the row of new-baked loaves and pies on a long work counter.

"You won't mind eating out here, will you?" asked Faye with a kind of innocent roguery.

"I'd like to bottle that fragrance," I said. "It would probably make me irresistible. Could I wash?"

"Right through here."

"Here" was a good-sized room off the kitchen—the farm office. On my way I saw the big rolltop desk by the windows, a filing cabinet, a bookcase of volumes that looked like textbooks, reference books, and bound reports. On the other side of the room there was a couch with a reading lamp beside it, and a stand with a newspaper and an open book. The bathroom beyond was modern, spotless, but plain white, even to towels. When I went back through the office I saw framed certificates on the walls, photographs of animals, and a case holding award ribbons and other trophies.

Faye was talking to an immensely dignified black and white border collie.

She introduced us and he touched my hand with his nose, then with his tongue, and went and lay down on a rag rug that was obviously his. His name was Jason.

She had set a place for me at a long trestle table of polished pine planks. "Here you are. Beef stew, still hot from the men's dinner." There was new bread to go with it, slightly warm.

Faye sat down with me and had a cup of coffee and a thick heel of bread slathered with butter and plum jam.

"My undoing," she said cheerfully.

"You can carry it," I assured her euphorically. With about thirty pounds off she would have been striking, but she was good-looking anyway. Her black hair was shiny and well-cut, her dark eyes thickly lashed, warm, and lively. She had a buoyant curiosity about life in New York, and about my job.

"I'm a great reader," she told me, "but you know something funny? I never gave any thought to how a book was put together, until Kitty told me you were an editor. So then I couldn't get it out of my mind, and I just thought, Well, I'll ask. I'll never get a better chance."

"I'll tell you anything I can," I said. "But we've got plenty of time for that." The food had simultaneously revived and lulled me. If I didn't get outside pretty soon I'd be falling headfirst into my plate. "Could I walk down to the cottage and not wait for the jeep?"

"You poor thing, you're probably dying for a nap," she said. "I'll point you in the right direction, and it's all unlocked and aired, ready for you. You'd better change your shoes, though."

Sitting on the brick doorstep I changed into boots. I took a small bag and my typewriter, and Faye and Jason walked with me toward the dirt lane.

I mentioned the lambs. "New babies all over the place these days," Faye said. "We're expecting a couple of bossies any time. Place is one big maternity ward. There's your road. Just follow it to the end. It's not long."

It curved off to the right down through spruce and birch and dead brown bracken left flattened by the snow. Birds flashed among the bare branches; I could at least recognize chickadees.

"You'll hear the brook before you see it," Faye said. "It's high right now, a real little river. I hope it doesn't keep you awake."

"Nothing will," I told her. "Nothing could."

# chapter 6

*I* heard the boisterous brook before I saw it, as Faye had promised. Then I saw it scintillating through the leafless boughs. It flowed noisily down the hill through the woods, boiled past the foot of the cottage lawn, and plunged down over glittering rocks in a miniature cascade, to be lost in woods again. It was Hopkins' "darksome burn, horseback brown, /His rollrock highroad roaring down"; I supposed that eventually it joined the stream whose bridge we crossed on the way to the farm.

The sliding, sparkling rush of it was almost hypnotic. With reluctance I turned my back on it, but instantly fell in love with the demure, folded-hands-in-lap presence of the small shingled cottage.

There was a sizable screened porch which made me at once passionately resent that fact that it wasn't summer. But there were other delights beyond the front door. The long living room was dominated by the fieldstone fireplace at one end, and by the upright piano set against the wall between kitchen and bedroom doors. The place was no decorator's dream; but there was something as comforting as a warm lap about braided rugs, the scarred sea chest holding wood, the morris chair, old rockers, and out-of-date but good overstuffed pieces. The bookshelves were also stuffed, as if everyone who had ever stayed there for the past fifty years had left books behind. They ranged from Gene Stratton Porter, Rafael Sabatini, Booth Tarkington, and John Galsworthy through some recent best-sellers, and there were at least two shelves stacked solidly with paperbacks, some of them very good ones, and enough mysteries to sedate a houseful of addicts.

The kitchen had a modern electric stove and refrigerator. It was well-equipped but no attempt had been made to turn it into a magazine kitchen. The bedroom was for sleeping and for putting one's clothes away. The chest of drawers was old, the double bed absolutely plain, but the mattress was superlative, and the sheets smelled of fresh air. There was a good reading lamp and plenty of pillows. The bathroom made no pretense of being dressing room, beauty salon, or adjunct to a seraglio. The back windows of the cottage looked out into a grove of thick-trunked white birches.

The place felt warm and dry; it was heated by gas radiators, from the hook-up of tall cylinders of propane gas against the back wall of the house.

The piano was a good one, as Mrs. Barstow had said. I sat down and played a few bars of Mendelssohn's *Spring Song*, in honor of April, and neither I nor the instrument sounded half-bad. The bench was full of music: song books, a hymnal, sheet music of all varieties, and, surprisingly, several opera scores that had been well-handled and marked for a coloratura.

Groggy with fatigue and letdown now that I was actually here, I was still intrigued by the scores, but when the notations began to get blurry I went for the bedroom like a drunk trying to walk a chalkline. I shed my clothes without picking them up, put on pajamas, drew the shades, and got into bed. The voice of the brook came into the house then, and bore me off to sleep on its swift and glittering flood.

The sound of an engine woke me, and I knew at once where I was, though I thought at first that it was the next morning. I sat up and peered out past the shade. A jeep was just jouncing out of the lane and onto the gravel turnaround under a big oak. A woman was driving, and she had to be Katherine Barstow.

I lunged for the warm wool robe I'd bought especially for April in Maine, knotted the belt tight, gave my hair a frantic lick and a promise with the brush, and was all the way across the living room when I realized I was barefoot. Too late now. I opened the door.

"Hello!" she said with a wide smile. "Welcome to Fourleaf Farm—oh, I'm sorry, did I wake you?"

"I'm glad you did," I said. "I think I'd have been there all night."

"It's the sound of the brook. When it's in flood it talks all the time. I've come down here to sleep when I couldn't close my eyes back at the house."

I saw that she had brought my bags, and I apologized and took them. She said, "They were my excuse for driving down. I was dying to get a look at you."

"I hope you're not disappointed," I said, flustered and not knowing why. "Come in, please." As she glanced about the living room as if silently checking, with a casual but non-offensive air of ownership, I decided that she flustered me because she was so immaculate; she made me feel absolutely sluttish, or at least unkempt. She was taller than I, big-boned but in such good proportion that she appeared slender in herringbone slacks and tawny suede jacket over a cream wool turtleneck. She had the high cheekbones, wide mouth, and long jaw that you see on the top models, but she was not gaunt, and she had a quick broad smile that was very likable.

"Do you think you'll be comfortable here?" she asked, straightening the oil painting over the pine mantel. It showed the brook tumbling out of the woods.

"I love it already," I said, and she turned to me with that smile.

"*Good!* That pleases me." Her eyes were blue, and when the smile narrowed them up behind the dark lashes there were fine sun creases at the corners. She had an outdoor look in spite of her elegant tidiness; I was never to see her without her lipstick or the tiny stones in her earlobes, but I was never to forget, either, that she was a working farmer.

She told me a few things about regulating the heat. "Now if only April gives us some decent weather. We can get a big dose of winter this month, and you're likely to fall out of love in a hurry."

"Not me, I'm taking it for better or for worse."

"Wait and see. You're a city sparrow, remember."

"Well, I'm not a born city sparrow," I defended myself. "It's just that my job's there." She looked so interested that I almost confided that my mother came from here. I hurried away from the brink. "I was wondering about a car. Renting one, or buying something for a hundred dollars or so. What would you advise?"

"Buying one would be your best bet. Reg Dunton handles a few second-hand cars. He keeps them out at his gravel pit on the Derwent road. I'll run you out there tomorrow."

"You're so busy I hate to impose on you," I said. "I thought perhaps I could get the man who drove me from the airport."

"He's Reg's brother," she said with a negating slice of one hand. "Between the two of them you'd be sold a pup for sure. If I'm along, Reg will mind his failings. Now, about groceries. Somebody'll be going to town to catch the late mail, so if you're up at the house at five sharp you can ride in. You can buy milk, cream, and eggs from us, of course, but that's your choice. We make our own butter. It's a fancy of mine."

"I'd rather get everything like that from you."

Again that decisive nod. "*Good*." She turned to leave.

"Thank you for coming down and bringing my bags," I said. "I'll walk to the jeep with you."

"Put something on your feet first," she said crisply. I went for my slippers, and when I came back she said, "I have to apologize for making motherly noises. I promise you I won't make a habit of it."

"I didn't mind. It sounded very natural. Did you see how guiltily I dived for my slippers?"

We both laughed. When we went out I raised my voice above that of the brook and said, "Does it have a name?"

"No, it's always been just 'the brook.' "

"It sounds too important to be anonymous."

"Name it then, if you want." When she settled behind the wheel she sat back and looked quizzically at me, almost smiling, but searching too; and I thought, *She's going to say it now, something about the Guilds. And I will tell her....* I felt as if I'd been running.

"I thought you'd be older," she said suddenly. "I didn't know editors came so young."

"You should see some of them. Fresh from the shell." Why should anyone here connect a fairly common name with someone they used to know? "Infant prodigies, that's what they are."

"It's just that 'editor' sounds—oh, you know."

"That's what I used to think too, 'til I got to be one. But I'm not so young. I'm twenty-four."

"And that's so very old, isn't it?" She regarded me with sad amusement. "What I wouldn't give to be twenty-four again. *Well*," she said briskly. "I must be off to my meeting." She started the engine. "Five sharp," she said, and I repeated it.

I stood on the lawn and watched her swing the jeep around and drive up the lane. Then I went back into the cottage, found a tin of teabags in the cupboard, and made myself a cup of tea. While I drank it I recalled how I had been tempted to confide everything at once, that I had seen her as a girl in the snapshots, that I was Helen's daughter... And if I had told her, if she'd given me the chance, I might have known by now who my father was.

But she hadn't given me the chance, and I hadn't made one, though I could have. I was trembly now with my narrow escape. Because I was really afraid to find out? No, I said emphatically. Because I want to put myself into the landscape. The time won't be right until then.

I made out a grocery list, showered, dressed in warm slacks and desert boots, and walked up the lane in the late afternoon. Behind me the brook's voice grew faint, but never faded out until I was all the way to the house, and even then when I stopped walking I thought I could hear it. Then animal voices coming from the complex of farm buildings and paddocks took over. The air was cool with an increasing chill, but had the fragrance of loosening earth and the tender grass greening close to the warmth of the house's foundations. A pick-up truck was parked at the end of the brick walk. I went up to it and said to the man inside, "Are you driving to town?"

"Yup," he said. He leaned across toward the other door and opened it.

I got in and said, "I'm Miriam Guild."

"Hi," he said, and didn't offer his own name, just started up the truck and we shot out like a torpedo aimed for the distant gate. Hanging onto the door handle, I was able to notice that the cows had left the fields for the barn, but there was no opportunity for pastoral musings about the quality of the late light over the fields and the deepening purple of the hills. I did wonder if the driver was the Barstow son, the one who could handle the bull. Presumably he had better communication with animals than with human beings. I tried to guess by sidewise glances (when I dared take my eyes off the road) if he was my age or younger, but I couldn't really tell because he wore a long-visored cap and glasses with those square, heavy, dark frames. He smelled not unpleasantly of the barn, and he chewed tobacco, spitting out of the window at intervals with what must have been an expert calculation of our speed and the wind's direction.

Everybody else had been so talkative so far that his silence seemed absolutely eccentric, and I amused myself gruesomely with wondering if the intended driver was unconscious and tied up somewhere, and I was being abducted by the local sex fiend. There'd been nobody stirring around the house, and for all I knew Faye and Mrs. Barstow had been knocked out cold too, or done to death by an ax.

This came to an end when we hurtled into the village and came to a surprisingly easy stop beside the common. The driver pointed silently at the grocery store, and went off across the green toward the post office.

The proprietor of the store was a dapper, youthful type, with rakish Edwardian mutton-chop whiskers. Cheerfully he bounced about his store collecting what I couldn't find. He knew my name, where I was staying, and what my job was.

A small boy who was a miniature of his father (except for the whiskers) carried the carton out to the truck, where my driver sat stolidly waiting.

"Hi, Ruel," the boy piped.

"Hi, Chuck," said the driver. He got out and took the carton and put it in the back of the pick-up because the boy was obviously too short to reach.

"Thank you very much, Chuck," I said.

"Oh, that's all right," he responded handsomely and strode back to the store, whistling. I surprised a grin on Ruel's weathered face as he glanced after the boy, and I also observed, apart from some missing teeth which gave him a jolly jack-o'-lantern air, that he was too old to be the Barstow son.

There was no conversation on the way back to the farm, but I didn't mind, and this time when we turned in between the stone posts it was almost like coming home.

The place was serenely beautiful and I went suddenly from euphoria to a kind of throat-squeezing sadness; it was as if I belonged here and had been granted a brief return from exile but must go away again. But I don't *have* to go, I thought desperately as the truck seemed to plummet down the dark tunnel of the lane and I braced both feet and clutched the door handle. I can get some kind of a job somewhere near.

Ruel carried my groceries in, and when I thanked him he said, "Ayuh." On the way out he added, "Kitty said be up at ten tomorrow to go look for a car."

When the sound of the truck died away I was alone with the brook and my first night in Parmenter. Not really the first, though, if you wanted to believe that an embryo is a human being from the moment of conception.

# chapter 7

*P*unctuality is the politeness of kings, I was always told so that I'd see some glamour in being on time. The glamour had worn off, but the brainwashing remained, so I arrived at the house just at ten, and nobody was in sight. I went around to the back. Between the brick walk I followed and the fenced-off outbuildings there lay a spacious drying yard and a freshly plowed good-sized plot that I guessed was the kitchen and freezer garden.

I heard the lambs again, a cow lowing, a persistent rooster. Somewhere out of sight a tractor started up. I was enchanted to see a gilt trotting-horse weathervane on the biggest barn. Swallows shot everywhere. A pond beyond the kitchen garden flashed back at the sun.

Outside the back door there was a low-slung, mud-spattered station wagon, and a neat little yellow Saab. A kitchen window was open and I could hear Faye singing along with the radio; Jason rose up blinking and amiable from a sunny doorstep. While I was talking to him Faye called from the window, "Go on out and see the lambs if you want to."

"The day I wander out into that wild kingdom will be the day the bull bursts all barriers and comes after me."

She laughed. "He's way over in the Far Meadow today. With cattle the expectant Pa doesn't wait just outside the delivery room. Go on."

"Thanks, but I'll wait until someone's willing to take me on a guided tour. I don't want to poke around and get in the way. Besides, Mrs. Barstow's taking me to look at cars today."

"Come on in then," said Faye. "She's out in the barn with

the vet. A case of milk fever. You've got time for a cup of coffee and a molasses cookie."

The kitchen smelled gorgeously of them. They were thin, hot, crisp, and golden. "How much baking do you do a week?" I asked.

"If I start to add up, it scares me. Or else makes me think I should have my own business." She rolled her dark eyes. "All I can say it's a good thing I like food because otherwise I'd be so sick of handling it by now I'd go on a hunger strike and love every minute of it."

We both laughed. Faye had a quality of ease that made me feel as if I'd known her for years. "What else do they raise here besides beef?" I asked.

She looked shocked. "Land of love, we aren't in the beef business! We've got a registered dairy herd! We also have eggs, some wool, apples, potatoes, squash for the cannery, blueberries—*and* we're tree farmers." She finished with a flourish of the rolling pin. "Do you know what tree-farming is?" Then she told me.

"The farm must be as big as a town in itself," I said.

"It's plenty big. It's four farms in one already, and there's a big parcel of blueberry land and pulpwood about to be tacked on any time now." She gave me a flashing sidewise glance, then shut her mouth with ostentatious firmness and began cutting a new batch of cookies. When she took out a sheet of finished cookies she slid the fresh ones into the oven.

Outside, a man spoke to the dog, and then I heard Mrs. Barstow's voice in the entry, pleasant but incisive in spite of the soft Maine intonations that made the other voices almost glide.

"Now, Henry," she said, "you know it would never work."

"I don't know anything of the sort," said Henry, "and neither do you."

"He's been trying to marry her for years," Faye whispered. She took two more cups and saucers out of the cupboard. Mrs. Barstow came in and registered pleased surprise at the sight of me.

"Oh, good morning, Miss Guild! I'm sorry to have kept you waiting, but this was an emergency. This is Dr. Cannon. Miss Guild is a book editor, Henry, what do you think of that?"

"What am I supposed to think?" He winked at me. He was a craggy, grizzled man who smelled of pipe tobacco. "Well, Faye, Dorothy's up on her feet. You'll have to take a look at her every so often and get her up if she's down."

"Ayuh," said Faye. "I've got nothing else to do but go out and twist a cow's tail every hour *on* the hour."

"Oh, it won't be that bad," said Mrs. Barstow. "The men'll be back by noon. I'd look out for her myself if I didn't have that luncheon meeting. Why I ever let them get me into the Improvement Association I'll never know."

"Because you wanted to be in it, Kitty," said the vet. "And what's more you wanted to be chairman. You know you love it."

"Well, at least the town has plenty to show for it," she said tartly. "The old cemeteries being cleaned up, and the scenic drive along Rollins Ridge all cleared and marked——"

"They should have at least named it Barstow Boulevard," said Henry, straight-faced. She flushed with what I took for instant anger, then laughed.

"That's what I thought, but I kept my megalomania to myself. Sit down and have a cup of coffee and try Faye's cookies, Henry. Come along, Miss Guild—oh, for heaven's sake, I'm going to call you Miriam."

"I wish you would," I said. "But, look, a car for me isn't important besides all the work going on here and the other things you have to do."

She held up her hand. "You are going to have a car. I've already called Reg. So come along."

I followed meekly out to the Saab.

The Derwent road didn't ever warrant a white line in the middle. There was nothing on either side but long stretches of alder swamp and spruce woods until we came to the gravel pit. About eight cars and trucks were parked in a line beside a wooden shack from which a fat man emerged, smoking a pipe, his hands in his pockets. He was clearly Ed Dunton's brother.

"Mornin', ladies," he said around the pipe. "I got something right here for you. Should be perfect. I just got it two days ago. Clarissa's old Chevvy," he explained to Mrs. Barstow. "And you know how she took care of it. All but had it in the house by the stove on cold nights."

"And of course you'll vouch for it," Mrs. Barstow said pleasantly.

"I've gone over her from stem to stern," he said. "There's nothing the matter with her except she's so old the list price is way down. But they don't make cars like that any more," he said fervently. "Look at her, hardly a speck of rust." He rapped a fender. "They don't use steel like that nowadays. Lean on these new jobs and they dent."

"Get in and try her out, Miriam," Mrs. Barstow said.

I did, and was suited. He asked $150, which she got down to $115. Being taken in charge by Katherine Barstow had its advantages.

She led the way to the farm home of the tax collector, who turned out to be the very young mother of two small children. In her little office off the kitchen I paid the modest excise tax and received my two slips to finish filling out and send to the Secretary of State in Augusta, unless I preferred to drive to the registry at Rockland. I chose the mail method, rather than use up a couple of hours away from Parmenter. Meanwhile I had ten days on the temporary registration.

When we left there Mrs. Barstow said, "Now the insurance. It's not compulsory, but it's a good idea anyway."

"I never thought about insurance," I said in dismay. "Will I be able to get any? Back home we always seemed to go through so much trouble when our cars got really old——"

"Fiddlesticks," she said robustly. "Get in and follow me." This time we ended up at one of the dignified old houses near the church, overlooking the common. A fussy, elderly man said, "What can I do for you, Kitty?" He sounded almost anxious. It hadn't taken me twenty-four hours to realize that Katherine Barstow was important in this town. With just half the presence that she had, I thought, I could convince most of MacKenzie and Thomson, Incorporated, that I was born to great things in the publishing business. Then I comforted my ego by reflecting that Mrs. Barstow had about twenty-five years' advantage on me in becoming a personage.

Now while I answered the insurance agent's questions I wondered about *him. Did you know my mother? Would you be thunderstruck to know who I was?* And I found myself tensely waiting for the question or comment. "Guild? There used to be Guilds around here." Or even: "We have some Guilds in town. You any connection?"

But it didn't come, though once the insurance man gave me a seemingly thoughtful stare. I decided it was because he was doing arithmetic in his head. Anyway, I came away from there insured, and pleasantly surprised at the rates.

"Can you find your way home from here?" Mrs. Barstow asked me.

"Yes, and thank you for your time and help."

She brushed that off. "Well, I'm off to my luncheon. Have a good day." We both got into our cars. She waved and drove off past the church and disappeared. I drove out of town the other way, back to the tax collector's house. She was giving lunch to her children and husband at the kitchen table. When she recognized me she looked worried.

"Did I make out something wrong?" she asked anxiously. "I wouldn't be surprised. I just started this job last week, and I wouldn't have been elected to it if the old collector hadn't decided to retire."

"You're qualified, so stop fussing," her husband told her good-humoredly.

"I know, Bud, but Mrs. Barstow makes me so nervous. She's *nice*," she assured me hastily, blushing. "She's always been nice to us. But she's so smart, and she's really kind of impor-

tant around here—she could have been on the board of selectmen but she refused to run——"

"If you'd let this girl get a word in edgewise," Bud said,
"you'd find out what she wants."

She grinned. "I'm sorry, I guess I do dither."

"All I wanted to know," I said, "is whether you have any
Guilds on your books. My people came from somewhere in
Maine—I don't know just where—but I thought it wouldn't
do any harm to ask."

Ardent with relief, she was already on her way to the office.

"I don't know any Guilds," Bud said, "and I've lived here
all my life. Peg's from away. You won't find any Guilds,
honey," he called after her. "Not for now, anyway. Might
have been years ago, long before my time."

She was reading out a variety of names beginning with G,
but no Guild. "I'm sorry," she said despondently. "I really
am."

"Don't be. It was just a shot in the dark, and I've had a
chance to admire your babies."

They were both pleased at that, Bud in a moderate manly
fashion. "Look," he said, "why don't you try Selma Hitchcock? She's the town clerk and she's got charge of the books
that go way back, besides what she'd know anyway from
being an oldtimer here."

Selma Hitchcock was the woman who had written to me
about the Barstow cottage. I thanked Bud for his suggestion,
and Peg for her efforts, received directions, and took off.

Selma Hitchcock wasn't at home. Three handsome cats
were sunning themselves on the doorstep, not at all alarmed
by a stranger. I stroked arched backs and blinked companion-
ably at cat-smiles, then drove leisurely back to Fourleaf Farm.
Sometimes I met a car or a truck, and once a man on a tractor
waved me past him. It was possible to stop to look out over
a stupendous view without causing a traffic jam. The few
who passed waved with casual friendliness and I waved back.
Guilds or no Guilds on the present tax lists, I was *home* and
knew it.

I decided not to break up my mood by stopping to ask Faye how Dorothy was. I parked the car on a flat dry ledge at the head of the lane and patted it affectionately when I left it. It was a nice little car that had seemed to enjoy trundling me about the country roads. One of my faults is to give personalities to my possessions, and then to feel responsible for having engaged their affections. Now I felt as if I'd come home with a small sturdy pony.

After lunch I walked upstream until the mixed firs and hardwoods thinned and I came out to a high field. It was empty of animals as far as I could see, and the only sound up here was the surflike rush of wind in the boughs, and in the field itself the faint rustle and rattle of dead grasses and dry leaves. On the far side, a stone wall ran along the sky. I was tempted to go up there but not enough to forget the bull; or even cows, who were not all like Stevenson's friendly cow all red and white.

It was getting colder anyway, low clouds were thickly moving in. I went back to the cottage and lit the fire already laid; I'd been too sleepy to bother with it the night before. Then conscientiously I loaded and started the tape recorder, and began to work through my old book of Czerny exercises. After an hour or so of that my fingers and wrists were tired, but I didn't want to stop. So I turned off the recorder, and took from the piano bench a thick book of *Best-Loved Songs*. These carried me back to my sentimental adolescence when I had lived vicariously the great romance which had produced me. *Tell me the tales which to me were so dear ... When other lips and other hearts ... Douglas tender and true ...*

I can carry a tune, which is the most I can say for my singing, and I sang now, going from the flowery Victorian songs to those which can still move by their timeless simplicity: *Drink to Me Only with Thine Eyes; Believe Me if All Those Endearing Young Charms; Passing By.*

*Passing By.* I'd first heard that at a charity pop concert, when I was about fifteen. I had found it beautiful—which it is—and by shutting my eyes as I listened I had blotted out the hall full of people around me, and the singer ceased to be Mr. Prentice with a couple of extra chins; he became a slim youth hopelessly in love with a vision.

I sang it softly now, listening to the other voice in my mind, and remembering the caramel-marshmallow sentiment of which I'd been capable in those days, though nobody who had ever faced me on a basketball court could have guessed.

> " 'There is a lady sweet and kind,
>     Was never face so pleased my mind,
>     I did but see her passing by,
>     And yet I love her—' "

I wasn't alone on the last line. A man's voice joined with mine, effortlessly took the lift on "her," leaving me behind, and sang the last three words in exquisitely modulated clarity.

" ' 'Til I die.' "

# chapter 8

The hair stood up on the back of my neck, gooseflesh stood on my arms, a chill ran down into my hands, but I kept on playing and the singer went on singing.

> " 'Cupid is winged and doth range
> Her country so my love doth change—' "

It wasn't the voice of memory; it did not remotely resemble that buttery high tenor except in that it was also a tenor. But my physical reaction was—to me—unanswerable proof of the presence of the authentic thing.

> " 'But change the earth or change the sky,
> Yet shall I love her 'til I die.' "

It ended. I sat staring straight ahead, listening to what had been left behind in the room. There'd been no affectations, no mannerisms. Just simple, unadorned quality.

Behind me a foot shifted. He said, "All right to come in?"

"You seem to be in already." I braced myself for turning. This wasn't a dream, so he'd be fat and going bald, or gaunt and bony with an Adam's apple sliding up and down. The frog, not the prince . . . Sliding around on the bench, I said, "Did you actually open that door, or did you sift through the cracks like fog?"

He was half-sitting on the center table. "I came through the keyhole. It's a little trick I learned from a door-to-door witch."

He was tanned almost to the same brown as his hair, and

a blue sweatshirt emphasized the color of his eyes. His smile compounded my disorientation.

"Well, it must be a very handy gift," I said, a little sharply. I felt as if I'd been taken advantage of because he *wasn't* the frog. "But anyone could make a nuisance of himself with a gimmick like that."

"She warned me," he said solemnly. "Don't overdo it, she said. People just don't understand. I could end up being burned on the common."

I laughed in spite of myself, which plainly gratified him. *Oh, we are really stuck on ourself and our voice*, I thought nastily. "Did you come to read the meter or something?" I asked.

"Like the lady in the song, I was just passing by." His speaking voice was pleasant, soft and unhurried. "On purpose."

"What purpose?" *This line must really kill the Parmenter girls*, I thought.

"To get a look at the new girl. Faye told me she was pretty. I didn't expect music too."

I might as well get it over with; it was what he was waiting for. "I didn't expect a singer, any more than I expected a piano this good."

"I'm not a singer," he said amiably. "I'm a farmer who likes to sing."

"And practice sorcery," I said. "Quite a combination." *Did the witch teach you how to handle your voice too?* I wanted to ask him. There was something familiar about the turn of his head and the set of his eyes between brow and cheekbone. "Are you Rory Barstow?"

"Ayuh," he drawled. "I be him, mum." He pulled at his forelock.

"You're the one who talks to the bull. Something else the witch taught you?"

"Oh, no, mum, Apollo and me's just close friends."

"Well, it's the first time I ever met anyone who was Old Buddy to a bull," I said. "How do you do? I'm Miriam Guild."

He stood up and gave me an oddly formal little bow. "Hello, Miriam. Welcome to Fourleaf Farm."

"Thank you," I said.

"I've brought you a welcoming present." He went out to the porch, moving without sound in moccasins. He was taller than I, with no extra flesh, no incipient little pot, but he was no gaunt rack of bones either. I hadn't been able to check on the sliding Adam's apple yet.

He came back. His gift was a brook trout, fresh-caught and cleaned. "There's a good pool right below here," he said. "That's where I caught it. Do you like to fish?"

"I don't know, I never had the chance to find out," I said.

He looked sorry for me. "Well, you'll have a chance here. I'll teach you. Do you know how to cook trout?"

"That I do know," I said firmly before he could take over. "My mother taught me. Somebody used to bring us fresh trout now and then." Come to think of it, it was Mr. Prentice. Of all people. I almost laughed aloud. To quench this slightly cracked (to me) impulse I said, "And my mother fished when she was a girl in the country. Fly-fishing too."

It was a mistake. It didn't put an end to the conversation; he was eager as a bird dog to know where she had lived as a girl. If I was vague, I'd sound foolish. If I said, *In Maine*, he'd want to know just where, so I lied. "Western Massachusetts. The Berkshires."

"Great country there," he said generously.

"Well, I'd better put this in the refrigerator," I said, and did so, wondering how to get rid of him. From the kitchen I heard him picking out a tune with one finger.

Viewed objectively he was a handsome creature who, with his looks and his voice, had probably been spoiled by every female in the community, beginning with his mother; he expected the proper response from me—both musical and biological—as surely as he expected the sun to rise tomorrow morning.

*Some day, chum, the sun won't rise*, I thought. "I didn't know farmers could take the time off to go calling at this time of year," I said, coming back. "Let alone fishing. Aren't you supposed to be plowing or harrowing or lambing or something?"

He looked up from the piano and grinned. "Calving. I'm on the night shift in the maternity ward. At this moment everybody thinks I'm sacked out catching up on lost sleep."

"You must have been up with Dorothy," I couldn't resist saying. "How is she?"

It was a mistake. He told me. I leaned in the doorway looking at the healthy sheen of him, and I just couldn't believe that this charming simplicity was all that ingenuous. And I wondered how many other women in this cottage had been brought "welcoming presents" while he looked them over. He was a character straight out of D. H. Lawrence, but did he know it?

When I'd learned more about milk fever than I really wanted to know, I asked brightly, "How do you happen to have such a good piano down here? And how does it stay in tune? So close to the brook, it must be damp and cold in the winter."

"Oh, a man comes down from Bangor once a year to tune 'er up. And we run the heat on low all winter." He picked out the phrase again, and I almost recognized it. "We had an opera singer here all one summer, about six years ago. She wanted a piano, so I drove her to Bangor and she picked this one out. Second-hand, but it was such a darned good find she was tickled silly with it."

*Was it only the piano she was tickled silly with?* I wondered cynically.

"What was her name?" I asked, wishing I had the courage to end this wasting of my time.

"Margaret Dundas." It was a throwaway. He didn't even look to see my reaction, but he must have felt it.

*"Maggie Dundas?* Are you *sure?"*

"Her manager made the arrangements for her under another name. She didn't want any publicity. But she was Maggie Dundas all right. My mother and I kept it quiet." He was serious. "She wasn't singing any. She'd had an operation on her throat that spring, and she thought she was done for. She came here to hide away."

I remembered. In my mother's circle it had assumed the proportions of a personal tragedy. Even when it hadn't turned out to be a malignancy, was that voice to be lost forever? There'd never be another such *Lucia.* . . . Those opera scores in the bench, pored over by a woman who thought she'd never sing again.

"Did she have anything to do with your singing?" I asked.

"Oh, I always sang," he said. "I can't remember not singing. Church, the Grange, school operettas, and I went through the guitar and folk song bit too. The summer Maggie was here I was big on country-Western stuff. I was eighteen." His grin invited me to be amused at his juvenile tastes. "You know—or maybe you don't know—the home-talent television stars with the fanciest Western outfits outside the rodeo circuit, and the Down East version of a Texas accent. Guitars, a fiddler, a couple of girls to sing the tearful numbers. You'd be on local TV once a week, and giving shows at every little town that could afford you. Days, you'd go on being a farmer or fisherman, or insurance salesman. But at night you'd be in show business. What a life!" He flung out his arms. "The world at your feet!"

"Did you actually *do* it?"

"It never got past the dreaming stage. I had my fiddler, but the other two musicians went and enlisted before they could be drafted. Girls were a problem, too. The best-looking ones either couldn't sing or their mothers wouldn't let them join. Or they had jealous boyfriends." He looked glumly into space and I thought, *I can imagine.* He roused himself and said, "But I had my stage name. Wow. Magnificent. I could see it in lights." He stood back and admired a blazing marquee. "It had everything. Originality, sparkle, a real clutch at the heart. *Montana Slim Barstow!*"

I collapsed on the sofa, laughing. He stood in front of the fireplace looking down at me, all alight somehow, and I thought, *Well at last he's got results*. But even I didn't have a law against laughter.

"Was the Queen of Opera properly impressed by Montana Slim?" I asked.

"I don't know about impressed," he said modestly. "But she came out to the barn one night at milking time, and heard me singing—the cows like it," he explained solemnly. "Then she asked my mother if she could give me some coaching, for her own sake, for therapy. It would be free, and it wouldn't take up too much of my time, so my mother agreed. She was always proud of my lung power. I take after my father. He used to sing at all the weddings. The Voice that Breathed o'er Eden had to be Cleve Barstow's or nobody's, and it was the same at funerals. Cleve had to see 'em all off."

We were both quiet, Rory looking down at his feet with the laughter suddenly gone from him, and I wondered if he was thinking of the father he had never known. For a perilous moment I wanted to reach out to him, to tell him that was how it was with me, and why I had come. Instead I said, "Did you really like music? I mean, *love* it? Or did you just enjoy singing because you could do it so well, and other people liked it?"

"I didn't know, until that summer with Maggie," he said. "It was like seeing the ocean for the first time and realizing how wide it was and how deep, and that it was what you were born for. . . . She was Scotch, you know," he said. "No, a Scot. She insisted on that. 'Scotch' is whiskey." He smiled. "She loved the old songs she'd grown up with and used to sing at school and church concerts, as I did. Those are the ones she taught me. Robert Burns and so forth."

"Did they knock the country-Western idea out of your head?"

"That, and the fact that I knew all along my mother wasn't ever going to consent to my ideas," he said dryly. "She was having a hard enough time holding me down then without letting me go barnstorming around the state. Hey, I'd better fix your fire."

"I can do it—"

But he was already crouching on the hearth. I said to his back, "The therapy must have helped. She made a wonderful comeback."

"She wrote to me once and said I'd helped. The lessons must have taken her mind off herself, that's all I could think."

*I'll bet they did*, I thought. A woman like Maggie Dundas, passionately despairing, hiding from the world and finding a handsome and talented boy, in love with life and dreaming of freedom.

He was absorbed in rebuilding the fire, as if that was all he was thinking of at the moment. I'd heard only what he would tell any interested stranger who spoke about his singing. What happened afterward, after she had gone? Had she made no mark upon him at all except in the way he had learned to phrase, breathe, and control? Was he really so simple that this was all it had been?

I suspected not by the way he had cut me off. Well, I'd never know, and I hadn't come here to be tormented by curiosity about other people. I had enough torments of my own to do me.

He had the fire going, and stood up. "A good birch back log, that's the trick. Let's see, now. I'm going to teach you fishing, and I'll show you some of the trails through the woods. There's one spot where if you're patient and quiet long enough you can almost always see deer."

I wanted to tell him I'd be too busy, but he was on his way to the door. There he stopped and gave me that smile. "Good-bye for now."

The sound of the brook and the peepers came in when he left, and the sharp piping of some water bird. When he had gone off the doorstep I went out to stand and listen. I stood in shade through which the brook ran like music. A cold air scented with earth and grass and water rose around me. The man had disappeared, so quickly that he seemed to have dissolved in the blur of shadows beyond the lawn. I heard the call of an owl from the woods behind the cottage, and I wondered whether it really was an owl, or Rory Barstow.

"And good-bye to *you*, Peter Pan," I said aloud, and went inside to my fire.

# chapter 9

Rory Barstow was a predator, even if he was as innocent about it as a fox or the owl out there in the woods. He had come down to look me over, he had tried out his usual tactics, and if they didn't work he would either adopt an alternate strategy or abandon the whole idea as a waste of time. The trout was delicious. I felt a little sorry for it, but no doubt it had been a predator too. I amused myself with thinking of Rory Barstow as a beautiful young trout, sleek and flashing, snatching at flies until one fatal day when he caught the one with a hook in it.

Sleep was a sensuous experience in this place. I went to bed early with my book, but could hardly stay awake to read. Putting out the light I lay by my open window listening to the soft flow and splash of the brook and the singing of the tree frogs, and without knowing it I slid gently under the surface with no sensation of drowning. I woke early in the morning to the brook again and the call of red-winged blackbirds.

By half-past nine I had three good hours' work done on the Andric manuscript, and I felt that when I read the section over that night I would be pleased with it. The morning was cool and very bright as I walked up the lane. There was a feeling behind my eyes like tears wanting to gather. All my childhood fantasies about my father and mother were just that, slain by reality as the dawn mists over the brook were slain by sunlight. Somewhere in this countryside my mother had been a young woman like myself, and my father had been as much flesh and blood as Rory Barstow. In the sparse beauty of early spring in New England they had never been more real than when they conceived me; and now I had the almost religious faith that I was going to find them both, that neither of them had left the place, that they were waiting for me.

My little car started on the first try. No one was in sight around the big house, but there were sheep and cattle on the sunny hillsides. The big black-and-white bull was in the strongly fenced field on one side of the drive. He watched me go by. He was an impressive beast, and I wondered if he were the only begetter of all the new calves or if he had a junior partner, a sort of executive trainee.

I drove to town, meeting on the way only an empty school bus (empty of children, that is) whose driver waved to me, and a truck with two big blanketed horses standing in the back, facing the way they had come. The two men in the cab waved as the bus driver had. On the door of the truck was printed in white the name "Windhover Farm." It sounded strange and beautiful when I said it to myself. And I met Ed Dunton, who blew his horn with the verve of a teenager.

In town I went directly to the grocery store. The sign said "Wyatt and Son, f. 1845." There was a telephone booth outside, and I'd call Mrs. Hitchcock from there. First I went inside and got a few more things for my grocery cupboard, and some picture postcards. The proprietor told me it was plain that country life agreed with me. I didn't know whether he was Son or whether the sign anticipated young Chuck's becoming a partner. On an impulse I said, "Did you ever hear of any Guilds around here?" I spelled it. "I guess in some places they pronounce it 'Gild.'"

He repeated it so alertly that I was positive he knew the name. Then he shook his head. "Nope, it doesn't ring any bells." My disappointment must have showed because he said kindly, "But you can't go by me. I didn't grow up here. I only came about fifteen years ago to take over the store when my uncle got sick. My wife and I decided we wanted to raise the kids in the country." He grinned. "I'm not even Wyatt, I'm O'Brien."

We both laughed. Then he said, "Tell you what, if I think

of it I'll ask any of the old folks that come in. And why don't you go around and see Selma Hitchcock? She's the town clerk."

"I was going to call her—"

I gestured outside, and he said, "Never mind that. Call from in here. Want me to do it?" He was already on his way to the back of the store. Mrs. Hitchcock was at home. They had some animated conversation and then I was sent on my way, with fresh instructions for locating the Hitchcock house from this direction, and since I was going there would I take along some dry mustard and molasses which she'd just run out of?

I would be delighted to. It made me feel almost like a native.

Mrs. Hitchcock and the cats were waiting for me. She was a large woman with thick gray hair braided around her head, glasses, a ruddy outdoor coloring. She thanked me heartily for bringing her supplies and asked me to have a cup of coffee. She'd been baking tarts to take to a bridal shower that night, and invited me to try them out.

"Well, now, how are you enjoying Kitty's cottage, and Parmenter?" she asked.

"I love them both," I said.

"We can still get snow," she warned me.

"I don't care," I said recklessly. "I've got an open fireplace, and plenty to read, and a piano. Anyway, the brook's not likely to freeze this late, is it?"

She laughed at that. "There's some who claim it's possible! Now what is it that you want to find out? Eddie's so full of blarney I couldn't make head nor tail of it."

"Did you ever know anyone named Fern Hopkins?" I asked.

She sat back, staring through her glasses. "Well, I never! Did *you* know her?"

"Not in person, but my mother had met her somewhere, and they used to write now and then." I felt so close now, my mouth was drying. When a cat jumped into my lap I was glad to have something to do with my hands. "To tell you the truth," I said, "her letters are why I chose Parmenter. I mean, the way she described it, it always sounded so wonderful. But since my mother died she hasn't written, and I wondered if—well, what had happened to her——"

"Oh, dear, poor Fern died of pneumonia, oh maybe two years ago. I've got the exact date in my records—she was stout, you know, and her heart just couldn't—" She shook her head and looked sadly past a windowsill of tomato plants.

I thought of the chubby little girl in the Easter photograph, the one in the clown suit; the laughing cheerleader, the 4-H girl showing her prize lamb, the high-school graduate trying to be solemn in white cap and gown. I couldn't really believe in a stout grown-up Fern dying of pneumonia and leaving grandchildren, even though my mother could have been a grandmother too.

"What about her husband, Ray?" I asked. "Is he still here?"

"Ray up and married a widow from Aroostook, of all places," she said. "She had a lot of potato land and wouldn't give that up, so Ray sold his orchards here—well, he sold to Kitty! I guess she was happy to get that land, it practically ties Windhover and Fourleaf together. My, yes." She seemed to have some thoughts of her own on that.

Then she returned to me. "Almost anybody'd be able to tell you about Fern. You don't need the town clerk for that."

"Well, I wanted to thank you in person for writing me such a nice letter," I said glibly. "But there was something else, because you've been town clerk for so long. Did you ever hear of any Guilds around here? My people were Maine people, but I don't know where they came from. I thought it might have been from around here, because my mother knew Fern."

"Didn't she ever tell you, dear?"

"My father died when I was little, and I guess my mother couldn't bear to talk much about the old days, after that."

Mrs. Hitchcock was sympathetic. "I can understand that. But I never heard of any Guilds anywhere in this whole region. Fern worked in Portland a while after she finished high school—she might have met your mother there. But I tell you what, when I've got some time I'll go through the records way back. It might be I can turn up some ancestor of yours in the births and deaths."

I could tell it was a kind gesture; she didn't expect to find anything. She insisted on my taking home three tarts, and told me to come again. She walked outside with me, pointing out her crocus and snowdrops, and the green spikes of daffodils. Then suddenly she asked, "What was your mother's maiden name, dear? Maybe I'll find that."

I was caught off guard. I almost said, "Why, Guild, of course." My sure instinct for self-preservation saved me. I said the first name that came into my mind, straight out of Rory Barstow's visit yesterday: "Burns."

"Burns," she repeated slowly. "I don't know. But I'll look. I won't have time till after the weekend, but then you've got a month here, haven't you?"

I assured her that time was no object, and drove away. I didn't feel like crying, I was too empty for that. Fern existed, but my mother hadn't. At least not in Parmenter. Yet there were the old snapshots; there was Fern, unmistakably, and the tall girl in jeans who might have been Katherine Barstow; Ed Dunton was in some of the pictures, and who knew how many other people whom I might have seen on the road or in the village?

I drove back to the farm. I had to wait outside the drive to let the milk truck come out, and by then the egg truck was approaching from the other direction. So I let that go in first. Sitting there leaning on the wheel I gazed bleakly out at the cloud shadows rolling across the shorn slopes and the dark blue velvet hills. I felt myself being watched, and looked around, indifferently curious. From the other side of the stone wall and the wire fencing, Apollo the bull stared at me with blank concentration. I didn't suppose he had ever attacked anyone, and it was hard to believe that he would do so even if he had the chance, he looked so massively calm and mild, gazing and chewing.

The northwest wind had dried my lane enough so I could drive down it, and I was moodily cheered to make the whole distance. "Great," I said sarcastically. "If it rains overnight you won't be able to drive *up* tomorrow." I got out and slammed the door. "Oh, the hell with it."

The little lawn was a well of quiet sunlight. Puffs of wind blew over it, but not into it. I brought out a heavy blanket and a pillow, and lay on my back watching the movement of the treetops against the sky. I cried softly in self-pity until I had to shut my eyes, and then I lay there like something flung up by flood waters or dropped by some giant bird of prey.

I knew I could walk up to the big house, carrying an album, and ask Katherine Barstow if she was the Kitty of the snapshots. I could say, "You knew my mother Helen. This tall quiet girl with red hair, who played the piano well."

I could, meaning that it was within the bounds of physical possibility. But I could *not*. This was no way to bring my mother and father to life, exposing them to old gossip, diffusing their essence and thus losing them altogether. The search had to be mine and kept to its narrow inviolable whole. When I'd completed it I would go away again, and nobody left behind would have guessed my real reason for coming there.

But to find out that even my name was neither my father's nor my mother's! In my distress I turned savagely on the woman who had done this to me. Why had she told me anything at all? Or why hadn't she done a complete job of lying, and created a background that would have left me feeling all of a piece, identifiable, and satisfied that there was no more to find out?

Ashamed, and weeping with it, I realized that my mother's real mistake had been to not burn Fern's last letters. If I hadn't found them, I wouldn't be in Parmenter now knocking at doors that opened into emptiness.

Then, after my headlong dive into the depths, I came up with a pearl.

*High-school yearbooks.* Somewhere, either in the high

school, the public library, or somebody's attic, there must be a collection.

Restored, I went inside and fixed up a lunch, carried it out on a tray, and had a picnic on the lawn. Chickadees were curious and friendly. Far overhead, gulls scaled on the wind, coming inland to forage in new-plowed fields.

After I ate, I brought out my work and became totally absorbed. What eventually dragged me back from the Montenegrin hillsides and the adventures of Ivo was the sound of a motor. Reluctantly I saw Mrs. Barstow turning her Saab around by my car so it would be pointing up the lane again. She looked so grim I wondered if Dorothy could be worse, or if perhaps more cows were down with milk fever. As deep in work as I was right now, she was the last person I wanted to see, and I didn't even know who the first person was.

# chapter 10

I ran my fingers through my hair and reached for my sneakers, but I gave up trying to get them on and stood up as she came toward me. She had a basket over her arm.

"Faye sent you some of her baking," she said. "Oh—am I interrupting your work?"

"I was just thinking of a break," I answered her deceitfully. As usual with Mrs. Barstow, not a hair was out of place. I felt like a hippie. I took the basket and sniffed the warm delicious odors coming out from under the napkin.

"Oh, *gorgeous!* Would you like a cup of tea or coffee? I'm going to have something."

She said abruptly, "My husband and I started housekeeping here, his people were still in the big house. I missed it awfully at first, after we moved up there. I hated leaving the brook. It's not always noisy, of course." She gave me a determined smile. "Yes, I'd love a cup of coffee, whatever you have."

We went into the cottage. I excused myself to go to the bathroom and wash my face in cold water and comb my hair. When I came out she had put the cinnamon rolls on a plate, and was standing at the back window gazing out into the birches. I set the tea kettle on to heat and took out cups and saucers. My breakfast dishes were in the sink, my lunch tray was on the drainboard. I wondered if she was thinking I was slatternly.

I took a sneaky look at her profile. It was like Rory's but thinner and finer, with the clear beautiful sculpturing of the mouth corners, cheekbone, and eye hollow that I'd always admired. It was also a very tense profile in its masklike stillness.

"How are all the mothers, both new and expectant?" I asked politely.

"What?" She gave me an unfocused look, then caught herself all together like a cat preparing to pounce on a mouse. "Oh! Everything going well so far."

"There must be a terrific amount of bookkeeping with farming these days," I said. "The tax situation takes up a lot of time, doesn't it? . . . Is instant coffee all right?"

"Fine, Miriam."

I made two cups of coffee and set them on the table, with paper napkins and small plates. "But I suppose where your son is your partner you can divide up the paperwork between you. . . . Here's some of Fourleaf Farm's best cream. There, I guess we're ready. I can hardly wait to try one of those rolls." I hoped I was beaming on her like a proud little hostess.

She refused sugar, cream, or a roll. Then, as if she'd reached some decision, she looked straight at me.

"Rory tells me he's been to call."

"Yes. He brought me a trout for a welcoming present." I laughed. "I thought it was awfully nice of him."

"Rory is very friendly. He always has been. Too much for his own good, sometimes. . . . Don't take that personally, please! I didn't mean it the way it must have sounded." Her smile took on an irony that made her look older. "You called him my partner. I wish I could say he was truly that. He has a feeling for the land and he's very good with animals, but, as far as the paperwork goes, he thinks it's the worst drudgery that was ever invented. He says he'd rather shovel manure than keep the books and the records. The Lord only knows what'll happen when I'm not here to do them."

"That won't be for a long time yet," I said. "He'll buckle down one of these days, wait and see."

"I doubt it," she said dryly. "Too much of his father in him. Cleve was always laughing and singing, as if tomorrow was of no account. Rory sings too, by the way. Very well. It's much more of a voice than his father had. But he's never taken it seriously; that would be too much work! It amuses him and entertains others, and that's all that matters to him. *Fun.*" She said it with contempt.

"Some people mature later than others," I suggested. "Another year may surprise you."

"My dear girl, he's almost twenty-five!" she said with a quiet but embarrassing passion. "And what if something happened to me in a year? Oh, I don't *know* of anything, but then I never expected my husband to be dead before he was thirty. So something could happen to me before I'm fifty. And this whole thing I've built up falling into that boy's hands! He could lose it in six months, and I don't believe he'd care!"

Her cheekbones were red. She lifted her cup and sipped, but only for something to do, I was sure. She tried for a natural laugh and did pretty well.

"What you must think of me, running on like this to a perfect stranger. But you seem such a sensible girl and not like what I'd expect, coming from New York, after some I've seen. Of course I know you're smart, you'd have to be in your kind of job. But having a brain is no sure sign of common sense."

I didn't know what to say, so I looked modestly at my plate.

"No, there's only one thing that'll save Fourleaf Farm for my son and my grandchildren," she said. "And that's his marrying the right girl."

My scalp began to tighten. What *was* this? Surely not a proposition coming. I stared even harder at my plate. My ears were hot.

"A girl with a good head on her shoulders," she went on. "With a proper sense of values."

This was incredible. The heat was spreading through my face and neck.

"A girl," she went on, "who's grown up in farming, who knows it inside and out, who can take up where I leave off, manage the farm and Rory both."

Suspense ended, I broke out in a light sweat and just stopped myself from wiping my forehead. "Do you have someone in mind?" I asked.

"I've always had her in mind, practically since the day she was born. She'll have property too, and between them they'll own about half of Parmenter." There was an almost religious intensity about her. "It'll be a perfect match," she said in a hushed voice.

"How does Rory feel about her?"

"He knows that she's always had an eye for *him*. But that doesn't cut any ice with him," she said bitterly. "Too many girls, and grown women too, have set their caps for him. By now he thinks no more of that than the wind blowing over his hand."

"Then how will you manage it?" It was blunt, but she didn't even look offended.

"Let him be alone with any girl long enough and he thinks he's in love. That's how it'll be managed. She's a very pretty girl, too—she was Miss Green Pastures one year, the Blueberry Queen another year, and she's got even better-looking since. If she'd make a dead set at him and really work at it, he'd notice soon enough. Trouble is, she's got her pride." She sounded mildly contemptuous. "If I'd worried about my pride I don't know where I'd be today. But I'm going to have a real campaign this spring to shove them together all I can. I know it'll work if"—her blue eyes met mine in unmistakable communication—"if there's nothing in the way."

I felt like saying, *Can't you keep him fenced in like the bull, or can he get the gates open by himself?* But I couldn't be annoyed. I could only admire the woman's dedication, and I understood it in a way; after all, I had my own dedication to a cause.

"I don't blame you for doing everything you can to secure his future," I said. (Yes, I actually said "secure.") She smiled radiantly at me, and in an instant of transfiguration I saw the young Katherine.

"You do have common sense, you see, and it's done me a

world of good to talk to you. I promise you I won't bother you this way again, but I was—oh, worked up today about one thing and another, and I can't blow off steam to Faye about some subjects."

Already having accomplished her mission, she saw no need to be gradual about departure.

"I'm glad if I was some help," I said demurely.

"There are times," she assured me, "when a good listener is the best help in the world." She stopped at the piano and looked at my music on the rack. "I'm so glad you're enjoying this. If you love music"—she turned that inwardly glowing look upon me again—"would you like to go to church with me this Sunday? Rory will be singing. That's one thing he does better than anybody else around here, and I can't help bragging."

I thought I wouldn't mention that I'd heard a little of that singing. And also that Rory had spoken as if he'd been serious about his singing once, if no longer. But perhaps she didn't know; often you confided in outsiders more than in your own people. And there was the delicate question hovering in space like a soap bubble: Had his mother *wanted* him to be serious about music, or just about the farm? That could have forced him to keep his dreams to himself.

"I'd love to go," I said. "I've never been inside one of those meeting houses."

"We redecorated the whole interior last year. I was on the committee." Of course she was. "It's too bad you missed Easter, but the music is always good. And not," she added with an unexpected twinkle, "just because Rory's in the choir."

# chapter 11

*I* stayed home all day Saturday, did my household chores, and worked on the manuscript. I was feeling a letdown after the strain and exhilaration of arrival and the first few days with their highs and lows.

In the afternoon I went walking, downhill along the brook bank through an alder swamp that soaked my sneakers, and where I saw jack-in-the-pulpit growing, a thick spatter of new violet plants pushing up through the wet mat of dead leaves, and tiny knobs of ferns starting. I found the trout pool, bypassed by the tumbling, rushing freshet. It was brimming golden-brown in the sunlight, almost black in the shadows. Red-winged blackbirds claimed the territory. I waited until I saw a trout snap at a floating insect and then walked back. Passing the cottage, I entered the cool aromatic shade of the spruce forest that climbed the hillside, and followed the brook up its stony, moss-bordered bed. This time when I came out someone was driving a tractor along a high ridge to the east. He wore no shirt, and his skin shone in the sun as if oiled.

Rory, I imagined. It would have been a more poetic sight if he'd been working with a couple of horses like the two I'd seen on the truck the other day. The Singing Plowboy. His mother was dreaming the impossible dream if she expected Miss Dairy Queen or whatever the title was to cut a permanent nick in that iron narcissism of his.

I walked home composing an earthy little drama. The chosen one would be invited for supper tonight and then Mother would say, "Why don't you two run along to the dance at the Grange Hall? I don't need you to keep me company. I'm going to spend a cozy evening curled up with the egg production records. . . . And if you really work at it, my dear, Rory will take you parking afterward, and with any luck you'll go home pregnant."

I fixed myself a large dinner, ate in front of the fireplace, then fell back in sottish luxury and tried to decide whether to lie by the fire and read until I was sleepy, or go to bed to read so I'd already be there when I felt myself sinking.

The sound of the brook masked other noises so I didn't realize a car had come down the lane until the lights shone in the end windows. Then they were switched off and a flashlight came bobbing across the lawn. *Rory?* I wondered with a mixture of dread and curiosity. After his mother's pitch I wanted nothing at all to do with him.

But when I opened the door Faye was there, and a stocky young towhead with a big smile and a musical Finnish name. They were all dressed up, and I couldn't tell which smelled the sweetest.

"I thought you might like to ride along with us to the dance tonight," Faye said. "You don't need to have a man of your own to take you, around here, and you wouldn't lack for partners."

"I'd love to go," I said truthfully. "When I get so I can stay up past nine o'clock without yawning my head off."

"Maybe next week then," said Faye. "My, you're real cozy down here, with your fire and all, and you've got the piano open, haven't you? Rory said you play. Could I hear you sometime?"

"Any time," I said.

"I'll take you up on that," she warned me, pointing a finger. "Leni and me both. Well, we're on our way, then."

"Thanks for the invitation," I said. "Wait a minute, tell me something. Where's the public library, *and* the high school?"

"No public library," Faye said. "The high school's in Fremont." She gave me brief, concise directions, then said bluntly, "Why?"

I was becoming entirely too good at giving plausible reasons. "I wanted to look at some reference books, and I thought they'd have some in the school library, if there's no public library. If I showed up with the proper introductions and so forth, will they let me use it?"

"Well, they should," Faye said. "The taxes Kitty pays, she ought to own half that school, and you're renting from her."

I went out onto the porch with them, thanking them again for the invitation to the dance. Halfway across the lawn Faye let out a piercing yelp. "Leni, you stop that! You might at least wait 'til we're in the car!"

Laughing, I went back inside to my fire, and having been shaken out of my grogginess I went to the piano and stumbled from memory through a couple of Chopin études. I was very bad. Back to Czerny tomorrow.

On Sunday morning, I dressed for church and walked up the lane. Only Kitty and the collie were home. "Rory went early, and Faye stays in town with her folks over Sundays. She's Advent, anyway. We're Baptists."

We didn't go to the church by the common, but to another one on a hilltop, the belfry aspiring to heaven and the bell ringing out over the countryside as we drove up. Cars parked in the yard where a flat slant of granite ledge showed through the worn turf. The cemetery sprawled beyond the church, a sunny place surrounded by shade trees, some of which already had their new leaves. I'd have rather stayed out there, reading the little stones in the old part of the cemetery, but I meekly followed in the wake of Kitty's discreet perfume as she progressed through the groups gathered around the steps. Occasionally I was introduced. I began to feel about ten years old, being taken in tow by a kind but authoritarian aunt.

Sunday school let out from the nearby parish house, and children were everywhere, exhilarated by the sunshine and mild air. The teachers, ranging from high-school age to the middle years, joined families or friends for the church service. One girl crossed the yard surrounded by her adoring class of little girls. She had the kind of healthy, sunny-blond good looks that everybody admires. She was a pleasure to watch, she seemed so happy.

Kitty's hand lay on my arm. "Eunice Parmenter," she murmured.

"Is she—?"

She nodded, her lips pressed together in a tight, triumphant smile.

The inside of the meeting house was airy and attractive in pale green and white, the carpeting and pew cushions dark red. Forced forsythia and Japanese quince blazed from the pulpit. A youngish man with sandy hair played Bach well on the small organ at the back of the raised choir loft. The minister, rangy in his billowing robe, his weathered face thatched with white hair, ascended the pulpit steps; the organist struck a commanding chord, doors opened, and the choir was coming in.

> *Holy, holy, holy, Lord God Almighty!*
> *Early in the morning our song shall rise to thee.*

And I was carried back, and singing my head off. Rory passed us, taller in the dark red robe than I remembered him. But the voice was the same, memory hadn't burnished it. The nape of my neck began to prickle again. I slid a sidewise glance at Kitty. She was staring straight ahead and singing hard, as if to even glance at her son would be to commit the sin of pride.

It was a good-sized choir for a small church, with as many men as there were women, and even a couple of excellent, strong basses. The one on the end, pacing alone, boomed out like one of those Russian specialties. He was a bearded monolith of a man, who looked about six foot seven in his robe.

I don't know when I had stopped believing in a personal God, but that had nothing to do with the way I sang the familiar hymns that morning. I *had* to put everything into it to try to compose myself, to keep from wondering if it was my mother's homesickness I was feeling. Where had her favorite seat been? Was she baptized here? Had she spoken pieces on Children's Day? Taken part in the Christmas pageant? Later practiced after school on the organ? And where was *he? Who* was he?

My back was sweating. I was appalled. I'd never fainted in my life, but I felt awful now. I looked out yearningly at the churchyard, wondering how quickly I could escape. Then like a soothing hand there was a familiar gentle introductory from the organ, and Rory stood up to sing the Offertory.

In the serene strength of Schubert's setting of the Twenty-third Psalm his voice flowed out into the church. I closed my eyes in instinctive self-defense and in greed too, not to let anything else interfere with the moment. Rory's voice became a series of images shimmering one into the other; a great bird gliding endlessly on the currents of air, like the gulls I'd seen yesterday; a stream rippling in calm beauty among the green pastures of Parmenter set in the blue rim of hills. The evening star, shining in the afterglow above the black pines like a message.

I didn't want the song to end.

When the last word was gone, and the organ finished as quietly as it had begun, I felt the slow cautious movements around me. Someone coughed, surreptitiously. Beside me, Mrs. Barstow stirred, I thought she sighed. I took a deep breath and opened my eyes. The minister was walking to the lectern.

The sermon was short, without pretensions of great erudition or inside information on world affairs. It was the message of a pastor to his flock. It was Communion Sunday and I left after the sermon, which wouldn't cause any interest because several other adults and some youngsters went out then too.

I walked around to the cemetery and strolled in the sun. A purple finch was singing with the same natural purity with which Rory had sung. I was still under the influence. No wonder Maggie Dundas had been excited. But I knew enough to separate the voice from the singer; I'd learned young about that, after a mad crush on a colleague of my mother's who played Chopin as I imagined Chopin must have played, directed a magnificent choral society, and turned out to be the first real lecher I'd ever met. A man might make the music, but music didn't make the man. I still saw Rory as a predator getting along on his looks and his talent, both of which were accidents of nature.

I wandered around reading inscriptions. No sense looking for Guilds; I'd already found out there weren't any Guilds here. But after what I'd felt back in the church, when I first went in, I couldn't doubt that this was Helen's territory. And if I believed that spirits walked I could believe that she was here, perhaps hoping that he too had returned, looking for her.

Well, it was a pretty little fantasy, and my mother would have been the first to laugh it out of existence.

Inside, the congregation broke fervently into *When Morning Gilds the Skies* and I walked back to the car. In a few minutes they began to come out. Nobody hurried in the warm noon. Little groups stood socially about, and I saw Miss Green Pastures with two other girls and a burly young man who'd been one of the ushers. Her hair blew lightly and gleaming.

Mrs. Barstow was crossing the yard with a big, fair, tweedy man. She looked very pleased with herself and the day. The man was grimly perturbed.

"You know what Tack's been through this year," he said.

"I gave him an extension, you know that. A generous one. Oh, there you are, Miriam!" She smiled at me. "Sam, come and meet my tenant. This is Sam Parmenter, Miriam... Miriam Guild."

"Hello." He gave me a choppy, distracted nod. He was angry, and determined to have his say. I turned tactfully away, and he said, "Why can't you give him six months more? See how he does with his blueberries? It's not like you needed the money——"

"How do you know what I need and don't need, Sam?" she asked softly.

"Dammit, Kitty——"

"*Sam!*" She was almost laughing. "Just out of *church?*"

I walked even farther away and studied the distant view.

Around me cars were leaving. Through the sound of engines I heard him say belligerently, "I suppose you're about to annex the Glidden place."

"My bid's as good as anyone else's, Sam. And so is yours. Are you doing anything about it?"

I turned around to drift back, trying not to be obvious, but saw in a glance that he was not so much angry now as speculative in the way he looked at her. "We don't need any more land," he said quietly. "I hear there's young folks interested in the Glidden Place. We need new blood around here, Kitty."

"Amateurs," she said with amused scorn. "They've got some romantic idea of living off the land. When they find out they can't even *begin* to put the place back into shape they'll be gone again. But they'll break the lake frontage up into cottage lots first, and they'll sell all the decent timber—Sam, that stand of beautiful pine!" Her voice softened. "Now don't you think one of us professionals ought to have the place?"

She had my vote, even if it was secret. Parmenter said curtly, "They can learn. There's too few young people interested in farming these days. Might be they'd do all right, and we need new blood, like I said."

"How old are Rory and Eunice? Going on ninety?"

"Good-bye, Kitty," he said formally. "Good-bye, Miss Guild." He strode toward a Thunderbird in which a woman sat waiting.

"Hello, Dora!" Mrs. Barstow called, waving. The woman smiled and waved back, brusquely interrupted by the abrupt departure of the car. Mrs. Barstow laughed and shook her head.

"Sam and I have been squabbling ever since we were kids," she said. "Whenever we have an argument—and that happens all the time—the years drop off us both. Sometimes I think he starts things on purpose."

I joined her laughter politely, but it didn't seem to me that Sam Parmenter had been merely indulging in a rejuvenating exercise.

As we drove out onto the black road I said, "I enjoyed the service."

"Wasn't that a beautiful thing that Rory sang? Of course he holds the choir together. I shouldn't say that, it infuriates him. There *are* a few others with half-decent voices. Oh, by the way, Eunice got up her courage and asked him home for Sunday dinner. He's so easy-going he couldn't refuse, so now it's up to her to make the most of the afternoon. She keeps saddle horses, and Rory likes to ride."

No wonder she was in such a luminous mood. The little chat with Sam Parmenter must have been the frosting on the cake.

"Sam's her uncle," she went on. "He runs Windhover Farm. Well, I should say they both run it, because Eunice is very good, and of course it's part hers. That was her mother in Sam's car. Dora. And a good name for her too," she added acidly. "She always reminds me of David Copperfield's child-bride, even now when she's been a widow almost as long as I have. Harry brought her home from somewhere like a re-triever bringing back a bird, dropped her in his folks' lap, and went off to get himself killed. When Sam came home from the service he took over running the farm from the old man. Now both the old people are dead, and Sam's stayed a bache-lor all these years."

"By his clothes and his car he looked like a swinging bache-lor," I said.

"Oh, Sam likes a good time still. It's a wonder nobody's caught him before this. But I'm sure he'd marry Dora like a shot if she'd have him. But no," she said sardonically, "she's the faithful widow of a dead hero, and she wouldn't shatter *that* picture for anyone."

She made a funny little snort, and I wanted to smile but didn't.

"Maybe she's still in love with her husband," I suggested, thinking *What about yourself?* Apparently there'd been no other man for her after Cleve Barstow.

"Oh, I know I sound like a shrew," she said ruefully. "Of course she could still be in love with him, or with his image, which probably isn't anywhere near the real Harry. I can't blame her for that." She concentrated on avoiding a stretch of road badly potholed. "Between frost and those pulpwood trucks of Dan Hall's, this road's about ruined. . . . It's just that Dora exasperates me so. Did you ever know anyone like that? Perfectly harmless, but they can make your hackles rise just by existing. She's so useless. She doesn't do one—darn—*thing*. I used to try to get her into things; but no go. I don't know how anyone can live like that, do you?"

"Well, yes," I said. "I mean, I couldn't, but I know some people can. It's a matter of metabolism, probably."

"That's just a fancy excuse, like people who say they can't help being fat, it's their glands, so they go on stuffing themselves. I take it back, there's one thing Dora Parmenter does to perfection. She makes believe the parlor at Windhover is a drawing room, and she pours tea. From her mother's heirloom silver, she claims."

We turned into the Fourleaf drive, and Fourleaf Apollo watched us from his field. Mrs. Barstow slowed the car to look at him; her expression was the same as when she had praised Rory's singing this morning. "He's been classified Excellent, you know," she said. "Officially. That's the highest rating given in type classification by the Holstein-Friesian Association. It means he's almost perfect in body conformation and coloring. There are a hundred points and he has over ninety."

"Even I can see that he's magnificent," I said, "and I don't know much about—uh—Holsteins."

She seemed pleased by that. We drove on toward the house. I'd worried about being invited for Sunday dinner, but it turned out that she never had big Sunday dinners, with Faye off on the weekends and the men off on Sundays until night. Today she was driving to Rockland to spend the afternoon with an old friend. I asked her if it would be safe for me to climb in the highest field I'd seen from the edge of the woods. "Apollo isn't likely to be up there, is he? Or any of the harem?"

"That's Bonfire Hill. No, you'll have the place to yourself," she said indulgently. "Just don't fall down in some God-forsaken corner and break a leg."

"Jason would have to come and find me," I said, scratching the collie's head. "You'd do that, wouldn't you, Jason?" He blinked amber eyes at me, tail slowly waving.

"Jason's been a great sheep dog in his time, but he never could double as a bloodhound, I'm afraid," she said. She looked affectionately down at the old dog. In the thin April sunlight softened by the branches of the maple trees she too was softened. As we stood by the doorstep she identified a birdcall for me, and pointed out the crocuses blooming in white, gold, and purple clumps under the windows.

"I love this house," she said unexpectedly. "I did long before I ever knew I'd be living in it some day. If Cleve'd had the handling of the place all these years, well—I don't know. That's why I worry about Rory."

There was nothing I could say, and I don't think she expected anything. But for the first time I was a little sorry for her, and the feeling stayed until I became absorbed in my own affairs that afternoon; they began with eating my lunch on the crest of Bonfire Hill.

# chapter 12

Monday morning was damp, raw, and gray. I found the district high school easily. It was new, one-storied, at least half windows, laid out amid playing fields and broad lawns spangled with young trees. There were few houses on this country road, but the place was encircled by a cycloramic view of meadows, dark woods, villages tucked away in cozy valleys, streams and lakes, and the encircling hills that seemed even more blue under a pewter sky.

It was lovely, but it was certainly not the high school my mother had attended. That was now the elementary school in Parmenter. Parking in the designated area, I had a chill in my stomach like the beginning of sickness. Surely they wouldn't be filing back copies *here* of yearbooks for Parmenter and the other towns in the district.

But I was here, so I went in. No one looked at me suspiciously. The girl in the outer office listened to me and said, "Why don't you talk to Mr. Davis about that?"

The principal was young and round-faced, with fluffy red sideburns I found almost endearing. He was not at all startled by my request to use the library, and he waved away my suggestion that Mrs. Barstow would vouch for me.

"This is unusual," he said, "but I don't think we're likely to start a dangerous precedent. I don't expect the civilians will be coming in droves wanting to use the library. We've had to brainwash most of the kids into it. What's your special interest? We're building up a good section on local history."

"Something like that," I said. "But you may not have what I'm looking for." I told him, and he tilted back in his chair and laughed.

"Do we have yearbooks! One old lady left us a bequest of Parmenter *Eagles* from 1884. Our kids find these fascinating, and so do I. Come on."

This first period there was nobody there but the librarian, a pleasant woman who found the Parmenter yearbooks for me and left me to myself at a table near the big windows. Outside it looked cold; in here there was modern heat and good lighting. The walls, drapes, and carpeting had the warm, subtle colorings that would come in early autumn to the world beyond the glass.

I held back from going straight to the 1938 issue. I leafed through some others, made meaningless notes, and decided what I would say if anyone pinned me down: I was making a study of rural high schools before and after World War II. The yearbooks would help me in one phase of the project.

Yes, that was very plausible. —Then, with a tremor in my hands, I picked out the copy of the Parmenter *Eagle* that should have had my mother in it. By some accident her picture might not have appeared; I had to recognize that fact.

Classes in the village high school had been small. Here were the graduates, twenty-seven of them. Except for the differences in hair styles, they looked like high school graduates at any time. Punctiliously I started at the beginning instead of scanning the faces in a sort of blind rush.

Katherine Adams led off, a lean girl with a pony tail, high cheekbones, and defiant eyes, refusing to smile for the photographer.

Cleveland Barstow appeared as a boy with dark crew-cut hair, freckles, and a broad grin. There was a ghostly resemblance to Rory which vanished if you tried to isolate it.

Ed Dunton wasn't there, but Reg of the gravel pit and the used cars was almost impossible to recognize in the big-eared knobby-chinned boy staring earnestly out at me.

I turned the page and there my mother was, in the photograph I knew so well. Nobody's mother then, but a child with a band holding back her hair smoothly from her clear wide forehead. Not a pretty girl, but not a plain girl either. Serious, contemplative, with an air of listening.

Helen Glidden.

*Helen Glidden.*

A name of this place; I'd already heard it in conversation. It clanged through my head like a bell, so loudly I could almost hear its echoes in the silent library. They made my head shiver and vibrate, or perhaps that was my speeded-up heartbeat. I had to hold myself in the chair, I wanted to spring up and run out of the library and go to Selma Hitchcock, to the insurance man, even to Reg Dunton, and challenge them. "I have roots here. I'm not just anybody, I'm somebody. You knew my mother. You must have known my father."

It was a queer thing that even in that clamorous moment of discovery I never thought of going to Mrs. Barstow. And after that first moment I didn't want to go to anyone else. It was too completely personal. Finding her name, finding *her*, was finding myself. Being born.

I sat very still, bent over the pages as if in deep study. The words on the page were all a shimmering confusion for a little while, then gradually they arranged themselves into intelligible sequences. So did my ideas. I looked for Fern and found Fern Osblom, a round pretty face with dimples and curly bangs, delighted with the occasion.

Harry Parmenter followed her, a good-looking blond boy. Serious, at least for that moment. I could see Eunice in him.

I studied the other boys in the class, wondering if my father was among them. Sometimes I thought I saw a resemblance to me, but it never held up when I came back to it a second time. Of course he needn't have been in that class, he could have been an earlier graduate, or he needn't have gone to Parmenter High at all. Maybe he'd gone away to school.

There were group photographs of the class officers, clubs, committees, the Student Council, the cast of *The Mikado* in which Cleve Barstow was an impish Nanki-Poo and Helen Glidden was one of the accompanists. Harry Parmenter was president of the senior class. Kitty was captain of the girls' basketball team. Fern was listed as one of the girls who'd made costumes for the operetta. Reg Dunton played baseball, football, and basketball. None of the boys belonged to the Chess Club. Helen belonged to the French Club and they'd spent a weekend in Montreal. In April of their last year, the entire senior class went to Washington.

Wishing I could be crooked enough to steal this issue of the *Eagle*, I put it aside reluctantly. After all, 1938 wasn't the crucial year for Helen Glidden, my father, and myself. I wouldn't be conceived until four years later.

I thanked the librarian for her cooperation and left. The principal was out of his office, at some far-flung spot in the school, so I left my thanks with his secretary.

I drove out of the school grounds and back toward Parmenter. Where had I heard the name Glidden, and how? Concentrating on that, I had a rough ride over frost heaves and into potholes. My little car wasn't going to hold together through much of that, so I tried to put my mind on my driving. I went down a long hill in a kind of slalom, and was blasted over to the side of the road by the horn of a dark green Thunderbird that rushed by me and disappeared over the next rise.

It looked like Sam Parmenter's car, and then I remembered. *I suppose you're about to annex the Glidden place.*

*My bid's as good as anyone else's, Sam.*

This Glidden place didn't need to have any connection with my mother. But I could go and look at it, couldn't I? I might recognize a building from the snapshots. Then I would have not only a name, but a tangible background. After that I would decide whom to ask about my father.

I drove into town and parked beside the common, and went into Wyatt's. Two women coming out smiled and said "Good morning" and went their way. Otherwise it was one of those lulls when for a few minutes the place seemed either spellbound or deserted; silent except for the loud whistling of blackbirds in the elms.

"Hi, there!" Mr. O'Brien greeted me. "You discouraged by the weather yet?"

"Nope!" I picked out a Hershey bar and paid him for it.

"Might snow tonight," he warned me.

"Who cares?" I took a bite of my chocolate bar. "I'd like it. I've never been in the country in a snowstorm."

"Well, I can see it's no use trying to plague you." He began putting packages of sugar on a shelf behind the counter.

"Do you know where the Glidden place is?" I asked.

"You interested?" He whisked around, alert as a robin.

"Not to buy, just to look at. I heard Mrs. Barstow talking about it."

"Oh sure. Kitty Barstow." His mouth quirked up at one corner but was quickly subdued. "She'd be bidding for it, sure."

"Who's selling the place? The heirs?"

"No heirs that anybody knows of. Looks like the last Glidden died about ten years ago."

Not my grandfather; my mother told me that when she finally left home both grandparents were gone, and she had signed over her portion to an uncle.

"Old Dick wasn't quite right in the head," Mr. O'Brien mused. "Never was, they say, from the time he was a baby. But he was a good and harmless soul. He inherited the place from a cousin, but after he set himself and it afire a couple of times the town stepped in and boarded him out with some decent folks. He was pretty happy the last few years, I guess."

"And he didn't have any heirs?"

"No, and he died without a will. Seems as if there was somebody who went away years ago, and the town's waited all this time for them to show up, but this last town meeting we got a couple new selectmen in, and they decided to put the place up for bids. In the old days, you could buy a place for the taxes due on it, but with what land's going for now they thought they could do a little better than that. . . . In the meantime they've been advertising the sale in the newspapers in Boston. Portland—Bangor too, I guess—just in case there *is* someone with a claim, but—" He shrugged and turned down the corners of his mouth. "I doubt if there is anybody."

"It doesn't seem likely," I said. I was glad to have the chocolate to eat, to cover up my nervousness. I couldn't even taste it, but I made it last as if I were savoring every tiny crumb. I kept warning myself, *It doesn't have to mean anything. It probably doesn't.*

"Speaking frankly, I'd like to see somebody else besides Kitty get it," said O'Brien, "and I'd just as soon say it to Kitty myself."

"Well, I wouldn't be talking to her about it anyway," I said. "She'd probably offer to take me, and I'd like to explore on my own, and not take up anybody else's time. Is it all right for me to go there, do you think?"

"Sure it is. Good Lord, the lovers have been taking it over for years, and kids go down and camp on the lake shore, and folks picnic there. You go right ahead." He drew a rough map for me on a paper bag.

When I went out, I walked across the common and looked at the Honor Roll again. I skipped over Parmenter and Dunton and concentrated on Jonas Moore, Toivo Laaka, and Robert Rollins. Moore and Laaka were names that came up several times in the yearbook. But not Rollins.

Where had Robert Rollins come from, to become one of Parmenter's soldiers? What was his work?

By now I should have been used to the physical manifestations, but always they struck me a weakening blow.

No sense going back to O'Brien; he wasn't here in the war years. I felt too feeble-minded at the moment to go on making up lies to cover my questions, and I knew that in the gray dank day I didn't want to look for the Glidden place, I was in no condition for ghosts; I'd spent the morning with those heartbreaking young ones in the yearbook, and I wanted warmth and comfort. Lacking a security blanket, I had a fireplace and a piano, and Andric's manuscript.

There was no one around the big house as I drove by. I

returned to the brook with a real sense of homecoming and stood listening to its multiple voices for a few minutes before I went in to my hearth.

No one came near me that afternoon, and I was glad of that. I was tired with a sort of finality. The search was almost over. It remained for me to take the last step, to tell who I was and ask *Who was my father?* Someone must have guessed, suspected, surmised. In such a small town it would have been impossible to carry on a secret love affair, especially one with such a result.

And now I wondered why I had been under such a compulsion. When I found out who he was—so what? Would I be any different, in myself, for knowing the name of a dead man? Would it make me someone other than Miriam Guild, to know whose genes and chromosomes I carried besides Helen Glidden's? Would I be pierced with rejoicing or regret? Or would there be just this nothingness I felt now?

My mother hadn't wanted me to know any more than she'd told me. I was the child playing with forbidden matches. But I had a choice: I could still stop before the flames flashed alive and devoured me.

Tomorrow I will decide, I thought, and I got up and went to the piano, and began to work.

# chapter 13

When I woke up in the morning the decision was made. Bright sun was cutting in through the eastern treetops, a woodpecker was tapping away on an old wild apple tree at the edge of the woods, and I knew I was going to find the Glidden place. I remembered yesterday's misgivings only briefly, and with distaste. I would go to see the place; it could do no harm, whether she'd lived there or not. I might *feel* something—

I could hardly wait to get started, and ate a sketchy breakfast. The car started with enthusiasm, and we were off.

Out on the main road I turned in the opposite direction from the way to town, and about a mile away I found the four corners Mr. O'Brien had marked, and the signs. One pointed south to Fremont, and I followed this. There were a few small places set in little clearings cut out of the spruce forest. Eventually I came to the cleared land and beautifully kept-up buildings of Seven Chimneys Farm, which was marked on the map. The white house with its many gables carried seven white-washed chimneys, I slowed down and counted them. A couple of small children rode tricycles on the black-topped driveway, watched by a German shepherd. They waved ardently at me and I waved back.

What did my place look like? I wondered as I drove on. Not kept up, of course, because it had been empty for so long. But how many chimneys, and how big a barn? Maybe it wasn't my place; I'd better stop thinking that.

I was watching for a turn-off to the left about a mile beyond Seven Chimneys, and I almost missed it, the trees and bushes were so thick. They brushed against the car on both sides, but the ruts were dry and the little car was valiant.

One of Old Dick's fires must have succeeded. Even cellar holes overgrown for decades would have been better than charred ruins. The sun that had cast glory on Fourleaf and Seven Chimneys spared me no wretched detail. —I remember seeing through blurred eyes that the big pines were there beyond an aldergrown pasture climbing a rise to the southwest, their needles glinting in the sun. I could hear the wind blowing through them like surf. I tried to say to myself, *I should find the way to the lake.* But I couldn't make myself move past the two elms that guarded the débris. I leaned my trembling body against a tree and shut my eyes.

If a voice out of a whirlwind had suddenly commanded "Seek no more," I wouldn't have been surprised. Finally I pushed myself away from the elm, and walked slowly forward. The chimneys still stood. Three. The barn had been a big one, from the size of the heap of rubble. A couple of small sheds that might have been chicken houses had escaped the fire. They looked as if they were sinking into the ground, they were so grown over.

The front doorstep was built from two slabs of dressed granite. Grass and soil had come halfway up the lower one. I sat down, feeling half-stunned. Yesterday's reaction was nothing compared to this one. I looked around me in a daze at the bare elms against the sky; at the woods through which I'd driven, at the winter-flattened overgrown grass of the once-lawn. And then, beside the granite on which I sat, I saw the flat green blades of new iris poking up from last year's sodden tangle.

Suddenly I had a picture of the iris blooming here year after year with no one knowing, except someone who came casually by on the way to the lake. But who would even glance at the house any more, now that there was nothing left to salvage? Year after year they grew, and multiplied, and bloomed purple and blue and gold, and no one cared.

But once a girl named Helen Glidden must have cut them and carried them into the house to arrange; a woman named Helen Guild had planted iris in a suburban yard. "I have to have iris," she said, allowing me my tulips. "Plain, old-fashioned iris, no fancy hybrids. We always had them."

I burst into tears, not for her, not for myself, but because of the flowers blooming on and on when everybody was dead.

I gave in to weeping as if it had been held back for years, and perhaps it had. It came up from my toes, wrenching at me all the way. My chest felt torn and my throat ached. I heard the noises I made, but there was no one else to hear them. The crows might have been curious, but the iris were certainly oblivious. I let myself go because there was nothing else left. I was at the bottom and now it seemed as if I'd been on the downhill slide for half my lifetime. And I didn't care; I was totally abandoned, groveling in woe.

Something struck my bowed head, lightly but enough to startle me even in my disgusting state. I caught my breath, then decided some chip or twig or charred fragment worn loose by the wind had dropped on me. But it was enough to jolt me out of the wallow. I looked around with wet blurred eyes, feeling in all my pockets for a handkerchief, and saw a figure before me.

It was an insubstantial dazzle, but still unmistakably there. Not a ghost. I was too wrung out to be afraid. Drearily I tried to rub my eyes clear and find out who'd witnessed my degradation.

"I didn't want to scare you," Rory said apologetically. "So I threw a spruce cone. It was supposed to land beside you, not on your head."

"What are *you* doing here?" I was too sodden to be crisp. It came out as a sort of adenoidal wail. "You're supposed to be farming." It was too much. "Can't I—can't I—" Whatever it was, I couldn't even say it. I wept again.

He moved fast and sat down beside me, put his arms around me, rocking me against his chest, murmuring, soothing. *He's very good with animals,* his mother had said. I wanted to ask him if he used this tone in calming and encouraging cows giving birth. This was all in one part of my mind while the rest flagrantly appreciated the comfort offered. I could not remember ever being held by a man while I wept, and this was another way I had been cheated out of not having a father.

This was the precise moment when I began to think of Rory Barstow as a man.

"What's the matter, Miriam?" he said against my temple. "What did you come way out here for? Tell me. If you've got some kind of trouble I'll do anything I can."

"I don't suppose you've got a handkerchief," I said thickly. He did, and it was clean. After I'd stopped snuffling and gasping, my embarrassment was profound. Every explanation I thought of sounded foolish or downright psychotic, and I wanted to cry again from self-pity. All the time he kept one arm around me and maintained a serious and sympathetic silence.

He was of my generation; we had that much in common, and I wanted to tell someone so I wouldn't feel so alone. So I told Rory. He didn't interrupt. When I finished he tightened his arm and said, "You poor kid."

"For heaven's sake, don't pity me," I said, "or I'll dissolve altogether. And it's so foolish. I'm no worse off than I was before. I simply thought if I came to Parmenter and saw where my mother lived and grew up, and found out who my father was, it would complete something for me, and I could stop thinking about it. I didn't expect all these emotional complications on the way. I mean, I thought I'd keep my cool no matter what."

He spared me any kindly masculine explanations of the feminine psyche. "Didn't she tell you anything at all that would give you a clue?"

"Only that he died in the war, and that she knew him here . . . in Parmenter. And I think this is the farm, because of the iris. Oh yes—I just remembered—I think I saw the pines in a photograph, behind the house."

He rubbed his chin thoughtfully, contemplating me with those dark blue eyes. "Well, look, if you identified yourself to just about anybody her age, they might be able to tell you something. What about my mother? You say she was in the old snapshots."

"No!" It was instinctive, and startled us both. "Not yet," I qualified it. "Look, I could make real trouble for someone. He must have been married already, that would be the only reason he couldn't marry her. So there may be people around town who'd be affected in some way. And what if he isn't dead? He might have been listed as missing, and then came back home. He could be living here now, and he wouldn't be at all overjoyed to meet his illegitimate daughter."

"Come on, let's get out of here." He stood up and hauled me up with him. "There's nothing makes me feel worse than what's left of a burned-out house. We'll walk down to the lake."

We walked around the ruins and along a well-worn track through the alders toward the pine grove. Soon we were in its cold shadow with the wind blowing above our heads and scattering flakes of sunlight over us. We went up a slight rise on damp red-brown needles, then the path tilted gently downward and at the end was the azure sparkle of the lake.

At least it was an azure sparkle where the ice had gone. There were still great pale translucent floes and patches. "It will go all at once," he said. "You think it'll never melt and then suddenly it's not there."

I couldn't think of anything to say, and he didn't seem to expect anything. We walked along the narrow rim of sand between lake and pines, and he went on talking about the lake; the loons who lived on it, the ducks and geese that stopped on their migration, the deer he had seen drinking at dawn, a moose family feeding in the shallows. It was tranquilizing; I could feel the storm ebbing away from me.

When we came out where the sun could strike us, wonderfully bright and warming, we sat down on a boulder. There was a small patch of open water here and the ice was jade green.

"Are we still on Glidden land?" I asked.

"No, this belongs to Seven Chimneys, the Rollinses."

I must have made some quick movement, because he said, "What's the matter?"

"I wondered about Robert Rollins, that's all. But I'm not going to think about it any more!" I said angrily. "I'm done with it. *Period*."

"Look," he said, "I might have known my father's name, but I never knew him, and I've missed him like hell all my life."

"Oh, I know I sound self-centered," I said, "but I've thought about one thing for so long that the withdrawal symptoms are something fierce. I'll survive. I guess it's pretty awful for a boy to grow up without a father."

"And to be grown-up without one," he said with a grimness that put years on him. "After having been told every day of your life as long as you can remember that everything is done for *you*, that *you* are her sole reason for carrying on, and that it's supposed to work both ways. My God, I used to pray for her to get married again, but she wouldn't look at another man."

"Because she was still in love with your father," I suggested. "Mine was until the day she died. But she always expected me to make my own life. And her work was her own world, I wasn't involved with it as you are with the farm. But I have to say, to be completely fair, that if you've been made to feel responsible for your mother she's probably always felt the same way about you." I remembered the way she'd talked about him that day.

"But listen—and I don't usually grouse on like this, but you told me what your hang-up is, so maybe you can understand mine—put yourself in my place; be young Rory, rarin' to go, and hear someone say to your mother, 'Kitty, you're still young, you're attractive, why don't you look around you, or at least go out with somebody now and then?' And hear her say, 'I don't need anyone; I've got Rory.' And Rory's heart falls into his boots." I saw sweat on his forehead, and it wasn't that warm. This was really an emotional concern with him.

"Maybe she thought you'd resent another man being brought in."

"Hey, be a little biased, huh? Just to make me feel good?" He grinned. "Look, I used to try to rig things up to get her interested. She knew it. But she didn't want any man to help her either with raising me or running the farm; she didn't want any man telling her. I was her *little* man, so she could tell *me*." He shrugged and spread out his hands. "So where does that leave us now?"

I could have told him, but he probably knew. At Eunice Parmenter's gate. I wondered how soon he'd accept the inevitable, and marry the girl.

"I'm sorry," I said. "Sorry for her, building so much around you, and sorry for you with all that weight on your shoulders. But she seems like such an intelligent woman—couldn't you have a talk with her, person-to-person instead of son-to-mother?"

"No matter who it is, it's always person-to-Kitty." He got up and walked restlessly around on the sand. "I'm beginning to think that life with your mother wasn't only good, but simple. You were lucky."

"I know that. I'm knowing it more all the time. That's why I'm going to leave well enough alone, to coin a phrase." I got up off the rock. "My feet are cold and I'm so hungry I can't stand it."

He linked arms with me as we started back. "Thanks for listening to me. I've never said that much before and I probably won't again," he said.

"Thank *you* for listening to me. You're absolutely the only other person in the world who knows what I told you."

He laced his fingers through mine and squeezed gently. "Unless your father's still alive and knows you were born."

"He might not know. Maybe she never told him, if she thought he had burdens enough."

"I can imagine your being like that," he said seriously. "Proud and honorable."

To say thanks would have been either cynical or coy, but I was touched just the same. And I thought how much more I knew of him now, since the first day. I knew that he was kind and sympathetic, and also that he was living under a strain which his mother didn't see; she saw him as a cheerful type who never worried about anything. It was as if he wore his easy manner as a disguise.

We came back to the burned ruins, now in full sunshine that made them all the more stark and tragic. A song sparrow sang steadily from a broken beam. Something whisked off into the woods on the far side of the clearing and I caught a glimpse of glowing auburn.

"A fox," Rory said.

"Oh, where'd he go?"

Rory said, "He's long gone.... This is your place, you know. You must be Dick Glidden's heir. The last Glidden of that line."

"*This?*" I said stupidly.

"Not just a pile of cinders," he said. "But about two hundred and fifty acres of pine grove, some lake shore, and a lot of overgrown pasture and blueberry land."

"But I never thought of that," I said.

"It's valuable enough so my mother wants it."

"I'm not thinking of value." I wasn't. "I'm just thinking of me owning anything. This ground I'm standing on. Those elm trees."

"The iris," he said.

I laughed foolishly. "Yes, the iris. And maybe that fox's burrow."

"A perfectly good barn cellar, a pigpen and a chicken house full of spiders, and hey! deer droppings under the apple trees. Woman, you're *rich!*"

I clasped my hands against my breast. "Oh, never in my wildest dreams did I ever expect to be owning deer droppings!"

"*Glidden* deer droppings."

"Yes." I couldn't laugh any more. Glidden ground. Where

Helen Glidden had walked. I stared around me through a haze of wonder that even took the cruelty off the burned site.

"Are you going to claim it?" Rory asked.

Still preoccupied I said absently, "I told you I wasn't going to make waves. Let sleeping dogs lie, let the dead bury the dead, and any other cliché you can add to that." It was too wrenchingly private here; I wished him out of sight but of course wishing wouldn't make it so.

"You don't have to make waves," he was saying. "You're Miriam *Guild*. Half the people who remember Helen Glidden will think she married and had you, and anybody who knows the truth can't be sure whether you're that child or not. And suppose they *do* think it's you?" He took me by the elbows and shook me gently. "Sure, they'll be interested and curious, some of them, but nobody's going to run around saying, 'Don't speak to her, she's a child of shame.' Nobody's going to burn a fiery cross on your doorstep. My mother won't evict you. People will say hello just the same when they meet you. And, if you don't make an issue of finding out who your father was, anybody who knows the truth can keep quiet— including him. See how easy it is?" He tightened his fingers. "Miriam, if you go away from here without making a move, you'll be sorry for the rest of your life. And so will I."

There was a profound sincerity about it that reached me even in my new chaos.

"Why you?" I asked.

"Because I don't want to lose you before I've even known you. Haven't you ever felt like that about anyone? —I'm not making a pass at you, Miriam."

I looked away from him at the ruins and said, "If I *am* the one, what would I do with it? Hold two hundred and fifty acres for sentimental reasons, when somebody else could make them productive? You and your mother, for instance."

He grinned and shook his head. "Leave me out of it, it's my mother who grabs everything she can get her hands on. I think we've got plenty." He spoke seriously. "You could make it productive, Miriam. Sell some woodlot, or a couple of house lots, and then you can have a small place built here for yourself on the cellar of the old house. I know at least two men who'd clean up and burn off the blueberry land for the next year's berries, and after that they'd pay you for the crop. You could tree-farm. You could rent the house and have a camp at the lake for yourself, or build a couple of cottages and rent those. You'd make enough to keep the taxes and insurance paid up, anyway."

"You're going too fast," I protested. "I've got too many things to think about."

"Then think about them," he urged. "Go on home and make a pot of coffee, and put your feet up and *think*. And what's wrong with sentiment, huh?"

"I was thinking of wasting the land. Sam Parmenter mentioned some young people interested in farming it."

"You see, you've got land in your blood, and you didn't even know it!"

"Is land in your blood worse than sugar? Sounds sludgy to me."

"What a rotten sense of humor," he said admiringly.

It was a good way to leave. We turned the car and the pick-up truck around on a dry hard area of the dooryard, then he drove out and I followed him. I felt so strange driving back to Fourleaf. Everything I had seen on the way here was now illumined with a different light that had nothing to do with the hour of the day. I had seen the fox, smelled the sweetness of new grass, seen the pines seething silver in the wind. . . . Seen the charred relics of disaster too, but sat on the granite doorstep and discovered the iris.

# chapter 14

W hen he approached the house, Rory stopped the truck, which stopped me. He got out and came back to me. "Ever seen a brand-new lamb?" he asked. "Or one about twenty-four hours old?"

"Only in pictures," I said.

"Come in and see one. She's one of triplets and the ewe won't own her. Happens every year."

"Do I look all right?"

"Great. Not a trace of tears." I left my car and rode around to the back of the house with him. A robin's-egg-blue Volkswagen was sitting in the driveway, and when he pulled up behind it he sat there for a moment, regarding it with a curious blankness that could have masked resignation, exasperation, or even pleasure, for all I could tell.

"You've already got company," I said. "I can see the lamb later."

"One of the neighbors, not company," he said shortly. "Come on." Jason came to meet us, and went into the house ahead of us, directly across the kitchen to a large carton set in a corner near the stove. He stood looking into it and wagging his tail in gentle undulations.

Only Faye was in the room, rolling out piecrust. "Well, look who's here!" she said loudly, and gave me a tremendous burlesque of a wink. "Where'd you meet up with that character?"

"Are you asking him or me?" I said.

"She's asking you," Rory said. "Around these parts I'm known—disapprovingly—as the Playboy of the Western World, or its Parmenter equivalent."

"Now, Rory, *I* don't disapprove of you," said Faye.

"Does that mean we're engaged?" He swept her into his arms.

She let out a yelp. "Mind my piecrust!"

"If it's only your piecrust you're worried about, not your virtue—"

Mrs. Barstow appeared in the office doorway. She smiled indulgently at Rory and Faye, and said to me, "Where *did* you run into that character this morning?"

"Out front," I said ambiguously, and quickly enough to surprise even me. "And he told me about the lamb."

Eunice Parmenter joined Mrs. Barstow in the doorway. "Good morning, Eunice," Rory said with one arm still around Faye. "If you came to ask for my hand, you're too late."

"I can see that. And to think I never guessed." Her amused smile included me.

Rory said, "Faye, what do you and Leni do when you're alone?"

"Play cribbage, what else?" Faye burst out laughing. Rory grinned, kissed her cheek, and released her.

"Rory's really the incarnation of a flea, you know," Mrs. Barstow said to me. "Now you see him, now you don't. I thought he was in the sheep barn, but he'd disappeared completely, truck and all. Next time I see him he's in the kitchen trying to seduce Faye."

"What do you mean, *trying?*" protested Rory. "She's already mine, all mine. Eunice, this is Miriam Guild. Miriam, Eunice Parmenter of the town of the same name. She owns it."

"Hello, Miriam," Eunice said. "I saw you at a distance last Sunday."

"I saw you too. Hello, Eunice. I never knew anybody before that owned a town."

"It was named after my great-great-great-grandfather, that's all."

There were tiny bleatings from the carton and Jason made a faint whining sound and looked appealingly around. "It's time for her feeding," Mrs. Barstow said. "I'll warm the bottle."

"Come on," Rory said to me. We went to the corner and leaned over the box. He lifted out the leggy little black creature, watched intently by Jason. I was unprepared for the tenderness the scene aroused in me, not only because of the lamb's helplessness but the dog's concern and the way the man's hands held the small body reassuringly against his own. I handled a miniature hoof, stroked the head, had my fingers nuzzled, felt the little puffs of warm breath from the infant nostrils.

For a moment it was as if Rory and I, the lamb, and the dog pushing his head in between us were alone in the room. Not quite in the room: In some fifth-dimensional, time-traveling way we were back at the Glidden place.

"Eunice is going to feed her." Mrs. Barstow's voice seemed unnaturally loud and jolly. At sight of the nursing bottle in Eunice's hand the lamb cried out and wriggled in Rory's arms. He went down on his heels and set the lamb on its feet on a square of old shag rug. Hungrily it fastened onto the nipple and began to suck, legs braced and tail wagging.

"I never get tired of watching that," Faye said, stopping her work. Eunice wore an expression of maternal tenderness; Rory, still hunkered down, said, "Pull for the shore, sailor." His mother, leaning against the work counter, had a softened look, but whether it was for the lamb or for Rory and Eunice so close there was no way of guessing, until she glanced over at me and then I knew what I was supposed to see and comprehend too.

Some until-now-unknown perversity arose at once in me and I gave her a bright, brainless grin and said, "What's her name?"

"Oh, Dora will name her," she said. "Eunice is taking her as a gift for her mother."

"She always wanted one," Eunice said. Even seen close she was an extremely pretty girl, with a glowing skin and the little light freckling that does actually look like sprinkles of gold. "I expect this one'll be a nuisance after a while, a cosset lamb always is, but my mother will love that. She should have had about ten kids after me, so she'd have young ones now." She looked back at the fiercely sucking lamb. "We don't have sheep, and every spring whenever we'd drive by a field with the ewes and lambs, she'd wish for one. She'd be crazy about any lamb, but a black one will send her."

"It's time the Parmenters had a black sheep in the flock," said Rory. Kitty made an exasperated sound, but Eunice laughed. "We *are* a dull bunch, aren't we? Damnably virtuous, Uncle Sam says."

"Doing his best to correct the impression," said Mrs. Barstow.

"Sam's a swinger, or thinks he is," said Rory. "Hey, leave a little milk and let Miriam feed her. She's never been this close to a new lamb before, let alone feed it."

"There'll be other feedings before she goes," his mother began, but Eunice had already put the bottle in my hand and moved out of the way.

"Sit here, Miriam," she said. The lamb grabbed at the nipple and I forgot all about the undercurrents, if indeed there had been any. Later I doubted there had been. When the lamb was back in her box, drugged with warm formula, I said I was going home. Mrs. Barstow urged me to stay for coffee before Rory could. Eunice began asking me about my job while she took mugs out of the cupboard. Faye got her pies into the oven and cut a coffee cake into large squares. Three men came in from work smelling of hay and animals: Leni, the taciturn Ruel, and a long-haired youth with an Indian band around his forehead.

He immediately said to Rory, "Where'd you vanish to? Went out of sight like one of them genies."

"That's me," said Rory, "Genie with the dark brown hair."

Kitty Barstow having coffee at the long trestle table with her hired men: I remember her like that as strongly as I remember the other brilliant facets of this diamond. Elegantly

lean in her tailored slacks, bright stones in her ears, lipstick
fresh, she carried on a highly technical discussion with Ruel
about a new type of spray for the orchard, the pros and cons
of a certain antibiotic for the cattle, and the possible merits of
organic feeding.

Ruel was no longer taciturn but extremely knowledgeable,
Eunice put in a comment or question now and then; Leni sat
next to Faye and said not a word, just grinned broadly most
of the time. Rory and I and Tip, the long-haired boy, talked
together, at least Tip talked, asking me questions and studying
me with a curiosity too candid to be annoying. When he
asked me how old I was, Rory said, "You doing an interview
for the *County Clarion*, Tip?"

"Nope, just interested, that's all. How old *are* you, Miriam?"

"Twenty-four."

"That old, huh?" Tip looked bemused.

Rory and Faye burst out laughing. The others looked
around from their end of the table.

"Yeah, she's too old for you, kid," said Rory. "She could
be your mother."

"I like older women," said Tip seriously.

"Time you went back to the barn," said Ruel. "Hard
work's the cure for what ails you, sonny."

"Who said I wanted to be cured?" Tip inquired. "So long,
Miriam," he said to me. "See you."

"See you," I said, lifting my hand.

When the men had gone out Mrs. Barstow said, "If Tip
does show up, just tell him to go away. He won't have time
during his work day, but he might decide to come calling in
his spare time, and he could be a nuisance."

"I wouldn't want to hurt his feelings," I said.

"That's impossible," said Rory, getting up to follow the
men out. "We've all tried it."

"You and Eunice ought to gather up some of the men who
must be dying to meet Miriam by now," his mother said.

"But how many of them would Miriam be dying to meet?"
asked Rory.

"Well, there's Sandy," said Eunice. "He's musical, so at least they'd have that in common ... Look," she said eagerly, "let's get together next Sunday afternoon over at my house. We can go riding if it's fit, or——"

I raised my hand. "The one time I tried to ride, my horse kept trying to scrape me off on a tree. I've had a block about riding ever since. Sorry," I said apologetically.

"Don't apologize, for heaven's sake," said Eunice. "I've had a block about New York ever since the last time I was there, and you've got the courage to *live* there."

"Not all that much courage. I'm scared to go out alone at night."

"How about a hike up Revelation Mountain?" asked Rory. "That's where Moses Parmenter received the Ten Commandments," he said to me. "Then he founded the town."

"Oh, you're just jealous because Peter Barstow didn't get here first," said Eunice. "How about it, Miriam? Are you a good walker? It's not a real mountain."

"I'm a marvelous walker," I said, suddenly feeling marvelous. Whether it was natural resilience bouncing me back after the early upset, or the result of warm food—I always did respond to that—or the charm of the hungry black lamb, or just the aura of good fellowship in the kitchen, I didn't know. But I decided to leave while I was ahead.

I took a walk downstream, and sat down by the dark glass of the trout pool to begin wondering how I could put in a claim for the Glidden place. At this point it was all hypothetical. I couldn't imagine myself possessing it; I couldn't really believe, when it came to that, that I had a right to it. But I wouldn't know until I asked, so how could I prove who I was, just in case I did ask? ... Not that I was going to.

First, I'd have to prove that my mother was Helen Glidden. For that I would have to send to City Hall in Boston for my birth certificate. Even if she had called herself Mrs. Guild back then, her maiden name should appear. I'd never thought of that before.

I had the albums of photographs, one of her graduation pictures, and the impeccable witnesses from our town in Connecticut to swear that the Helen Guild they'd known was the Helen of the photographs. She had told me about making her share of the place over to her uncle, so that should be recorded in the county registry of deeds, along with her signature.

Sitting on a boulder by the trout pool, I watched the morning's events as if on a private screen inside my brain. Then, just in case I was being too sentimental, I thought quite cold-bloodedly of land values today; perhaps I'd be a fool not to claim what was my own and then sell it to the highest bidder. How much would Kitty Barstow be ready to offer, anyway? How rich was she? Or was she actually land-poor? Maybe accumulating more land was her addiction.

I drove to the village and from the telephone booth outside Wyatt's I called City Hall in Boston to ask how much money I should send for a copy of my birth certificate. While I was talking, Eunice came out of the post office. She stopped to pat a Labrador on the steps and spoke to a girl with a baby carriage. She bent over to talk to the baby.

I liked her. I didn't blame Kitty Barstow for wanting her for Rory. But Rory was struggling, and what I'd seen could have been only the tip of the iceberg. He had called me free, and I, looking for my ghosts, hadn't believed him. But now I did. I was free to move, to choose, without hurting anyone but myself if the move or the choice were wrong.

I knew better than to attempt instant analysis. But the sweat on his forehead hadn't been theory. It had been real, whatever its cause.

# chapter 15

In the morning I woke up with the fixed idea of going to the Glidden place again. This time I'd be prepared for the fire, and also for the iris. I wanted to walk over the same ground with some sort of objectivity. —I took an apple and some crackers and cheese. If I was lucky, Rory wouldn't see me drive by; besides, he couldn't very well disappear from his work two days in a row. Or maybe he could; maybe that was just one of the things that bothered his mother.

Anyway, I'd been grateful for, and had even enjoyed, his solace yesterday, but that was in the past. Today the desolation was gone, and so also was my pleasing picture of myself being calmly objective, because yesterday I'd missed the size of the buds on the lilacs, and a bright yellow dandelion blooming in a pocket of warmth. The song sparrow was back. I found daffodils coming up beyond the iris, and spent a happy half-hour digging around with my bare hands. I went down to the henhouse huddling beneath apple trees, found it whole and wondered how anybody would get the ineffable aroma of hen out of it, just in case anybody wanted to camp out in it. *Just in case.* The way I wanted my birth certificate.

I walked down to the lake. The air was much warmer than yesterday, and among the shrinking ice patches the water was a twinkling sapphire. More birds must have arrived from the south; there was a good deal more singing. I walked around the shore to the sunny patch of beach where we'd sat yesterday. Our footprints led the way, since there was no tide to erase them.

Eating my crackers and cheese with slices of apple, I tried to be hard-headed and realistic. *If I'm going to do anything about this*, I thought, *I'd better do it soon.*

I used up several hours all in all, first awed by this pure solitude and then savoring it like a gourmet. What infinite privilege to move through time and elegant space and silence, enhanced rather than marred by the sounds of nature; to be unafraid; to know beyond a doubt that nothing could harm me here; that if there were ghosts they were mine, and that I loved them.

When I returned to the cellar holes, I picked up some rotting wood in the grass and made a tidy heap of it, collected broken branches for another pile. I sat on the doorstep a while, and left reluctantly when there was nothing else I could do around the place.

When I got back to the farm, the mail driver had just stopped at the box, and handed the mail to me. It was all for the main house, so I had to stop there even though I'd planned to go straight down to the cottage and get to work.

I went around to the back door. No Jason this morning, and the animal and poultry voices were drowned out by the machinery of the bulk feed truck.

Faye was alone in the kitchen, ironing. "Hi! You look mighty pleased with yourself this morning!"

"I am," I said, putting the mail on the table. "It's a fabulous day."

"It's the best April we've had in years. I hope that doesn't mean a wet May."

"Oh, don't borrow trouble, Faye," I said. "Just take what Fate or the gods may give."

She gave me a quizzical look. "You in love, by any chance?"

"I'm always in love with something or someone. Right now it's Parmenter, and the cottage. . . . Where's the lamb?"

"Oh, Eunice took her home yesterday. Wanted her mother to have the fun of tending and feeding her while she's real tiny. Sit down. Pour yourself a cup of coffee first, there's some fresh." She hung the white shirt carefully on a hanger and suspended it from the drying rack. "Rory and his white shirts. He's singing at a wedding tonight. Around here, it isn't a real wedding if Rory doesn't sing at it. I wonder who'll sing at his."

"When's that?"

She shrugged. "Just as soon as some folks can manage it. Sometimes they act like having him still loose is like knowing the bull's out again. Not that he's dangerous, but——"

"Valuable," I said.

She nodded vehemently. "Well, I don't blame Kitty for wanting to see him settled. Don't you want some coffee? Kitty'll be back in a minute. She's out there while they unload, as if they couldn't dump that feed without her standing by."

"She's so lucky to be so well and strong that she can be everywhere at once. She moves like a teenager."

"Oh, she's tough," said Faye with admiration. "Those wiry ones are. She'll be going strong when she's ninety."

"Knock on wood," I said, and we both did so, half-serious. My own mother had been one of the wiry ones. "I'll take a rain check on the coffee, Faye. I've been out all morning and never even made my bed before I left."

"I'm shocked," said Faye. We both laughed. I was halfway along the brick walk to the end of the house when a sort of Valkyrie whoop from Faye stood my hair on end.

"Telephone for you!"

It was Mrs. Hitchcock, the town clerk. So much had happened since I'd seen her that I'd forgotten my visit completely. Faye was ironing close by the wall, where the kitchen telephone was installed, and she couldn't help hearing that energetic voice.

"I'm sorry, dear, but we couldn't find any Guilds on the books. But my husband says years ago there used to be Guilds over in Fremont. Now those might be your folks. You go over there and ask. There's always a bunch of old coots sitting around the store, and I'll bet you dollars to doughnuts you'll find out something."

"I'll try that, Mrs. Hitchcock," I said, "and thanks very much for all you've done."

"I just wish it could've been more, dear."

"You've done plenty, and I'll let you know what I find out."

When I hung up Faye was too intent on ironing a pillow case. "I always heard that the Guilds were Maine people," I said, "so just for fun I asked Mrs. Hitchcock if she'd ever heard of any around here. It's like asking somebody from New York City if they know your friend that lives there. But it did no harm to ask."

"After all, stranger things have happened," said Faye sagely. "What was that she said about Fremont?"

"Oh, there used to be Guilds over there, ages ago."

"You gonna follow it up?"

"Maybe, just for fun."

"You ought to. Maybe that was why you were made to come to Parmenter. I don't know how you feel about stuff like that, but *I* believe in it."

"Believe in what?" Kitty asked. She came in with two grinning men behind her. "What have we got to go with coffee, Faye? I hope both you men are happily married, because if you aren't you'll want to marry Faye after you taste her baking."

Faye looked martyred but without much conviction, and disconnected her iron.

"And how are you this morning, Miriam?" Kitty greeted me. "Are you going to have a cup of coffee with us? ... I'll write that check out now," she said to the men, and strode into her office.

I smiled at the men so they wouldn't think I minded having coffee with them, and said, "I was just leaving, so I'll keep on going."

"Don't go!" Kitty called. "Or if you must, come in here for a moment first, will you?"

I went into the office. Kitty beckoned me close to her desk. There was a sparkle in her eyes; they reminded me of the lake this morning. "You remember what I told you the other day?" she asked in a low voice. "What I've been hoping and working for?"

I nodded.

"Well, Rory spent Sunday afternoon and evening over at Windhover. He's taking her to a wedding tonight, and he seems quite happy about it." Her smile became mischievously conspirational. "Let's hope some of it rubs off on him."

"Perhaps it will," I said, and then added for one of those arcane reasons one hardly understands, "After all, it's April."

She tipped back in her chair and looked up at me. Or past me at something else, invisible. Her smile was gone, leaving only a faint impression around her mouth, like the image of a flame left imprinted on the eye after the candle's blown out. "I read something the other day, maybe you know who said it or wrote it. I'm no intellectual, but it stuck. 'April is the cruellest month.'"

"Yes," I said. "T. S. Eliot, an American poet who lived in England."

"April *can* be, you know, and not only to the new lambs." The weather lines deepened at the corners of her eyes.

"Any month can be cruel when a person's unhappy," I said.

"That's true." Then she picked up her pen and said briskly, "Well, I must pay the man, mustn't I? Thank you for listening, Miriam." Her smile dismissed me.

"Oh, you're welcome," I returned cordially.

Going down the hill to the brook I decided that I had just been warned again. It was either a tribute to my powers of seduction or, less flattering, a warning of Rory's.

It was too bad Rory didn't have the courage to leave, at least for a while, and see something else besides Parmenter, besides Maine. But I couldn't condemn him for lack of courage; he was a partner in the farm, and that was big business around here. He couldn't in all decency walk out on his responsibility here, and perhaps that was the reason for the sweat that day.

Thinking of Fourleaf Farm made me think of mine. Yes, I was beginning to think of the Glidden place as mine, even though I had not yet consciously decided to do anything about it. But if I should—and Mrs. Barstow had her heart set on acquiring it—I hoped I'd be able to convince her that I had come to Parmenter only with the thought of seeing where my mother grew up, and hadn't the faintest idea that there was any property.

I don't like to be regarded as a cheat or a liar. But to tell her now seemed a little too soon, when I wasn't sure yet that I was the only heir, or a heir at all.

I mulled over that through lunch and only got rid of it by getting to work on the manuscript. In the late afternoon I went out for a walk, and when I came back, pleasantly chilly and hungry, Rory sat on the piano bench picking out *Gentle on My Mind* with one finger. Without looking around he said, "Do you always come crashing in as if you're raiding the joint?"

"Do you always walk into somebody's place when they're not there and make yourself at home? Aren't you supposed to be at a wedding?"

"Not till eight o'clock." He turned plausibly earnest. "Are you really mad with me? I swear I haven't been anywhere but at this piano. I never even glanced at your work." He waved at the table.

"I didn't leave a fire going."

"Oh well, I knew you'd be cold when you came in. See, you're warming your hands at it while you're giving me hell."

"I am not giving you hell," I said in measured tones, then gave in and laughed. "All right, thanks. I appreciate it."

"And I came on business."

"Don't sound so smug. Why didn't you put the tea kettle on while you were being so handy around here?" I went into the kitchen and did so, and he followed me.

"One for you?" I asked, reaching for mugs.

"I can't stay that long, dammit. I've got to be early at the church. Look, Faye told me about Selma calling you up. Did it ever occur to you that your name might really be Guild?

Maybe your father didn't come from Parmenter, but from Fremont."

"But these Guilds were in Fremont long years ago. *He'd* only be about fifty now, so a lot of younger people should know him. Mrs. Hitchcock said to ask the old men."

"Oh." He looked disappointed, then brightened. "Have you been thinking about claiming your place?"

"I don't know if it's *my* place," I said. "But I've sent for my birth certificate." I hadn't intended to admit that much; saying it aloud made it much too definite.

"*Good.*" It reminded me of the way his mother said it. "Look, the minute you get it, let me know. I'll take you to see Barney Knox. He's the first selectman."

"*If* I decide to go through with it."

"What do you mean, *if?* Look, you're the heir and you can't simply let the thing dangle. You'll have to make some disposition of it. Even if you don't want it you can take it and sell it, for a darned good price. You'll have to pay the back taxes first, but they won't be too bad; taxes around here only shot up in the last couple of years, after the new high school was built."

"Well—" Dreamily I stirred my tea. "I've got until the certificate arrives to think about it. In a way it's like being unexpectedly proposed to, and I'm awfully tempted because I'm crazy about the man on first meeting. But how deep does it go, how long will it last, and do I want to take a step that will change my life?"

He laughed, but he was stubborn. "Do you want to haul back into your shell and play dead? Look, Miriam, even if you do, *I* know who you are. I can tell the selectmen an heir exists."

"Is this a kind of power play between you and your mother?"

"No, no, *no!*" He swung his head around impatiently. "First, what I told you back at the lake is true: I don't want you just to go away and never come back again. You cried in my arms, Miriam, and in a way I cried on your shoulder. That makes us something besides casual acquaintances, doesn't it?"

"What?" I said warily.

"Friends, at least. And as your friend I'm telling you you'll be sorry forever if you let the place go. And cold-bloodedly I'm telling you you'll be responsible for the damndest legal tangle you ever heard of. What if you marry and have kids, and they find out some day about the place, which in the meantime has been sold to somebody else? And they come charging in to claim their rights?"

"They'll never have to know——"

"Your mother never intended you to know."

That was a stunner. We were both silent. I felt both tired and lonely, sitting there staring down at my tea and not wanting it. Rory moved around behind me and his hands came down on my shoulders, kneading gently. "I'm sorry, Miriam, I shouldn't have said that. But because I know the truth do you think I could let anyone, my mother or somebody else, take on that property? *No*, you'll have to make some disposition of the place. It won't be a millstone around your neck You can still be a free soul."

I had my eyes shut, basking in the strength and warmth of his hands. I wondered if this was part of his technique; no matter, I was immune, I'd just enjoy. Be a hedonist. "All right," I said. "But once I've taken the step I may be hooked. Because I spent this morning there and I know I love it."

"Good. I hope you *are* hooked." One hand brushed the hair off my neck and rested for a moment across my nape. Then he smoothed the hair back down again and said, "They'll be out beating the woods for me."

I could still feel his palm on my skin, and a reluctance to turn my head and lose the impression. *Very nice*, I thought dryly. *Goes with the beautiful scenery*. I got up and went to the door with him. "What are you singing tonight?" I asked chattily, to show I wasn't in a spell.

"*If Ever I Would Leave You*, and *Because*. ... Well, good-night," he said abruptly, and left. My own good-night followed into the dark after someone already invisible, as if he hadn't ever been there in the first place.

# chapter 16

*I* tried not to think about the Glidden place any more that night, but its sunny and sparrowy fields and the pines seemed to fill the cottage. *My* pines, *my* lake shore, *my* orchard ... They went round and round in my head, and I had to make up my mind to forget it all until the birth certificate arrived. I exorcised the whole thing finally by going back to work. Supper on the rug before the fire, the dictionary handy, the manuscript spread around me, and a scrupulous dedication to the placing of commas.

I finally leaned back against the sofa to stretch and rest, and think about myself. My mother had been willing to settle for life with a piano instead of a man, because she had known the man and possessed him always, in me and in her memories. But so far I was as unfledged as a new-born bird; I hadn't yet had what I considered a genuine love affair. I liked men in general, had liked a few very much, and had always believed that if I could get this blank portion of my life, or rather my origins, filled in, I would get around to living as the free soul Rory told me I could be.

I remembered now how he had said it, with a kind of greed. I wondered if he were singing now, and I thought, *Is the voice as good as I think it is, or is it just part of the emotional fog that surrounds me in this place?*—But there'd been the fine hairs standing up on the back of my neck, the chill down the spine ... Ah, well, he was wise to stay here with it, to use it for his own pleasure and that of others; whatever his secret problems, he had a kind of primal innocence that would have been beaten to death in the world outside the hills.

I played the piano for a little while before I went to bed, and the concentration tired me out enough so that I slept without dreaming, and woke up to a gentle rain. I worked on the manuscript all day except for a few walks through the thickest part of the spruce woods where the rain could hardly reach me. Nobody came down from the farm and I didn't go up there.

Friday morning was warm and foggy, fragrant with earth and water smells, loud with peepers and birds. I spent most of it outdoors. The brook foamed by with a new torrent. After lunch Rory brought the mail down. There was an envelope from Boston City Hall, and he held it up so I could see it, but I didn't reach for it.

"Take it, it's not one of those letter bombs," he said.

"I'd forgotten about it." I took it reluctantly.

"I know. You've been running away from yourself," he said severely. "Look, I can't take you to Barney's tonight because it's choir rehearsal, and Barney's our best bass. But I'll make a date with him for tomorrow night, before they take off for a dance."

"Don't you and Eunice go to dances?" I couldn't resist it. I got a grin back.

"Sometimes. Not together. What do you think about Eunice and me?"

"That you make a lovely couple."

He laughed. "We might, but we aren't. Regardless of what anyone says." *Kitty?* "Hey, would you like to go to choir rehearsal tonight? It's not what you'd call a far-out idea, but we have to take what we can get around here. And I'd like you to meet Sandy, and for you to hear him play."

"I've been to church here once," I reminded him. "I heard him. I was impressed by his quality." *Not as much as by yours*, I thought.

"He should be somewhere else, in a bigger place, but I don't know what in hell we'd do without him." He wandered away from me toward the front windows. "I don't know what I'd do, anyway," he added as if to himself.

"He's played for you for a long time."

"Since high school. By now we don't even need words to communicate. Did you ever have a friend like that?" He still didn't look around.

"Yes," I said to his back. "Once." It wasn't exactly the truth. I'd had chums but never one that close, but for some reason it seemed important at this moment to agree.

"Well!" he said energetically, and spun around, all business and meeting my eye a little too steadily. "We'll have to figure out a way to keep this quiet. Would you mind driving to the village tomorrow night? I'll meet you at the common, by the Honor Roll, and take you to Barney's."

"Isn't that right in the middle of everything?"

"Not on Saturday night. The drugstore keeps open till nine, but otherwise, all the action is at the Grange Hall or down to Rockland." He was half out the door. "Tomorrow night at seven," he called back, and swung over the railing.

I tried to settle down to work, but he kept interfering. No steady girl at his age, no girl at all (unless she was a well-kept secret) in spite of his line and his hinted-at reputation . . . I didn't much like what I wondered now about the sweat on his forehead the other day, but the premise wouldn't have been impossible. And if it was so I was even sorrier for him than I'd been before. He had all the more reason for feeling trapped.

The envelope from Boston lay where he'd dropped it on the table. I looked at it for a few minutes before I picked it up, wondering in squeamish suspense what it was going to tell me. I'd never had a need for a copy of my birth certificate; now I saw it as a source of information that had been within my reach all the time. She might—just possibly—have named my father.

If she did, she had patently named a phantom. Rodney Guild, birthplace Oldtown; occupation (when he wasn't being a soldier) an electronic engineer. Plenty of those around. Inventing a name and a business for a man, even inventing his death, didn't make *him*. But here she was, as she'd been all these years, if I'd only known; Helen Glidden, born in Parmenter, Maine.

With a sense of anticlimax I put the copy in my bag.

Rory was right about the common being quiet. Sometimes a car went by, and across the square there was moderate activity in and out of the drug-and-variety store, but I stood isolated in the soft dark. The Honor Roll was illuminated by a light at the top, and standing in the shadows I could read it again as I waited. It was like straining for a glimpse of a phantom in the fog, the phantom father on the birth certificate.

A car entered the square, cruised slowly around the common, and stopped behind mine. A car door opened and shut, and there were footsteps behind me. I said without looking around, "Do you know who Robert Rollins was?"

"A Marine killed at Tarawa. The oldest of five kids at Seven Chimneys farm. Not married."

"I wonder what the Rollinses look like. Because I don't look a bit like my mother."

"You don't look a bit like the Rollinses either," he said roughly. "Come on, Barney's waiting." He took my arm to hurry me.

Instinctively I wanted to resist the pressure forcing me on. The whole situation made me queasy. I had a sudden revelation, as I got into his car, that some day I would wish that I had never come here. *Some* day! I wished it right now. Why didn't I tell him I didn't want to go on with it? But I couldn't find my voice to say so. It was like trying to shout in a bad dream as we went rushing down a strange road in the dark. In the dim light from the dash I saw his face alien and set, like a sculpture cast in iron. My stomach began to knot with cramps. Hadn't I enough problems of my own without colliding head on with somebody else's misery and taking it to my heart? Cleopatra and the asp, I thought crazily.

I remembered Barney Knox as the bearded bass who'd brought up the end of the choir. Tonight he was as impressive, but more vividly so in wine slacks, yellow shirt, and bittersweet tweed jacket. Rory was as colorful in rust corduroy Norfolk jacket and tartan slacks. The two made a handsome pair of peacocks, and I felt mousy, or should I say henny, beside them.

Ann, Barney's pretty wife, also dressed up for an evening out, was introduced, and then retired to the kitchen with the two young teenagers. "Sonia's to have *The Margot Merrill Show* and Scott the movie, is that clear?" she was saying. "And anybody who doesn't want to watch the other program is to keep still or go stay in their room."

"Or I'll throw the TV to hell out," Barney said softly but carryingly after them. The kitchen door shut. He swung back in his chair, tipped his fingers together, and looked benignly at us. "Well?"

"Got something to shake you up a mite, Barney," said Rory with a grin. I held out my birth certificate, and I knew when he got to the name *Glidden*. One of his eyebrows went up. He gave me a quick look and went on reading. Then he sat back in his chair and said again, "Well," but with a different intonation.

"We think she's the heir to the Glidden place," Rory said. "At least *I* do."

"I have other proofs of my identity," I said. I felt awkward and shy, trying to push forward in a way that was foreign to me. My mouth kept drying. "I have my mother's collection of pictures."

"I dunno if it shakes me up, Rory," Barney said, "but it makes me think. Your mother know about this?"

"Nobody does," said Rory. "There didn't seem to be any sense in talking about it before Miriam knew anything for sure."

"Funny thing," Barney mused, tapping his thumbnail against his teeth. "I used to keep an eye on Old Dick, even after we moved him out, go and see him now and then. He'd ramble on and on, not make much sense sometimes, but he used to talk about a little red-head cousin who could play the piano to beat the cars."

"My mother was red-headed," I said. It scratched my throat. "Look, she'd only be fifty—no, not quite that—if she were alive. There must be plenty of people in town who knew her—Rory's mother, for one. It's just that I don't want to make a big thing about it, explaining why my mother or I never came back till now, and what my history is, and all that."

Rory took my nervous hand in a comforting grip. "She didn't even know about the place; she just came here to get a look at her background."

"No need to say anything yet," Barney said. "I'll have to talk to the other two selectmen, but they'll keep it quiet. Your mother'd be before my time, but Heck Robbins is around fifty—lived here all his life. He'd know her and where she lived. If you can produce the pictures and then some proof that you're the daughter on the certificate, there shouldn't be any trouble." He smiled at me.

"I can do all that." I stood up.

He laughed and shook his head. "You don't have to to-night. I'm going to the dance. But don't worry, we won't auction the place off behind your back. I'll call a meeting for Monday evening, if I can collect the other two, and you be here with your documents."

"She'll be here," said Rory.

"Why don't you two come along with Ann and me now?" he suggested. "Or maybe I shouldn't say anything." He looked remarkably unembarrassed. "You have your own plans most likely, not including double-dating with a couple of old marrieds."

Feeling a little giddy by now I said, "As you can see, I'm not dressed for any kind of a date except maybe a hike in the woods, but Rory looks as if he had a date. Two or three, in fact."

"There's more than two or three girls in town'd like to go out with him tonight. My daughter's scared foolish he'll be married and settled down before she's grown up. Meantime she's real religious; won't miss church for anything."

"By the time Sonia's through high school," Rory said, "she'll be wondering what she ever saw in that old man." He took me by the arm and pointed me at the door. "Let's get going so the town father can go raise a little hell. Good-night, Ann!" he shouted toward the kitchen door. "Good-night, Sonia, Scott!"

There was a chorus of answers, and the little girl came and stood in the doorway; she had Alice-in-Wonderland hair, and she was skinny as a flute in striped bellbottoms. She managed to get out the beloved name separate from the other voices. " 'Night, Rory."

"Sonia," he said, giving her a long straight look. "Let me know when you're eighteen, and *we'll* go to a dance."

"Five whole years," she mourned blissfully.

"Yep, you'll be all dried up and blown away like an old leaf by then," her father said.

When we got into Rory's car I said, "Everybody loves you. Such popularity must be deserved."

"Oh, it's nothing at all. Scatter a little sunshine as you go, it doesn't cost a cent." He talked about Barney and Ann while we drove back to town. At the common, he walked me to my car and opened the door for me.

"Thanks for tonight, Rory," I said. "Have a good time at the dance."

"Oh, I'm not going, I just dressed like it to get out of the house without any questions. The line of least resistance." He tossed it off flippantly, stopped, then said in a quieter way, "I'm going over to Sandy's. . . . Want to go?"

Sandy, the friend he couldn't do without. He was obviously being polite, that's all. "No, I think I'll go home and sit in front of my fire and dream a little." With an involuntary impulse to make some contact with him in the secret places of his isolation, I put out my hand. "Thank you, Rory, for everything you've done."

He took my hand and held it. "What have I done?"

"Listened, and comforted, and helped me make up my mind. Otherwise I'd still be dithering around, or running away like a rabbit."

He tightened his hand. "That's what I wanted to stop. The departure of Molly Cottontail."

# chapter 17

Sunday morning showed a silver sun wading in a snow-drift. I hoped it would really snow, one of those silent falls in which I would go up through the woods to the high pasture to see hills turn white. And coming back I would watch snowflakes drop into the brook and disappear in the flood. Like a child I watched impatiently for the first sign of snow while I ate my breakfast, but it didn't come.

Kitty Barstow hadn't invited me to church again. Maybe she thought that after her warnings it would be unkind to dangle delicious Rory before me. She was probably complacent this morning, if she believed he'd taken Eunice out last night. Of course we'd be together this afternoon, but in a group, and Eunice would be there to take care of herself.

*He may be safer than you think, Kitty,* I thought. At least from women. I hadn't anything tangible to go on, but I'd been fooled once before. I'd even fallen for the boy, and then I'd been shocked and revolted by the truth. I was nineteen. Now, neither believing nor disbelieving, but simply considering the possibility, I felt only pity for both Rory and his mother. He was already living under a strain that was stretching his nerves to an intolerable degree. Her bad time was to come.

When he called for me in midafternoon, it was spitting snow and I'd been so busy on the manuscript that I'd missed the first flakes. "Shall I dress for climbing that mountain?" I asked him.

"*Today?* What are you, a fitness freak?"

"Good God, no," I said piously.

He seemed utterly carefree, and I took my cue from him and resolved to enjoy myself.

The white gates of Windhover Farm were fastened hospitably open, and the house sat among maples and birches. It was of the same period as Fourleaf, but a couple of wings had been built on, and a long ell at the back. In the sheltered corner where the ell joined the main house, birds were clustered unafraid around loaded feeders.

Eunice and Sandy and two collies came from the open barn doorway to meet us. Eunice in yellow seemed to be walking in her own sunlight. Sandy was Alexander Gilchrist. He was lanky and quiet, his hazel eyes friendly behind his glasses.

"Shall we go see the horses before we go in the house?" asked Eunice. "Or would you rather not, Miriam?"

"I love to look at them, even if I do think I give off some aura that turns them carnivorous."

"Stick with me, Miriam," Sandy said. "I have the same trouble. These two don't believe it exists, but we know, don't we?"

"We do," I said solemnly. "And we know about cows, don't we?"

"I'd sooner face a pride of snarling pianos," said Sandy.

Eunice and Rory looked back, laughing. Her arm was through his, their shoulders touching, a sight to make Kitty Barstow's heart rejoice.

There were five Morgans in box stalls, all nuzzling and nudging. Eunice had brought lump sugar and apples, and I dared to feed a gentle mare round and heavy with foal. Then we visited two enormous oxen, indentical twins and very old.

"My grandfather's pride and joy," Eunice said. "And those are their names—Pride and Joy. He raised them from calves. They've won about a dozen blue ribbons. Now they live like retired royalty." She took my arm. "Now come on in and meet Mother and see how the baby's grown."

Mrs. Parmenter was in the old-fashioned summer kitchen off the main kitchen. She was feeding the lamb. Eunice stood back to let me go in first and her mother looked up when I came in. "Why, hello!" she said with happy surprise. Then the smile of recognition faded to apology. "I'm sorry! For a minute I thought you were somebody I knew."

"Who, Dora?" Rory asked.

She shook her head. "I don't know, dear. It's gone. Oh, you know me, always seeing things."

I'd given up expecting anyone to react to the name Guild, but Mrs. Parmenter's first greeting had shaken me, and I concentrated on the lamb while I repaired my poise.

"Have you named her yet?" I asked, on my knees beside the oblivious and hard-sucking lamb.

"Yes, she's Phronsie." She had a gentle manner that I found very appealing.

"From *Five Little Peppers*?" I asked. "My mother had her mother's Pepper books, so I grew up on them."

"Really? They were my favorites! I used to imagine there were six little Peppers, and I was the sixth one. But Eunice was always too busy racing around outside to read much, especially anything so tame. Oh, I wouldn't have had Eunice a bit different," she assured me. "Even though up to the age of fourteen she thought the smell of horses was the most beautiful fragrance in the world."

"What happened when she was fourteen?" Sandy asked.

"She got a bottle of lily-of-the-valley cologne for Christmas, and she fell madly in love with her dentist."

"Well, it's time you all knew the truth," Eunice said. "I went underground. I still think the smell of horses is beautiful; I just wear Muguet du Bois to deceive the world."

"What about the dentist?" I asked.

"Oh, I gave him up in six months. I decided it wasn't fair to take him from his wife and children. . . . It was Dr. Davies in Rockland," she said to Sandy. "He's still my dentist, and he has six sons."

"You'd better git ye one of them," said Rory. "If sons run in the family you'd have a passel of boys to help you with the place."

"I'll find out how old the oldest one is, maybe he'll do." She was good, laughing as if it hadn't touched a sensitive spot, but I felt entangled in tensions as if in invisible wires, and looked uncomfortably away. I met Mrs. Parmenter's eyes. From Kitty's contemptuous description I'd expected someone vague and colorless, but she was neither. Her topaz eyes were gentle enough, but perceptive. I wondered just what they perceived in me. Competition with Eunice? Or was she simply observing a girl with an unusual job in a world so far removed from Parmenter that it could be Jupiter?

"How do you like Parmenter, dear?" she asked me. The lamb breathed on my fingers. The black ears were like stiffened velvet.

"I love it," I said.

"If you love it in April you must come in June," she said. "Or September. Or even December."

"That's what I keep trying to tell her," Rory said.

"Come on, Miriam," Eunice said, "I'll give you the tour."

The old house had been restored and preserved with loving respect, good taste, and comfort. A big money cat slept on Eunice's bed, and another one blinked at us from Sam Parmenter's chest as he napped on a couch in his den, amid drifts of Sunday papers. There were photographs here and there in the house. Harry Parmenter wasn't excessively present, but still he was there. There was a particularly attractive picture of him beside Mrs. Parmenter's bed, where she must have seen him the instant she woke up in the morning, and the last moment before she put out her light at night. I thought of my mother's iron composure, never giving in to the compulsion to save out at least one separate picture of my father. And I wondered too how many pictures of Cleveland Barstow there were at Fourleaf Farm; Kitty had spoken with such scorn of Mrs. Parmenter's devotion.... Perhaps she could not bear to look every day at the beloved face. How would *I* feel?

When we came back to the spacious square hall of the main house, Rory and Sandy were playing pool in a masculine kind of room across from the living room. There was a fire in the fireplace and the dogs lay before it. I was fair at pool, but Eunice was very good.

"Instructed from the cradle by her Uncle Sam, who's really Minnesota Fats," Rory said.

"If farming fails we're going on the road," Eunice said.

Later we went across to the living room. "Mother will have tea ready," Eunice said to me. "You could have a drink if you'd rather. What about you two?" she said over her shoulder to the men.

"Don't ask Sandy," Rory said, "you know he's a secret lush. Keep him on tea, for God's sake."

"Listen," I said. "If you think that I have cocktails every afternoon at five, you're in for a great disillusionment." After Kitty's remarks I was ardently looking forward to tea at Windhover Farm. I wouldn't have missed it for the world, and I was almost euphoric at being here in the long living room with its birch fire burning under the white-paneled mantel, its African violets, flowery slipcovers, the dogs waiting with patient good manners for handouts; and outside the windows the green-bronze fields and smoky blue hills, and snowflakes blowing on the wind.

Sandy played and everybody sang. Even Sam rumbled with enthusiasm through *John Peel*. When we were dry, and drinking fresh tea, Mrs. Parmenter asked Rory to sing *The Rose of Tralee*.

"Harry loved it," she said. "He couldn't sing for sour apples, but he'd pick the tune out with one finger and try anyway, and his father would always call out, 'Give that calf more rope!' " She had a merry, youthful laugh. I didn't think she'd been a nonentity when Harry married her.

Rory neither rushed to the piano nor had to be coaxed. "Go on eating your cake, Sandy," he said. "Miriam can play for me."

"I'm rusty," I protested. "Besides, I've never accompanied anyone."

"You've accompanied *me*. Remember? *Passing By?*"

"That was an accident. And I don't know the music for *The Rose of Tralee*."

"We've got it," Eunice said. She opened the book and set it on the rack, and gave me a bright smile. It struck me as a little too bright, a little too steady. Rory and I had already been together and she hadn't known, and she was trying not to show anything now.

It could have been upsetting; I decided to be annoyed instead, and as a result played well enough to make my protests seem coy and artificial. Besides, the niggling little sensitivities all dissolved like the snowflakes in the brook when Rory began to sing.

There was a brief silence afterward. Then Mrs. Parmenter said, "Thank you, dear. Harry always said he should have been born Irish. Especially after he'd had a few drinks."

We all burst out laughing. Sam said, "Good Lord, I can see him yet—and *hear* him!" He laughed again, shaking his head and wiping his eyes. There was palpable relaxation in the room, though perhaps only I had been aware of strained suspense. Maybe Eunice hadn't given a thought to my playing for Rory, maybe she was too confident about herself and their long friendship, maybe I was the oversensitive one. But Kitty Barstow was to blame for that, she'd been so damned obvious about warning me off. Oh, well, that too was past like the snowflakes in the brook. I asked for more tea.

"You play so beautifully, dear," Mrs. Parmenter said.

"Thank you." I took another slice of lemon loaf.

Sam poked the fire and took over the hearthrug. "Rory, I see the foreclosure on the Harkins place is in the paper. What's your mother planning to do with it?"

"I don't know. We haven't discussed it." Rory was trying to balance a piece of cake on a collie's nose.

"I take it you weren't in favor."

"Sam!" Mrs. Parmenter protested. "Isn't the day bad enough outside without talking over that grim business?"

Her brother-in-law ignored her. "I suppose she's already got her bid in on the Glidden place."

The cake fell off the collie's nose and he caught it with a snap before it reached the floor. "You moved," Rory accused him. "On purpose. You'll never be able to take Lassie's place. You're ruined in show business." He looked up at Sam with bland innocence.

"I don't know that either, Sam. I'm not only the silent partner, but the blind and deaf one as well."

"Oh, I'm sure she told you, Rory," Eunice said. "You probably let it go in one ear and out the other. I've seen the glazed look when you aren't listening."

"Oh, he's listening all right," said Sandy, "but to something else."

"A different drummer?" I suggested.

"Thoreau," Sam grunted. "No farmer."

"But, Sam, didn't he plant a lot of beans?" Mrs. Parmenter asked earnestly.

Later we moved back to the piano for more singing. Later still I went out to the summer kitchen with Mrs. Parmenter for Phronsie's next feeding, and took turns holding the bottle. After that the older people settled down with supper trays in the living room to watch a TV program to which they were both addicted, and we ate in the kitchen, talking and joking like teenagers; laughter seemed to well up easily in this house, like water filling every footprint on damp sand.

# chapter 18

When we left in midevening, Mrs. Parmenter asked me to come again. Sam was cordial in his own unornamented fashion, and Eunice repeated the invitation when we said good-night at the car. Sandy drove off ahead of us. The snow had stopped, and the black road glistened with wet; the air was warming rapidly and the peepers had started up again in every swampy spot along the road.

"What a nice day this has been," I said. "You've got good friends. I like them all."

"They liked you too. They'll be glad if you get the place." He laughed. "Sam especially. It'll be a wipe in my mother's eye."

"She says they're friendly rivals, always have been. . . . Look, Rory, if everything goes all right tomorrow, I'd still like to keep it quiet for a little while, to get used to the idea. Do you suppose the selectmen would mind not saying anything right off? Just that they'd heard from someone about it, that's all."

"Sure, they'll keep quiet." We drove through the village, around the common, and took the now familiar route out to Fourleaf Farm. I was beginning to feel peacefully sleepy when he suddenly spoke. "You've probably gathered—you couldn't miss it—that my mother has got some pretty fixed ideas about Eunice and me. I haven't done anything to convince Eunice it's a sure thing, but my mother's all but proposed to the girl in my name."

"I know," I said. "Your mother told me. She came down to the cottage one day."

He made a fast involuntary gesture and then his hand fell hard on the wheel.

"Well, it's a tribute to your sex appeal, Rory," I said. "She probably expected me to fall in love at first sight."

"I can't see it as all that funny! Eunice is the only one who isn't damned blatant about it. Even Sam's been giving me this fatherly, or uncle-ish——"

"Avuncular," I said helpfully.

"Whatever the hell it is, it's the only thing he and my mother agree on."

"What about Mrs. Parmenter?"

"Oh, Dora's still too wound up in her own marriage to worry about Eunice. You see how many pictures of Harry there were around? I think she *talks* to him! In our house the only picture of my father is in my room."

"Your mother probably couldn't bear to look at them," I said. "My mother couldn't."

"Maybe so." He sounded bleak.

We were crossing the bridge where the brook splashed noisily beneath us on its downhill plunge toward the lake. "Rory, do you think that if people weren't trying to push you and Eunice at each other, you might—" I let it trail off.

"Make a fetch of it? I doubt it. I grew up with her, I love her like a sister, but that's it."

"She's in love with you," I said, "and nothing sisterly about it."

"I know that." He was angry. "But what in hell am I supposed to do about it? I'll be damned if I'll marry somebody just because *she* wants it, but how can I ignore her? Or say to her, 'Look, you're a wonderful girl, and I know you're in love with me, but I'm not with you and never could be.' What would that do to her pride, for God's sake?"

"It's honest," I said. "It might take off some of the pressure. Maybe she'd like you to bring it out in the open. But that's just my opinion. Look, why are you so sure you never could be in love with her, given time and no interference?"

"I know, that's all!" he said irritably.

"Because you love somebody else?" The ground was delicate; it could be quicksand. I'd gone too far and blushed in the dark for prying into forbidden territory. So his spontaneous laughter caught me off balance.

"What gives you that idea?"

"You're a healthy young male," I said. "Biologically complete, presumably."

"Me and Apollo!" He was still laughing. We turned in between the gateposts. "You got anything to eat down at your place, or shall we stop and steal something out of the freezer?"

"You mean you're still hungry after all you ate tonight?"

"Yep, I sure be, ma'am."

"I can scramble some Fourleaf eggs."

"That'll do me."

We drove by the house. The only lights were in an upstairs bedroom. "Kitty's reading in bed," he said. "Faye won't be back till the last gun's fired. Jason's in the kitchen."

"He'd give you away if you burgled the freezer."

"We'd steal him too."

At the cottage he got a fire going in the fireplace while I attended to the food. He ate with such a good appetite it made me hungry to watch him, and I ate more than I intended to. "Good eggs we raise up on the hill," he said, "but then you do a real fancy scramble."

"That's one of the prettiest speeches I ever heard."

"And that's only one of them. You ought to hear what else I can come up with."

"I'm listening."

"How's this? Good coffee, too."

"Thanks. I opened the jar myself."

It was witless, easy fun. There was a comfortable at-home-after-the-party mood; it was as if we had known each other for a long time. Whatever his problems were, and whatever mine, we were effortless comrades that night, all the battles out of mind. I enjoyed watching him, convinced now that he wasn't trading on his good looks half as much as I'd first suspected.

When we finished he began to clear the table and wouldn't let me help. "Go play something while I wash up."

"If you'll sing something later. Or do you save your voice?"

"For what? Go play."

Paradoxically I was both keyed up and relaxed enough to do well; it was one of those magical times when one's hands have a life of their own. He came into the room applauding. I stood up and bowed.

"Oh it was nothing, nothing," I said modestly. "And I mean it. Sandy's the real artist. He's got such strength and virility——"

"Let's not talk about Sandy. He's my friend and all that, but I don't want him here tonight. Get off the bench." I did, and he began going through the music. "Maggie liked the old Scotch songs," he said. "She grew up on them, and they made her homesick. She taught them to me."

"Let's have them, then." I put the song book on the rack and opened at random. It was *Bonnie Doon*. "Know that one?"

He said mischievously, "She used to play that for me with tears running down her cheeks."

"I shan't weep," I said, "but I'll tell you one thing. Whenever you mention her I have gooseflesh, just thinking of her here at this piano. Now I think I'm too intimidated to play for you."

He put his hands on either side of my head and turned my face gently toward the music. I played the introduction, and then came the voice—

" 'Ye banks and braes o' Bonnie Doon,
    How can ye bloom sae fresh and fair—"

And I knew why the woman sat there playing with tears running down her cheeks. I think Robert Burns would have wept too. My own eyes began to smart. It wasn't a superficial sentimentality; it was because I was taking part in something of such simple but flawless beauty.

When we'd finished I began feeling in my pockets, hoping I wouldn't have to snuffle, and Rory leaned over and looked at me. "Crying?" he inquired with a pleased smile.

"Sorry to disappoint you," I said, "but I save my tears for sad movies. If, however, I wept about music, I'd be weeping now. Does that satisfy your vanity?"

He patted my head. "How about *Sweet Afton?*" We did that, and *Loch Lomond*, and then we came to *My Love Is Like a Red, Red Rose*. We used to sing the other two in school from the early grades on, but I had hardly heard the last one, so perhaps that was why the impact of the words, in this place and in my situation, smashed me down. Not physically. I kept on playing, professionally appreciating the way he handled the old song.

> " 'And fare you weel, my only love,
>     And fare you weel a while!
>   And I will come again, my love,
>     Tho' it were ten thousand mile.' "

The last note went into infinity like a bell's sound. That was what did me in, finally. Whether it was the thought of my father, Eunice's, all the young men who expected to come back but never did, added to the impact of the music itself, I don't know. But I gave up, excused myself, went and washed my face and blew my nose. When I came back, he was putting more wood on the fire. In the dancing light his face was serious to the point of austerity.

I sat down on the sofa. "Tell me something, Rory. Did you ever want to do anything special with your voice, or do you take it for granted, the way a bird sings?"

"We don't have to talk about that tonight, do we?" he asked the fire in a perfectly polite, perfectly flat tone.

"We don't ever have to talk about it. I'm sorry I mentioned it." I had the horrid sensation of having jabbed someone in a very sore spot. I went back to the piano and began turning over pages. I hardly saw the staves and the notes. I was suddenly worn out, wrung out, remembering almost with nostalgia the cozy ignorance in which I'd lived snug as a snail in its shell. Everything was too much to be borne, and I wished that Rory would get out while my back was turned.

"*Miriam*," he said. One word, no more, but the one word made the back of my neck prickle. He was there, behind me. I looked around at him and saw something like strain or anguish cut deep into his face. The sight seemed to cut off my breath.

"What is it?" I asked faintly. The next instant we were in each other's arms.

I'd been attracted to men before, but I'd never in my life felt anything like that. I felt as if I'd drown in a minute, and the terrifying fact was that I didn't care. I wondered if this was anything like the famous rapture of the depths—a killer. I had to struggle against both of us to loosen his embrace.

"Listen," I began, "it's the music, that's what did it——"

"No." He was neither speaking in his sleep nor with the exhilaration of conquest. "I love you, Miriam."

"You can't, not this quick. *I* can't——"

"Don't talk." His lips moved across my cheek.

"I'm only trying to be——"

"Don't say *objective*," he warned me. "Don't say it."

I gave up luxuriously to the moment. We separated again for lack of breath, but still kept hold of each other with entwining fingers, smiling giddily, wet-eyed, and shaky. "Come on, let's sit down before we fall down," he said, and led me to the sofa, where we settled against each other as if we already knew how we fitted. We talked as lovers have always talked.

"Did you ever feel this way about anybody else?"

"No. Did you?"

"Never!"

"Anybody back there in New York? Or in that town where you grew up?"

"I thought so a few times, but it wasn't anything like this."

"I know what you mean. But we're grown up now. It's real."

We sank again, rose for air, and I said, "When did you *know?*"

"The first time I saw you I knew something was happening to my life, but I wasn't sure what."

"If I hadn't been playing the piano," I asked mockingly, "would you have known?"

"All right, then," he said. "Because it's part of you, part of the whole picture, the essence, whatever you want to call it. It was going to prejudice me in your favor anyway, right? Like anything that makes a man look twice at a woman. Now tell me *when* you knew."

It's a wonder I didn't blush with guilt for what I'd wondered about him. "I don't know," I said truthfully. "I was on guard against you that first time. A little cynical about all that charm, and the voice thrown in——"

"Hey look, no hands!" he said. "Showing off for the new girl."

"That's what I told myself. But maybe I was really on guard against myself."

"You asked me something a while back. Before the sky fell on us." He squeezed my ribs. "I didn't want to talk about it. Didn't intend to talk about it."

"You don't have to," I put in hastily.

"I want to. You're supposed to know. You told me what drives you, so you have to know about me." He took his arms away from me and crouched on the hearth rug to replenish the fire. "You know how pearls are made?" he said as he worked. "But we can't even make pearls of our troubles. We just have to try to live around them somehow."

He returned to me, and put one arm around me. He took my chin in his free hand and we looked at each other in silence. His eyes were so dark a blue they looked almost black in this light. "Maggie wanted me to go away to study," he said. "Before that summer I took singing for granted, as you said. Like a bird. But after that summer, with what I'd learned about myself and about music—then I wanted to go."

He spoke without drama. I had the conviction that he'd steeled himself to this and was trying to get it over with as quickly as possible. "She told me it would be hard work, hard as hell, and full of frustrations and disappointments. She didn't pull any punches. But she'd get this man to take me as a pupil, she'd grubstake me, and after that it would be up to me."

He took his hand away from my chin, and I reached up and closed my fingers around his. "Why didn't you go?" I asked. *He's never taken it seriously*, his mother had said.

"My mother," he said without expression, and I wasn't surprised. "I was still a minor. The farm was for *me*, I wasn't going tooting off to the city on any such foolishness. I could sing around here all I wanted; she was proud enough when she saw them all weeping and blowing their noses at weddings and funerals. But I could put anything else out of my mind." The hand in mine twisted until it could squeeze my fingers in an unconsciously brutal grip. "Maggie'd been all right to take my mind off being Montana Slim. She might have sung for kings, but all she meant to Kitty that summer was a babysitter for me and a damned good rent on the cottage to help pay the taxes. If I had any crazy ideas about running off, she'd have the police bring me back. She said a few more things about Maggie contributing to the delinquency of a minor, but Maggie was great. She just didn't hear it. Talk about royalty —the real thing must be like Maggie Dundas."

And Kitty Barstow is a liar, I thought. Whatever her reasons—jealousy, fear of losing Rory, an old resentment of his father's singing—she is a liar. By a lie she is trying to cut out the heart of his life.

He released my hand and laid it on his knee, stroked it finger by finger. "We knew we'd never have a chance to speak alone after that. So she told me, in my mother's presence, that whenever I made the break I should write to her, and don't mess around with any voice teachers in the meantime. She left the next day, and I went to Rockland and enlisted in the Army. That was one thing Kitty couldn't control. She'd been pretty sure she could keep me from being drafted, with all her contacts, and a little blackmail here and there. But I got our local draft board off the hook by enlisting, so I guess they'll always like me for that." He grinned. "And I made my break, even if it wasn't in the direction I wanted."

"Vietnam?"

"No, I was lucky. I drew Korea. I was there three years." He brushed it off like an annoying fly. "It took me past my twenty-first birthday, and I celebrated that by writing to Maggie and telling her I was on my way. My mother celebrated by writing to me."

He stopped. When the silence began to have echoes I said, "Naturally. Or didn't she write to you all the time you were there *until* your birthday?"

"Oh, she'd written, all right. Nice newsy motherly letters, so if anything happened to me she wouldn't have it on her conscience that she wasn't speaking to me when I left home. But she'd never written one like this." His forehead was suddenly wet, as I'd seen it once before, and he took his hand off mine and wiped the palm on his pants leg. "She wanted me to know this before I came home, because she didn't think she could tell me in so many words. She was still so shaken up— *terrified* was more like it. She'd gone into the hospital thinking she had a simple ovarian cyst, and they'd found cancer."

"Oh, *Rory!*"

"I know. She was so scared it scared the hell out of me, I can tell you. I threw up," he added, a little shamefaced.

"I don't blame you. I would too. But Rory, when *was* that? She seems so well, so full of life, not like somebody under a death sentence——"

"Well, it happened quite a while before that letter—she didn't tell me till I was due to come home." He looked absently into the fire. "She said the surgeon said he'd gotten it all. But she'd seen too many people die of cancer, and she couldn't believe she wouldn't. Neither could I. I wrote to

Maggie, and my letter crossed hers. She was expecting to see me, and she talked about a scholarship. I was sick, Miriam. Oh, God, was I sick." He groaned, and gathered me into his arms. "But I had to come back here. You can see that, can't you? Mad as I'd been with Kitty, when we both thought she might be dying I had to come back."

"Of course you did. You'd have been a monster not to. But listen, Rory, have you ever talked with her doctor?"

"No." He mistook my meaning. "Oh, she's not keeping anything from me. I know she's felt for a long time as if she's walking the high wire, but she wouldn't lie to me if something happened to scare her again. We've never discussed it—that's why she wanted to tell it all in a letter so we wouldn't have to talk about it. But we know it's right there. She'd never lie to me," he repeated. "She never has. Her theory is that the truth can bear its own weight anytime, even if it's enough to crush you to death. At least you die undeceived," he said dryly.

"Yes," I said. I moved away so I could put my hands on his cheeks. "So you gave up your plans because you thought, under the circumstances, you should be here. And anybody'd agree that was right."

"Even Maggie did." He turned his mouth into my palm.

"But it must be at least four years, Rory. Maybe the surgeon was right, even if she doesn't believe it. That's why you ought to talk with her doctor. Get it straight from him, what there is to worry about—*if* there's anything to worry about."

*If she really had cancer.* The phrase blared so loudly in my brain I was startled for fear I'd spoken it, but he looked just the same, holding my hand against his mouth, his eyes shut.

"Twenty-five isn't too late to start, Rory. Or thirty, or even thirty-five. People have come to it from other careers. Ezio Pinza was a racing driver. The point is, do you still believe in yourself?"

"*Yes!*"

"Then find out if it's all right for you to go. She's a strong woman, Rory. She's still young. She's involved in everything.

She loves the farm. She'll survive, and she'll be proud of you."

"I never thought of going to Doc Pierce." He hit his forehead. "My God, how could I have been so thick? I've just gone along feeling like a fox in a trap—my God, the time I may have wasted—*no!* I was waiting for you."

"You know," he said later. "My father must have disappointed or disillusioned her somehow. Or maybe she just never forgave him for dying like that. I used to think she wouldn't look at anyone else because she was still in love with him, like Dora with her Harry, but for a long time now I've been thinking it's something else. That business about the pictures. . . . Well, I told you that." He gathered me up again, and nuzzled in my hair. "Never mind. I'm born again," he said jubilantly. "You did it. You just gave birth to a one-hundred-fifty-pound healthy boy with good lungs. How do you feel?"

"It was nothing at all," I said. "I can go right back to hoeing potatoes."

# chapter 19

It took us quite a while to part for the night. Once he was gone I was dizzy with reaction, and fell into bed without washing my face or brushing my teeth. I slept heavily but woke around four to reality like a slap in the face with a wet towel. I couldn't truthfully call my new state happiness. There was too much all at once. My stomach was upset, I couldn't eat, my coffee tasted terrible. My mind bounded deliriously from one subject, one face, to another. I hadn't gone through the looking glass. I'd been caught in a revolving door, or maybe a demented engineer's highway, a succession of cloverleaves from which there was no exit. Cloverleaf . . . Fourleaf . . . Fourleaf Farm, and Kitty bright as stainless steel. A stainless steel lioness with one priceless cub.

I worked, but it was as exhausting as ditch-digging. I had chills though the day was mild, and even working in the sun I kept bundled up. I thought with a kind of drunken resignation that I was coming down with something; all I needed was a virus infection to make the mad dream complete.

Yet when Rory came around seven that evening health overtook me like a sunrise. He himself wore a sheen like the best grade of spring morning. He took me into his arms—or I took him. I remember only the fervent rapture of those first embraces, and the unspeakable thankfulness that went along with them like prayer.

I said finally, "What's the news? You're radiant."

"It's because I'm in love and I've got a good firm holt on ye."

"Did you see the doctor?"

"No, dammit. He's off for a week on his annual spring fishing trip. So we'll have to wait. But it's funny—after I talked to you about it, all the scare went out of it. God, what an ignorant jackass I've been, not to go to see him before. And that wouldn't have violated my promise of secrecy, because he'd know all about it anyway. You've let me out of jail, Miriam."

"You've let me out too, so we're even. And look," I said, "if she ever did get sick, for *any* reason, or have an accident, you'd be only a couple of hours away by plane."

"And if Maggie says the scholarship idea is down the drain —I woke up at three this morning composing a letter to her— and nobody else wants to take me on because voices like mine are a dime a dozen, I'll be right back anyway. The Singing Plowboy returns, battered and disillusioned." He grinned as if it were a tremendous joke and nothing like that could possibly happen. "If she's disinherited me we'll farm your place."

"Let me go and straighten myself up." I tried to disengage myself but he held on. "I love you all rumpled and flushed and with that look in your eyes."

"Do you want the selectmen to see me like this?"

He laughed and let me go.

*My place, my darling,* I thought, as I went to tidy myself, *is going to be sold to finance you in case there's no scholarship....* This inspiration had come to me on awakening. He had a good bank account of his own, but he didn't know how fast it could melt away when he had to spend it for subsistence. Even with a scholarship it would have to be used. If Maggie Dundas had given up on him, there were teachers, good ones, to take him; I would have sworn on my life that such voices *weren't* a dime a dozen. The only doubt I had, when I allowed it, was about his temperament, whether he had the necessary toughness. But I hardly knew him, I couldn't judge whether or not he had the essential diamond-hard core of dedication. Maybe he didn't even know himself. But we would find out. And, if I had been led to discover him instead of my father, well, perhaps that was as it should be. My mother would have said so.

Not that I still didn't want to know. Now it was less of an unhealed sore than a maddening concept of infinite emptiness.

Barney Knox greeted me as a friend and introduced me to the other two selectmen; one was a raw-boned type like a good-humored Ichabod Crane, and the other a stout, placid, pretty young woman who was knitting a child's sweater. They were open-minded and hospitable. I said I could get references from our doctor and minister, and they decided to check them in case any questions arose; but they had already accepted me on my portable evidence. No one asked me anything about my father; Barney had already told them that he had been killed overseas. The raw-boned man had known my mother.

"We always wondered what became of Helen when she left here," he told me earnestly. "She had real talent, that girl. I always figgered she'd go far. Kept on with her music, did she? I'm glad of that."

"We hope this means you'll come back to use the place," the woman told me. "It's nice to know it'll still be in the same family."

In the face of such welcomes I must have shown some discomfort because Rory said quickly, "Look, how about keeping this quiet for a week?"

"We'll just have to say the bids are off," Barney said. "Mentioning no names."

"You'll want to do your own telling," the woman said to me. "I know I would."

*Especially where Kitty Barstow is concerned.* I thought I could read that, but I may have been mistaken.

"Could I have a tax bill as soon as I'm accepted as the official heir?" I asked.

"Oh, you'll get that soon enough," Barney assured me. "The assessors'll be on your trail like beagles."

"Just you remind them," said Rory, "that the place hasn't been farmed for God knows how long, the pastures are full of alders, the blueberry land full of juniper, and there's no house and barn."

They all shook hands with me when we left, welcoming me home. My guilt nearly swamped me, but once back in the car with Rory, and in his arms for a quick embrace before he started the engine, guilt, apprehension, and everything else disappeared in the flood tide.

When we drove past the lighted windows of the main house I said, "Where are you supposed to be tonight?"

"I could be shooting pool at the firehouse, playing chess with Ron Hitchcock, working out an arrangement with Sandy——"

"And another arrangement with Eunice," I suggested.

"Shut up," he said. "I love you. Do you love me?"

"It's either true love or plain old biology," I said. "I lay awake all night wondering if my hormones were making a fool out of me."

"And what did you decide?"

"If you can't beat 'em, join 'em." We had stopped on the turnaround by the cottage. The sound of the peepers chimed in our ears, and the brook's voice pervaded everything. I said, "It's almost as if there's an influence here outside of ourselves. I don't mean spirits, but something left behind that can't ever die, and we've taken it, or it's taken us. . . . I want to show you something in the cottage—why I had to come here in April."

I had brought the book with me, but I hadn't opened it until tonight, when I read him the first three verses of Swinburne's "Relics." The third was the one that had run me through:

> Dead memory that revives on doubtful ways,
> Half-hearkening what the buried season says
> Out of the world of the unapparent dead
> Where the lost Aprils are, and the lost Mays.

He was quiet for a few moments. Then he said, "All my Aprils were lost until you came. And we won't let any more be lost, will we? *Will* we, Miriam?"

"No. Never."

It was hard to separate at night. But music saved us more than once. At that point we were still in good control, moving warily though with delight through the strange, paradisiacal rain forest.

The next day was as warm as early June and I worked outdoors again. In midafternoon, when I'd given up and was lying on the lawn on a blanket listening to the birds and the stream, watching the ragged April clouds blow over the spruce tops, Faye and the dog walked down the lane. She had brought some fresh cupcakes, and I made tea, and we carried it back out to the lawn. We talked about one thing and another, Faye being anything but dull, and then—I don't remember just what the approach was—she said, "Rory's mighty happy these days. Might be just spring, of course, and it might be love. It ought to be, at his age." She gave me an oblique, luminous glance. "I'm not gossiping, now. But Kitty seems to think he's spending a lot of time with Eunice these days."

"She's a nice girl," I said enthusiastically.

"And a good one. But she's like her mother; one man is all there is."

"It's the same with Mrs. Barstow, isn't it? I'm not gossiping either," I said with a grin. "But she's never looked at another man, from all I hear."

"I guess Rory'd have liked it better if she did," Faye said. "I'm still not gossiping."

"My mother was widowed early too," I said, "and she was always faithful to my father. But if she'd met someone else I hope I'd have been reasonable about it."

"Rory would be, I'm positive. It's hard on a young one to feel he's got the whole responsibility. Not that Kitty acts clinging or dependent, but—" She let it trail off; perhaps for fear that at last she was gossiping.

If I could have been flagrant enough, I'd have asked her then what she knew about Kitty's surgery. But I couldn't do it. Anyway, even if I had the effrontery, it was too late. Faye was going on.

"I haven't seen Rory act so happy in a long time. Though he was always a great one for fooling. He could make you laugh till you cried, sometimes. Even as a tyke. But then—" She puckered her forehead in a frown of recollection. "When he started to grow up, well, he was pretty happy the summer that singer was here, because he's so crazy about music and she was teaching him. But in the fall he went into the Army, and when he came back he was different. Just like they tell you about veterans coming back. He'd have spells when he wouldn't talk, you'd never hear him whistling around the place the way he used to, and do you think he'd *sing?* Not on your life. Well, it stands to reason, after all the hardship and poverty he must have seen overseas. Must make him still brood sometimes, soft-hearted as he is."

She handed me her cup and I refilled it. "It was Sandy got him back to music. He came from Bangor to head up the music department in the new high school, and the Baptists here hired him as organist. The choir wasn't much account and he set out to build it up, and somebody told him about Rory. So somehow he talked him into it. The best thing in the world for that boy. *I* was worried about him, now I can tell you!"

"Wasn't his mother worried too?"

"Not so you'd notice it. Oh, Kitty can keep things in," she added hastily. "She's proud as Lucifer."

*Kitty wasn't worried,* I thought. Never mind if the thrush didn't sing, she had him back in the cage. . . . No word of the cancer operation; Kitty must have sworn Faye to secrecy too, or perhaps Faye thought the operation was for something else, too minor even to be remembered. Or perhaps there'd been no cancer.

But Kitty doesn't lie. Rory swears to that. . . . She could have still been terrified back then, which would have quenched him; that and his awful disappointment, for he admits he was frightened too.

"I've been running on like that brook," Faye said, "and forgot what I came for. Kitty wants you to come up to supper tonight. It's at six. She's off to an F.H.A. meeting today, and I was supposed to tell you this morning, but, what with cooking for a gang of extra help this noon, I never got to it. It'll be more like dinner, it'll be in the dining room."

# chapter 20

I put on a dress for dinner, sensing that slacks would not be the thing for a meal in the dining room at Fourleaf Farm. The dress was a slim straight little article in a leafy pattern that reminded me of the woods around the cottage. I walked up the lane in the early evening sunshine. There was a serene and understated beauty about this time before the rush of blossom that would come later. I felt the quiet in myself, a time to get my breath before the future took me like the brook in freshet.

I needed to be quiet all the way through, so that when I saw Rory for the first time in twenty-four hours I wouldn't give myself away. *Don't blush*, I willed myself sternly as I went in the back door. *Don't light up like Times Square.*

All of which was unnecessary, because he wasn't in the kitchen. The men were just leaving after their supper, calling back compliments to Faye, and she was enjoying it. "Nothing I like better than honest praise," she told me. "I can't ever hear enough of it. My mother says she should have named me Vanity."

"Why not? It's quite pretty if you say it often enough. Like Citronella, and Scarletina."

In the office Mrs. Barstow said, "The trouble with you, Rory, is that you won't pin yourself down to anything that requires brainwork."

He answered in good humor. "To me farming is crops and animals, not a computer system."

"Well, if you simply want to be a herdsman and not run your own place as a paying business," Kitty began acerbly, and then made an obvious effort to tone it down. "Oh, Rory, you're just being perverse."

"Hey, watch it, Mum. Even in the Army they never called me that, and I had plenty of chances."

Eunice laughed, and Kitty said with humorous exasperation, "Don't encourage him, Eunice."

"I'd better go out," I murmured to Faye. "I'm a little early." But she waved me to a chair.

"This goes on all the time. It's no secret how he hates all the bookkeeping." I sat down reluctantly. At least I could make conversation to keep from listening in, but I couldn't think of a darned thing to say. I kept stroking Jason's head and scratching behind his ears. He laid his chin heavily on my knee and we began hypnotizing each other with long stares.

"Some day," Kitty began, and Rory picked it up. "Some day, son, all this will be yours, and if you don't know how to keep the books you'll lose it all to the I.R.S. or in a crap game."

"Which is more truth than poetry," she retorted. "You're like your father, scared foolish by a record sheet. Listen, my boy, if you want to stay in farming these days you've *got* to know the whole operation. But here you are, a man grown, and there are 4-H boys in this town who know more about it than you do."

"When you're gone, Kitty my love, about a hundred years from now, I'll hire me a couple of bright 4-H boys. And girls."

There was a smothered chuckle from Eunice, and Kitty said acidly, "I didn't build up Fourleaf Farm to what it is for you to make bad jokes about it. As long as you've got an audience for your so-called wit you're happy, and the farm can go to hell, *if* you'll excuse my language, Eunice."

"Oh, Mrs. Barstow," Eunice said, "you know how Rory loves the farm."

"I don't know anything of the sort!"

"Tell me the truth, Mother," Rory said, "You've had the

time of your life building up Fourleaf, haven't you? Oh, I know it's supposed to be for me——"

"It *is* for you, not *supposed* to be!"

"All right, love, it's for me. But would you give up any of the satisfaction you got out of it? And don't you like the paperwork too, and everything else that goes along with it? You love it, admit it."

There was a short silence and I had a peculiar and probably false picture of Kitty Barstow at bay. Then she said, "I admit it. I have loved it, I do love it. And that's what makes it harder to think you could lose the whole business. Dribble it away by poor management, ignorance, or just plain indifference."

"Thanks for a straight answer," Rory said. "Now what makes you think I'm fool enough, and unfeeling enough, to throw all your work away? That damned bookkeeping nearly splits my head open, but I'd hire someone for that."

"Unless," his mother said, "you made the proper marriage and got yourself a real partner. Someone who saw the farm as something personal, not just an employer."

"Well, there's always that," said Rory amiably. "We can't tell, can we?" He came out into the kitchen, leaving silence behind him. When he saw me, he didn't say my name, but I was glad Faye's back was turned so she couldn't see his face or mine either, for all my good resolutions not to illuminate. At almost the same moment a car stopped at the back door and Jason's throat vibrated against my knee. He turned his head to listen, ears pricked.

"Here's Sandy!" Rory called. "Miriam's here too. Time to eat!"

It sounded as if I had come when Sandy did, and Faye didn't correct him, but I saw her eyes shift from him to me and back again.

The dining room paneling was painted that pale robin's-egg blue seen in so many old houses. There was a genuine primitive of a big-eyed child over the mantel. "Peregrine Barstow," Kitty introduced him. "Rory's great-great-great-grandfather."

"Was this the Barstow farm then?" I asked.

"Oh yes, though this isn't the original house. The first was a log cabin, then there was a small frame house. That one burned. This was built in 1800. The Barstows and the Parmenters owned just about the whole valley in those days." She gave Eunice a smiling nod.

"And Mother's been busily trying to get back all the original Barstow lands," said Rory. "We may end up owning Augusta some day."

Mrs. Barstow wasn't amused, but Eunice was. She was extremely pretty tonight, her hair sparkling in the lamplight as if interwoven with gold threads. She and Rory made a startlingly handsome pair. Kitty's eyes linked them again and again, too guarded to show her passion, but insistent enough to show her determination. I couldn't blame her. Here was a healthy and good-looking girl who had sprung from this valley and adored it, who could manage the farm and produce children to carry it on. Even I could see the perfection of the match.

The trouble was what lay between Rory and me. We didn't dare look at each other across the table for fear of looking too long and becoming lost in it. Then I worried for fear we were too obviously ignoring each other. It seemed sometimes as if the truth were written on our foreheads in letters of fire.

The meal came to a close with a superlative lemon meringue pie and good coffee. When we went into the living room I wondered how long before I could decently leave. I decided that by nine I would say I was tired—I could always use my early-morning working hours as an excuse. As if we'd been through it all before, I knew that Kitty would instantly delegate Sandy to walk me home, before Rory could offer. That didn't matter. I had to get out of here as soon as I could.

The general conversation split into fragments of more concentrated interest when Eunice asked Mrs. Barstow something technical and incomprehensible (to me) about her meeting today. After politely trying to follow, I found that the men were discussing Sandy's problems in staging a high-school performance of *Pinafore*. This was intelligible to me and a lot more interesting.

They went from that into planning the Memorial Day music at the church, and the women went from farm management into knitting. I'd never progressed beyond the little squares of garter stitch we did in Brownies, so I wandered around examining the knicknacks collected by some sea-going Barstows. I was looking at a shelf of tiny ivory figures when Rory said close to me, "If you like that kind of thing, come into the back parlor and I'll show you more." His fingers brushed my bare arm. His lips moved in silent words. No one could see his face, but mine was exposed to the others in the room.

"Oh, do you have more?" I exclaimed idiotically. "They're fascinating!"

Kitty said, "Sandy, Miriam's quite a musician too, I understand."

"Come and play for us then," Sandy said. He was trying to get his pipe going.

"You're the real musician here," I said.

"Thank you, ma'am." Sandy pulled a forelock. I didn't look at Kitty. I'd moved away from Rory, which was clearly her wish.

"All right, Sandy," Kitty said gayly. "*You* give us a tune."

"By some strange coincidence I just didn't happen to bring my music," he quipped. "Rory, come on over here and sing something. I'll play for you."

"Amateur night at the Strand The-ayter," said Rory. He didn't want to sing, I could tell by a thinning of the lips that made him look older, strained and tired. He too had been working hard this evening to maintain a façade. "It's too soon after all the pie. I may be good, but not that good." He dropped into a chair and lay back with his hands behind his neck and his legs stretched out.

"My, everybody's being awfully shy tonight," said Kitty in an edged tone. "If Eunice or I could perform we wouldn't have to be coaxed, would we?"

"Oh, I'd probably be madly temperamental," said Eunice.

"Hey, Eunice," Rory said lazily, "I heard your Uncle Sam bailed Tack Harkins out. Tack stopped me by the mailbox today and told me."

"He'd been up here with his money," Kitty broke in. "Couldn't wait to come up, all of a smirk. And I couldn't wait to call that Sam and give him a piece of my mind. I told him it was just throwing sand down a rathole, and do you know what he said?"

We all waited, Rory with a suppressed quiver around his mouth, Eunice apprehensive, Sandy and I polite.

"He said that was his hobby! Imagine it! He was just trying to rile me up with that juvenile sense of humor of his. I told him if his hobby was throwing away money he could come over here and dump a load on my front lawn any time." Her cheeks were burning; she was feverishly handsome, exhilarated by rage. "*Then* he told me he'd put in a bid on the Glidden place trying to undercut me—and Barney refused it. Sam says they must have turned up an heir, or at least a claimant. Fiddlesticks! It's one of his practical jokes that he's so proud of."

"What makes you so sure there can't be an heir?" Rory asked. Head back, he watched her from under almost-shut lids. "Seems to me somebody or other mentioned a Glidden girl in school with 'em——"

"Why?" asked Kitty sharply. "Why would they mention it?"

He shrugged. "*I* don't know. I don't even know how it came about. Or maybe I saw it myself in an old yearbook. You ought to know something about her. Was she before or after you?"

I was lightly sweating down my back. Those letters of fire

on my brow had changed to something else; my own name was burning me up.

Sandy said in complete innocence, "When I first came here quite a few older people mentioned her to me, because she used to play the organ at the Baptist church sometimes. They thought I'd be interested."

"Maybe she wasn't of the same family," Eunice said helpfully. She and Sandy alone were blamelessly curious. I was trying to look nonchalant while my stomach roiled. Rory yawned as if he weren't really interested in what he'd started. I could have shot him.

"Oh yes, she was of that line," Kitty said. "The last of it, except for her uncle Matt and Old Dick. They'd run out, the Gliddens. Gone to seed. Matt never married, Dick wasn't quite all there, and Helen went away—oh"—Kitty shrugged and spread her hands out—"twenty-five or more years ago. She studied in Boston, but where she went from there, I don't know. As far as I know, she was never heard of again. She must be dead," she said authoritatively. "I'm sure of it. She was always so thin and white, she had to be anemic."

"Did she play as well as they tell me?" Sandy asked.

"I guess so. Had no time for anything else. Or *anyone*," she added reflectively. "But she wasn't the type men looked at, anyway. She was odd. Skinny and intense, all music. She'd put a man off. If she hadn't played for just about everything all through high school, no one would have even *seen* her." She laughed reminiscently. "I can be sorry for her now, but at that age—well, youngsters can be cruel. If they're riding high they don't give much thought to the ones that aren't."

"Did she ever play for my father?" Rory asked.

"Oh, yes." She dismissed that casually. "The operettas and so forth."

*It's my mother she's talking about*, I thought in fascination. *Or a girl who turned out to be my mother. I don't recognize her, but then why should I?* And after all, how much did Kitty know about the reality of Helen, except that she played the piano well?

"I wonder if she ever married?" Kitty said reflectively. "She must have had some crushes, but as I said she wasn't the type they'd look back at."

"So you don't think she could have written to the selectmen?" Rory sounded merely curious.

"No." She dismissed that with a wave of her hand. "She's dead, I'm sure of it. Fern Osblom was her one great friend, and if I'd thought of it someday while Fern was still living I'd have asked her if she knew anything about her. But Helen Glidden wasn't anyone you'd think of when she'd been out of sight for years. I haven't thought about her from the time I last saw her until you asked about her tonight. . . . No, your uncle's trying one of his jokes on me, Eunice," she said good-humoredly. "And if I know him, he's frantically hoping he's outbid everybody, especially *me*."

"I can't see Sam frantic about anything." Rory yawned. "He already has plenty to leave his favorite niece, hasn't he, Eunice?"

"I don't know who his favorite niece is," said Eunice demurely.

"She's going to have a handsome dowry, whoever she is," Rory went on, gazing sleepily at the ceiling. "Parmenter money—Parmenter land—Parmenter, period."

Eunice had poise. She showed nothing but the same ingenuous amusement. But Kitty, who must have been simmering all day about losing the Harkins farm, suddenly cracked with anger.

"Rory, your bad manners are only exceeded by your bad taste."

Rory didn't move. Only his eyes slanted toward her, glistening under the lids. Eunice's expression grew fixed. Sandy slid onto the piano bench and began picking out a tune with one finger. *Show me the way to go home*. I felt as if I were about to burst into manic laughter.

Kitty stood up and spoke to me with incisive dignity. "Sandy and Eunice know Rory well, so they'll probably excuse his conduct. But an apology is due you, Miriam."

"Not at all, Mrs. Barstow," I said, getting up myself. "I'm afraid I haven't even been listening. I ran into some trouble with my work, and I can't get my mind off it." I smiled reassuringly at her.

She gave me an almost bewildered look and put her hand to her head. She looked gaunt and driven. "I've got a headache. I don't get them often, but this has been a terrible day. I know you young people will excuse me."

The rest stood up. Three of us murmured politely and sympathetically. Rory went to his mother, pulled her arm through his, and walked out into the hall with her. We three began talking all at once, so I don't know what any one of us really said. In a few minutes Rory came back, wide awake now.

"What'll we do? It's too late for movies and too early to break up."

"Why don't we go down to the cottage?" I heard Miriam Guild say.

# chapter 21

We walked down the lane by flashlight, laughing and talking with exuberance as if we'd just been freed from some oppressive influence—which of course Kitty was, at least for Rory and me. Jason went with us, pleased about everything, frisking youthfully ahead. Sometimes we were strewn across the lane, sometimes along it singly, and then in twos. I avoided making a pair with Rory. I didn't think we could be that close without touching, and after several hours of being in the same room with him I didn't even trust the small sensuality of brushing hands.

But just at the end, when we were crossing the lawn, Rory turned around to whistle to Jason, caught my hand, squeezed it hard, and dropped it.

The instant we were inside, with a lamp turned on, Sandy underwent a metamorphosis. He set a straight course for the piano and gave a swinging, brilliant performance of pop classics, beginning with the title song from *Cabaret*. He enjoyed it even more than we did. At the finish we applauded, whistled, stamped, and shouted. He stood up grinning and bowed deeply.

"And he can look so pious on Sunday mornings," said Eunice.

"I have to play like this for my father every so often," Sandy said, "so he won't think I've prematurely aged. I've got another assortment for my brothers and my schoolkids, just to convince them I'm not over the hill. But I'll spare you that."

"You don't know how lucky you are," Eunice said, "having brothers and a father." She spoke without envy; like me, she was accustomed to her half-orphanhood.

"Amen to that," said Rory. "I used to think a lot about the kid brothers I might have had. Another boy or two in the family could have changed my whole life. Then I think of *him*, my father. Trying to see a guy my age who never got any older. Going out to harrow that day and never knowing he wouldn't see the night come. Sure, he knew he'd been classified 4-F, but he'd never felt sick, he couldn't believe anything was wrong with him. . . . But there it was, waiting out there in a field of squash plants. I keep hoping it was so quick with him he never had a chance to know what it was."

"I think of my father a lot too," Eunice said, "but more of my mother—I guess that's natural. A girl would identify with her mother. I'd like her to marry again, but she's never seen anyone yet who could come up to him." Her glance warmly took me in. "She says he was wonderful, and I guess he was, because other people say so too. When I was younger I'd look at his medals and study his picture, and I'd think he was a kind of—of knight, or even a warrior prince." She laughed at herself, blushing a little, but I guess my expression reassured her; I knew exactly what she'd meant, even though I'd had no picture or medals to contemplate.

"Miriam belongs to the club too," said Rory.

"I guess I've been lucky," Sandy said.

"Well, don't be so damned apologetic," Rory said. "Next thing you'll be offering to shoot your old man so you'll be one of the group. How about some cheerful noise around here?"

"It's Miriam's turn," Sandy said.

"And she's not getting away with that false modesty act, either. Listen." Rory switched on the tape recorder. At first it was scales and exercises, and then a very creditable performance of *La Plus que Lente*. Sandy leaned sharply forward. Listening objectively I thought, *Not bad at all. In fact, pretty good.* —Rory was enjoying Sandy's reaction. I became aware of Eunice's immobility and, innocently vain, thought it was because of the music until I glanced toward her. She was looking at Rory with a puzzled expression, a tiny frown between her eyebrows. It dawned on me, about the time the piece finished, that Rory was being very familiar with the tape recorder.

On the last note I reached over and shut off the machine. The next would have been Rory singing *My Love Is Like a Red, Red Rose*. And that was for no one else to hear.

Sandy's eyes were alight behind his glasses. "You don't really have to go back to New York, do you?"

"Why don't you marry her, Sandy," Eunice suggested, "and make sure of her?"

"That's a thought. Are you bespoke, Miriam?"

"Yes, she is." Rory said it so fast we were all taken aback. I saw the beginnings of shock in Eunice's sudden parting of the lips, the widening of her eyes. But Rory went easily on. "She told me all about him. He's a poor but honest youth, but underage. His parents won't sign him off."

"He gets a nice little fortune when he's twenty-one," I said. "I'm waiting for him to grow up."

"Like the boy in the song," said Rory. He sang the line. "'He's young, but he's daily a-growing.' What have you to drink in the house, Miriam?"

"If you're not teetotal I've got beer and wine. I've also got tea, coffee, and hot chocolate. Make up your minds." I went out to the kitchen. Eunice followed me to help.

Perhaps I was hypersensitive, but I knew all the signals, and she was flying them. I was sorry for her. I had turned into the Dragon Lady before my own eyes, remembering how once I tried to save face at a party while the boy who had brought me flirted shamelessly with another girl who knew, as all the rest did, that I adored him. She had been cruel in her power.

It had been agony for a seventeen-year-old girl, but I'd been over it, and him, in a month. Eunice and I were women, and it was life we were trying for, not dates and a prize.

For a peculiar out-of-focus instant she and I were drawn together in wordless alliance against the egotistic and arrogant male. Then it passed, but she had flawless good manners and we talked in conventional girl fashion as we set out glasses and dishes.

We stayed away from music for the rest of the evening. They had questions about publishing, and I entertained them with stories of our more eccentric authors, including the elusive Miroslav Andric. In an hour or so we broke up, calling our good-nights across the lawn above the voice of the brook. Then I was abruptly lonesome for Rory, and too nerved up to think about sleep.

I lay down on the sofa before the fireplace to use up the rest of the fire that glowed in the scarlet hearts of the birch logs. I'd turned off the lights and lay there watching the flickering red light and lively shadows in the room around me. Just about the time I decided this wasn't going to relax me either, someone very quietly crossed the porch.

I had never bothered to lock the screen door at night, I had never felt a moment's uneasiness at being alone here; now, in an instant, I was crouching on the sofa, gazing at the door and wondering if I could get across to bolt it before it opened. Visions of a deranged character inflamed by drunk or drugs, plotting to ravish and/or murder me, danced not like sugarplums through my head. Weren't all these outwardly tranquil villages supposed to be seething with unsuspected psychotics?

While I huddled there on the sofa hypnotized by my idiot fancies the door opened and the sex fiend came in. The fire sprang up again in a little burst of ruddy light in which Rory appeared like a figure in a painting, burnished red-gold against the dark.

"*Good!*" he said. "You're still up." He dropped onto the sofa beside me and with a groan took me into his arms, in a large, tight, and unsubtle hug as if I were a giant teddy bear. "Good God, what a night! I wanted to tell you I'd be back, but I couldn't get a chance. After a while I thought the hell with secrecy, but I didn't know how that would go with you."

"Very badly," I said, "especially in front of Eunice. She's

mad about you, and she's so sensitized to everything about you that she was picking up plenty tonight. Especially when you made so free with the recorder."

"You know," he said against my cheek, "she was always a good kid, but if she joins everybody else in putting the pressure on the old friendship's going down the drain."

"Didn't you ever give her anything to go on?" I tried to make it loverlike teasing. "You're breaking my neck, and putting a permanent bend in my rib cage, and cutting off my wind, and——"

"Here, let's get comfortable." I was roughly rearranged and tucked into the crook of his arm. "Now was that about Eunice?" He began kissing me. It was good and began to get even better. I fought my own inclination to come in with the tide and said, "Tell me about Eunice. If there was any under-standing at all between you, open or otherwise, I'd like to know."

"I took her out on a few dates in high school. I also took out some other girls. When I went into the service, that was the end of it. There wasn't anything between us then except those few dates and some necking that never got very far because she wasn't that kind.... After the summer studying with Maggie, I'd outgrown Eunice somehow." He was silent, looking at the fire while I looked at him, wondering what he saw instead of the flames. "Not just Eunice, but everything around here. There was something big I wanted to do. Well, you know all about that.... I've never led her on, if that's what you're afraid of. Not even a little fooling around for auld lang syne."

"Did you take her home tonight?" I asked, moving away so I could see him better.

"Yes," he said. "I went and got her too. My mother made the plans, then told me. Girl can drive a tractor and ride a stallion, but she wasn't able to drive from Windhover to Fourleaf and back again on a clear spring night." He made a sound halfway between a snort and a growl. "I think Kitty hoped I'd have my way with the girl between here and there.

Well, I handed her in and out as if she was fine bone china, and delivered her at her door in a state of unblemished chastity. I saved all my baser impulses for you."

He seized me with a roar. I squawked in spite of myself, and we fell off the sofa and into a strenuous and amorous wrestling match.

It was something I'd never done before, but I liked it. Loved it, in fact, and I wasn't any easy loser. We were both panting when by a trick he flipped me onto my back and half-covered me with his body.

"Nobody would know if I didn't get home tonight," he said very softly, as if we had listeners. "If I was making the coffee up there at four in the morning."

"Jason would know." It was hard speaking, and not because of his weight on me.

"Oh *hell!*" He rolled off. "I should have brought him back with me. I just let him into the kitchen and didn't shut any doors. He's likely to go prowling around two in the morning and wake Kitty up, and she'll be sure this is the time I've driven into the quarry."

"Unless she thought you were spending the night with Eunice," I suggested.

"Very funny," he said.

I rose up on my elbow, leaned over and kissed him, and he pulled me down on him. "Don't mention anybody else tonight, will you?" he said in my ear. "This is our island, our boat, our spaceship, whatever you want to call it, and we're alone on it." We were entwined and sinking again. I wanted to keep on sinking, but I was the one who pulled us out of it. We argued about it, without acrimony, while I made coffee.

"Aren't you sure I love you?" he asked. "Is that it?"

"I'm sure," I said. "I'm sure of me too. That's why I can wait till the time."

"When *is* the time?"

"We'll know." He was standing behind me and I turned and took his face in my hands. "Rory, go along with me on this. Please? I won't say, *if* you love me, because I'm not asking for that kind of proof, and you don't need any other kind of proof, either. Not right now."

He listened seriously, his arms around me. We leaned against the counter while the water boiled.

"It's all so new to us, and we have so much else to do all at once," I said. "Do you realize what's happened to me in the last few weeks? And to *you?* We're in the process of changing over our whole lives, Rory. Already we hardly know ourselves." I hadn't thought it out, but the reasons and the words for them were coming from somewhere, and the reasons were right. I was sure of it. "I'm so scared of getting sidetracked, drugged, even *lost*, when we have so many hard steps to take."

He hadn't taken his eyes off my face. He said, "And you're thinking about your mother. . . . I'm not going to leave you, Miriam. I'm not going to get myself killed. You won't have to raise a child without a father." His voice shook slightly. "I do solemnly swear."

"I know," I said. "I know." My own voice trembled. "That's what I'm trying to promise us." Suddenly I felt weak and wan, like crying on his chest.

He was laughing at me. "You're superstitious! Don't say you aren't!"

"All right, I'm knocking on wood and not looking at the moon through glass——"

"Over your left shoulder, don't forget that."

I nodded, beginning to sniffle with incipient tears. "Not walking on cracks and——"

"Not opening an umbrella in the house." He hugged me back to teddy bear status. "Not having three lights in a room——"

"Or singing before breakfast . . . No, it's a bargain with fate." I managed with some difficulty to reach for a tissue. "Or you can call it a sacrifice to the gods for a safe voyage."

"That I can understand," he said. "Listen, my darling, we've got time. We've got all our lives. If you feel what you say, down into your bones, you could be right. How do I know, maybe you're half-witch and you know these secrets? Who am I to go against magic?"

We came out of our trance to find the kitchen full of steam from a madly boiling teakettle. "Hey, who's for a sauna?" Rory asked, opening the back door. *I love you*, I said silently. *Oh, how I love you.*

# chapter 22

The next morning I woke early to drive to the Glidden place. I knew it would be a farewell, and I wanted to be alone there. In an allegorical way it was something like finding my father only to lose him again; I had owned the pines, the lake shore, the old apple trees, the iris, and hadn't known it, and now I was about to say good-bye. The thought squeezed me like a vise. But the pressure was instantly loosened by the invincible, omnipotent fact of Rory.

My secret visit to the place had its practical side. Rory wasn't going to easily accept my decision. He thought his money would finance him, but I knew better.

Occupied with material details, I found I'd missed Seven Chimneys Farm without my usual conjectures about the Rollinses, and was almost at my own turn-off. I went in off the black road and parked, and walked down the rutted drive, wanting to approach on foot. When I came out to the twin elms their leaves were bigger, translucent against the sun. There were a few daffodils open, and the iris buds were beginning to show some blue. I went directly down to the lake. Most of the ice was gone now, and the water was a pale summery turquoise. I heard the wild, fragile beauty of the loons' duet before I could pick them out. And there were deer hoofprints sharp in the damp sand. I found myself chanting silently but over and over the refrain from one poem of the *Child's Garden of Verses: Good-bye, good-bye to everything!*

It was almost unbearable. I walked back to the pines and up the hill among the thick old trunks. The chilly shade was warmed with freckles of sunlight. Some small birds unknown to me sang over and over in the tops. I had the sense of being cheated of time; I should have been able to walk over every acre I possessed before I gave it up. —But I had only to think of Rory and it was all right. Thus I came out into full sunshine on the brow of the hill above the cellar holes.

A girl and a horse stood between the maple trees. The horse cropped grass, the girl stood looking around her. It was Eunice, in levis and a white turtleneck sweater.

*Damn it!* I thought uncharitably. But she saw me, and waved, so I waved back and went down the slope among the alders and spreading juniper, startling up sparrows. Eunice came to meet me. "I was riding by and I saw your car," she said.

"I'm glad you did," I said. "I saw that turn-off leading away through the trees, and I couldn't resist it. It was an invitation."

"This is the Glidden place. The one we were talking about last night."

"Oh, really?" The words and the usual intonation are one of the sillier responses to a statement of fact. Eunice didn't bother to confirm the obvious.

"It's beautiful, isn't it? That wasn't a joke Uncle Sam pulled on Mrs. Barstow. I wonder *if* and *who*." She laughed. "Speculation's the chief indoor sport around here."

"Come and sit down," I said, gesturing at the granite doorstep. I didn't know what we'd talk about, but I'd be damned if I'd act uncomfortable and unfriendly. "You must have ridden for miles this morning, to be way over here."

"Coming through the woods it's not as far as you might think. The 4-H kids have a project for keeping most of the old woodroads cleared for hiking or riding, and for snowmobiles in winter." She began moving restlessly around with her hands in her pockets. A woodpecker drilled relentlessly on one of the old apple trees. The horse wandered peacefully a few steps at a time; the sound of his munching was very clear.

All at once Eunice turned around and came back toward

me. I knew that she had made up her mind about something.

"I rode to the cottage first this morning," she said. "You were gone."

"How did you know where I was?"

"I didn't. This was pure luck, unless you want to call it fate." Her laugh was hard with nervousness. "I didn't want to go home or up past the main house. I'd come down over the top of Bonfire Hill, and when I went back up I turned north instead of south. I went on and on and eventually I came out of the woods almost opposite this road. When I saw your car I could hardly believe it."

"Well, I'm glad you rode in," I said.

We were both smiling away as if the scene was exactly what the surface represented—if she'd stopped at the cottage it was a spur-of-the-moment thing, just because she happened to be nearby.

"I wanted to talk to you about something," she said.

"All right," I said. "What?"

"Rory." No hedging, no backing and filling.

"What especially about Rory?" Friendly curiosity on my part.

"He's been down to the cottage a lot, hasn't he?" It was humiliating to her, even painful; she flushed, and set her lips as if to will down pain, and her eyelids flickered until she could fix her gaze.

"Several times," I said. "It's because of music. He came by on an errand, and I was playing. That attracted him. It's natural." I tried not to sound amused or patronizing. This was taking all her pride.

"It would be natural in the first place, yes," she admitted. "But afterward——"

"For music," I said firmly. "I don't know how you are about music, but we——"

"Oh, I know!" she said with childish sarcasm. "You're a race apart, like artists and writers. You see things and feel things differently. So that explains and excuses everything."

"No two people see anything in the same way," I protested,

"but some have things in common. I know that's a beautiful horse——"

"Mare," she corrected; her smile was cold, but again it was like a child's contempt.

"You see? All I know is that she's beautiful, but someone who knew horses could immediately start talking about her in a language I couldn't begin to understand, and you'd be pleased and responsive, wouldn't you? If the person happened to be a man you wouldn't think he was making a pass, would you, just because he knew all about Morgans?"

The tawny eyes gazed at me. The breeze lifted the gilt fluff on her forehead. The mare blew softly and stamped. She said, "It's not as if Rory's starved for music. He gets plenty of singing and he could do a lot more if he really wanted to. He was asked to be soloist in a big church in Portland."

She couldn't possibly be that naïve. And how could I possibly be such a rat? "But this is music for pleasure," I said, "for himself, not for anybody else." I tried a joke. "The way some people drink."

"It's not for himself alone, it's for you, and you play for him. That's so, isn't it? It's a"—she went absolutely crimson— "a kind of lovemaking, isn't it?"

I opened my mouth, to say God alone knew what, but she spoke first.

"I've been in love with Rory ever since I can remember. I went out with other boys, but it was only when he went out with somebody else. They used to call me the Snow Queen and the Ice Statue because I wouldn't neck. Well, I couldn't! Not even for fun. Once I really tried to fall for somebody else. I really worked at it. You don't know what I—" Her eyes became beseeching. "Anyway, I couldn't go through with it."

"I never could either. It's nothing to be ashamed of."

"Oh, don't think you have to be kind to me!" she almost shouted. "This is hard enough without pity! Look, I *hate* the way Mrs. Barstow shoves me at him. I wish she'd leave us to manage our own business, and we *could* manage, I'm sure of it, if only you weren't here."

She stared at me as if expecting a blow or at least an angry outburst. I didn't say anything, because I couldn't think of anything to say but the truth. *You haven't a prayer.* If she didn't know it by now—hadn't known it before I came—I wasn't going to deliver that belly punch this morning.

She wet her lips and said, "We were always close friends, and I know that if we could just be together at our own pace something would happen."

"He'd fall in love with you," I said.

"Why shouldn't he? He may be half there already, but he won't admit it. I'm good-looking, I'm healthy, and I'm not frigid—not for *him*, I know that." She swallowed, and shut her eyes. "Just being in the same room with him, the way I feel, I have no pride, no shame." The words came in a whisper, and the back of my neck prickled. How well I knew.

"I think he was almost ready before you came," she went on. "People asked the two of us to a lot of things this winter, and he always took me and brought me home. Two people can't keep being together all the time without something happening."

Especially when one of them is burning up. Poor Rory, one affectionate kiss from him and he'd have been in bed with her before he knew it, and in church the next week with somebody else singing the wedding music. And maybe a third party begun behind the bouquet.

Who was I to scoff? I sat down on the doorstep again and began looking through the tangled grass for more iris; not to be rude, but because I couldn't stand much more of this naked anguish. She came closer.

"Why don't you go away, Miriam?" she demanded. "You're just amusing yourself with him, the way that singer did. She ruined everything once, and now you're ruining it again. You can't possibly want him, not to keep, not for a *husband*—a woman like you, with your kind of life. You'll go away when you're ready, and you'll have destroyed everything for us here, but it won't matter to you, will it? You'll never give us another thought."

I couldn't lie to her any more than I could tell the truth. But it's right, what Stevenson said: The cruelest lies are often told in silence. I felt simultaneously guilt, pity, anger, and the whole thing shot through with glittering little spears of triumph because I had him. The privileged girl who stood before me in her riding clothes had grown up knowing who she was, surrounded by adoring family and a town named for that family; Daddy was a heroic legend. She didn't need Rory. I did.

I sat with my chin in my hands, looking at her. *Did I appear vanquished?* I wondered.

She said, "I'll have a chance without you, and I *won't* need Mrs. Barstow."

"Eunice, I have things to do before I leave here," I said. "I can't go yet."

"I should think you could do that—that *editing* of yours anywhere it's quiet. There are plenty of other places in Maine." Suddenly her voice went small, tight, and high. "Go away, Miriam. *Please*."

"Not until I'm ready," I said softly.

She turned and walked to the mare. I watched her swing up into the saddle and ride into the lane. I gave her time to get to the black road and back to the bridle path, then I went slowly up the lane to my car. I felt rotten. *You need to hold on to your self-confidence*, I told myself. *You've got every right in the world to be happy. Don't let Eunice do this to you. She wouldn't let you taint her happiness, if she were the one. Go home, eat something, and get to work.*

# chapter 23

I couldn't stand the sight of the manuscript. I tried the piano but was all thumbs, and finally I went out and climbed up the rocky side of the brook, in hopes that the hilltop in the April wind and sun would blow or dazzle away her face and her voice. I sat on the topmost stone wall with the farm falling away before me. Crows rattled polished black through the crystal atmosphere and I counted them. One for sorrow, two for mirth, three for a wedding, four for a birth; five for the happiest day on earth. *And don't let another come to spoil it.*

Another one didn't come, and I was reassured. I knew that was infantile, but I needed all the support I could get. Some people took Miltowns, I'd count crows.

I wasn't taking Rory from Eunice because she'd never had him to lose. But her visit this morning to the place that was mine, however secretly and however briefly, was like the presence of the bad fairy at the christening. It was as if she'd set loose a sackful of bad influences. I almost thought *evil*, but that was foolishness. There was no evil here, but it was a battle of three women, and I wanted no such war with all its griefs and sulks and tempers, and wet eyes and trembling lips.

I wasn't used to conflict, either open or covert. It wore on my nerves. But at least I was ahead, I had Rory. And I didn't have to enter the battle; I had only to hold fast.

I returned to the cottage then, refreshed and hungry, and went to work on the manuscript. I didn't stop until mid-afternoon, when I went out for another walk again. I felt optimistic about everything. There was a capricious wind, red-winged blackbirds calling constantly from around the brook, bright green under foot everywhere and a green April scent to match. I went up the hill and as I followed the curve away from the main house I saw Eunice's blue Volkswagen turning between the gate posts onto the black road. Still insulated in euphoria I wondered if she'd been telling Mrs. Barstow about me, but I doubted that. She was too proud.

The mail driver came from the opposite direction as I reached the road, and stopped at the box. From behind the wire fencing Apollo watched us.

"Looks as if butter wouldn't melt in his mouth," the postman observed.

"He looks as if he's waiting to be patted," I said.

The driver cackled. "I met him head-on down the road one day. Well, not quite head-on. I stopped, but I didn't know as he was going to. I thought my car was going to be wrecked and Kitty'd have me up in court for damaging the champeen."

"What happened?" I gazed into Apollo's large lovely dark eyes with their ridiculous lashes.

"Well, I was fixed to set it out in one of them eyeball-to-eyeball confrontations, but then Rory came jogging round the bend, whistled to him, and the creature went to him clever as a kitten and follows him home. Well, more side by side they went," he added. "Shoulder to shoulder. Rory raised him. He's a young feller still, the bull is. He ain't fully realized his capacity for meanness, you might say."

He loaded me down with the Fourleaf mail, taking it for granted that was what I was waiting for.

"How'd he ever get out in the first place?" I asked. "He sounds like a show jumper."

"Oh, somebody leaves a gate open, or don't see if it's latched, and the wind gets it. This time I was telling about, a truck'd gone off the road in the night, smashed through the stone wall and broken down the fence. When the tow truck hauled it away the bull wasn't in sight, and nobody let 'em know at the house about the fence. So the bull just walked out the next morning."

"Well, I hope it doesn't happen again right off," I said. "It would be just my luck to meet him, and my car's a lot smaller than yours. And he might take an instant dislike to it."

He was enormously amused. "Ayuh, I can see him bouncing that doodlebug off the top of his head."

He went off with a couple of rakish toots of his horn, like Mr. Toad, and I went back up the long drive. Apollo kept sedately apace on his side of the wall. As I walked, I was calculating my chances of leaving the mail on the front hall table without being stopped when I heard a car coming from the house, and in a few moments Mrs. Barstow's yellow Saab came around the curve under the maples, going fast. She slowed at sight of me but didn't stop; I got a short nod, more a chop of her chin, and then she was gone. Apollo and I both stood gazing after her. Then our eyes met in solemn communication, I shrugged and said with a mystic lack of meaning, "Ah."

When I went in the front door I could hear sounds of high merriment in the kitchen where everyone seemed to have collected for a mug-up between jobs as soon as Mrs. Barstow was gone. I heard Rory laughing. I could have joined them and been welcomed, and I was tempted; but I had work to do, and Rory would be down in the evening. I left the house mail on the table by a green jug of forsythia that was twinned in the mirror behind it.

When Rory came it was as if we'd been parted for weeks. Then we settled down in front of the fire to talk. I told him I'd driven to the Glidden place that morning and taken a walk, but I left out Eunice's visit.

"What did you think while you were there?" he asked me. "Could you see a house again, a barn, the pastures cleared? Could you see *us* there?"

"Rory, the sale of the place could finance you," I began, but he hugged me to him.

"No. That's your place and your children's place. You can't sell it out from under them."

"*Our* children," I said.

"All right, ours," he said with a grin. "And, besides, if I don't make it in New York, we'll have the land to come back to. Money goes, but the land is always there if you're willing to use your two hands and your back."

"What about Fourleaf Farm? Isn't it two-thirds yours?" I asked curiously. "Not that I think you should push your mother around, but if we had to sell the Glidden place you'd still have land, wouldn't you?"

"Maybe legally, but morally it should all be hers. I've just ridden along."

"I'm beginning to think you only want me for my farm." I sat up haughtily. "You men are all alike. You want just one thing."

"Ha." He nibbled the back of my neck. "So at last you know the truth. Tell me to get out."

"I'm helplessly in the power of my glands and hormones," I said. "I know you're a fortune hunter but I can't help myself. But seriously——"

"Don't be serious," he mumbled into my hair. Then he was, a few moments later.

"Kitty got the news today about the place." I stiffened, and he said, "Not about you, but Barney called her up and said the bidding was off. Between losing that and the Harkins place, she thinks she's had a tough week. Eunice was over this afternoon, but my mother never even bothered to send Little Red Ridinghood out to find me. Which shows a real lack of fighting spirit."

"I'm sorry," I began, meaning it, but he gave me a vigorous shake.

"Don't be. It's only temporary. By suppertime she was thinking hard again. Scheming how to get around the mysterious heir when he shows up, I imagine."

"I think I should tell her the truth," I said. "It shouldn't come from anywhere else. I have no reason *not* to tell her except that she'll think it's strange I didn't tell her right away who I was. And she'll find it hard to believe I didn't know about the place when I came here."

"And she'll make you an offer," he warned me, "which you aren't to accept. That'll be the hard part; you're likely to hand the place over just to ease your conscience."

"Well, I don't know if I'm that much of a goody-two-shoes," I protested. "Still I can see why she——"

"Don't be so damned *reasonable*," he told me. "And let's not talk about it any more tonight. That's for tomorrow."

" 'Tomorrow to fresh woods, and pastures new,' " I quoted out of nowhere that I could remember, and he said, "I like these pastures myself."

It was well after midnight when we separated. Music had occupied us part of the time; usually I was the one who grabbed at it like a life ring when I felt us sinking. But, as Eunice had so perceptively remarked, music could be a kind of lovemaking too. It left us both keyed up and depressed, exhilarated and exhausted. We knew what we wanted, but it wasn't time yet; not before the battle, and there would be one as soon as we found out that Kitty wasn't living under the threat of cancer. I hadn't told Rory how sure I was, because he was so positive that she had never lied to him. But I was a woman and I could put myself in her place; though I believed I would be both too honest and too superstitious to lie about such a thing (*Don't tempt Fate*, my mother used to warn me), I could understand how a desperately obsessive and possessive woman might use any means to hold on.

What Rory hoped to find out from the doctor was that there was no need to worry about his mother, that she was completely cured. If he found out that she'd never had cancer, then he should feel freed from any moral obligation, and it would be up to me to try to make him understand and forgive. It would do him and his voice no good to carry away an inexorable resentment.

It was all charging around in my head at one o'clock that morning, and at two, even after a long warm shower, a cup of cocoa, and one of those English-village mysteries. Then suddenly everything worked and I fell asleep. *Plunged* is more like it. I half-roused once to put off my light, and submerged again.

At first the pounding was a part of my dream. In it someone was hammering on a naked ridgepole against a clear blue-burning sky. At the same time I knew someone was at the door of the cottage. I wakened slowly and grudgingly, to damp gray light. Then I thought *Rory!* and unrolled from my tangle of bedclothes, and went across the living room pulling on my robe. The floor was cold under my bare feet.

It was not Rory, but Faye was too flustered to see my glad though rumpled welcome turn to surprise. "What's the matter?" I exclaimed. I stood back to let her in. I thought *Rory* again, but with terror, seeing a tractor accident or Apollo turning deadly at last.

Faye flopped heavily into the nearest chair. "Oh, what works we've had up at the house!" she panted. "What works!" She rolled her eyes up and fanned herself with a hand.

"Well, tell me!" I stood over her, nauseated with suspense. "Is it an accident?" Even as I got the word out, I thought, *Kitty's found out about me, the place, or about Rory and me. They've had a terrible scene. Yes, that's it.*

"Kitty's in the hospital!" Faye said.

"Is it the cancer?" I asked stupidly.

Faye went blank with astonishment. "*What?* Did you say——?" Like many people she couldn't utter the word. She was frightened. "Kitty told you something *I* don't know?"

"No, no, I'm all mixed up," I protested. "I was dreaming when you knocked, and it was about somebody I knew who had cancer. And when you said 'hospital' it was like being still stuck in my dream."

"Oh, I see. Gorry, I'm sorry I gave you such a turn. But then you gave *me* one." She hugged herself. "Someone walking over my grave."

"Tell me about Mrs. Barstow. What happened?"

"Could you give me a cup of coffee to tell it on? I've been up since before four and haven't had anything to eat yet."

"Start the water heating, and I'll go wash my face and get dressed."

It was only a little past seven. When I came back out the coffee was dripping and she had the table set. "How about scrambled eggs?" she asked. "You've got some bacon here too."

"All right, if that's what you'd like." My stomach was sore with nerves, but at least Rory was all right, unless he'd knocked his mother down or given her a heart attack. . . . I almost doubled up with nervous pain behind Faye's back.

Together we got breakfast on the table while Faye gave me the story. A little before four she'd been awakened by a terrible crash and a cry. She was out of bed and in the hall before she was fully awake, putting on lights. There was nobody on the front stairs, and she found Kitty crumpled up halfway down the steep and narrow back stairs. The fact that they turned a corner had kept her from plunging straight to the bottom and possibly killing herself.

As it was, Faye thought she was dead then, because she was unconscious. Without touching her she ran back upstairs to Rory's room to wake him; he was always a heavy sleeper, so she wasn't surprised that he hadn't heard anything. But he wasn't in his room, and he hadn't been to bed.

At this point I had another belly cramp. He'd left me a little after one. What had happened to him between here and there?

"So I ran up to the third floor to get the men. My word, I don't know where I got the wind to run like a deer, but I did. Ruel sleeps like a cat, he was down in about three minutes and all dressed. But that Leni, he'd had five beers last night, and he was snoring to beat the band. I hauled him out of bed by main strength—him in a nightshirt, but to hell with modesty at a time like that! And all the time no sign of that cussid Rory. I *wanted* him to go chasing girls, but this was too much!"

"How'd you get her off the stairs?"

"Well, I didn't know if it was right to move her, but the

way she was all bent up there, and in a draft too, didn't seem right. I must say those two did real good, once Leni got his eyes open. Gentle as if they was handling eggs. Got her onto the mattress from the office couch, and they kind of eased it down the rest of the way. Then I settled her in the office with a hot water bottle and a couple of blankets tucked around her."

She stopped to eat a little. "I didn't think I'd ever be able to eat again after the shock and all, but this tastes good. Can't *you* eat?"

"Later. Just tell me the rest of it."

"Well, of course, her doctor *would* be away fishing, and I was just calling the town ambulance, when Rory comes strolling in the back door, him and Jason, as if it was noon in summertime. Said he couldn't sleep so he'd been out prowling around. Well, he took one look at his mother and turned feather-white. He rode in the ambulance to Rockland, and he just called up and said as far as they knew there wasn't any concussion or skull fracture, or anything else broken. A lot of bumps and bruises. They're keeping her a couple of days for observation, just in case of something internal. But she's conscious and says she's fine." She smiled proudly. "That's Kitty for you."

"Well, I'm glad," I said truthfully, and selfishly. A serious injury could send our plans a-glimmering.

"Thanks for a great breakfast," Faye said.

"You fixed it, and thanks for coming to tell me. Can you get a nap now?"

"Lordy, no, I've got those men to cook for. The work goes on, no matter what. She'll be having a fit down there in the hospital, for fear we're all sitting down playing cards and watching TV while the place goes to hell. What about these dishes?"

"Oh, forget them, for heaven's sake."

I went to the door with her. The day was raw and lowery, even the birds seemed quenched by the pressure of the sky. But Rory was all right and his mother probably was, so I built a fire in the fireplace, and decided to have some solid food after all.

I worked all morning. By noon, Rory came. He slammed the door behind him and took me into his arms, wouldn't let me speak, hugged me until I thought he'd crack a rib, buried his face in my neck as if it were a warm cave he was trying to crawl into.

I guess my side of the embrace was pretty frantic too. Sometimes at the sight of him my basic insecurity would burgeon into full bloom, as if unconsciously I believed I was never meant to have this other, more fragile flower: the condition of love between Rory and me. It had happened so suddenly and was so devastating.

I got partly loose after a while. "How is she?"

"All right. Nothing broken, but she's sore all over. And she's ugly as sin. She won't speak to me." He grinned, took my hands away from his face and kissed one palm and then the other. He did these things with such grace that if I'd been soured on men I'd have suspected him of practicing on a good many palms before mine. . . . He sniffed loudly at my fingers on my right hand and shut his eyes. "Your blue pencil has a rare old bouquet with delicate nuances of woodsmoke and orange peel. What vintage was that?"

"I can't help it if you didn't give me time to bathe in mare's milk and attar of roses," I said. "Why isn't she speaking to you?"

"It's not just me. She's mad as hell with everybody. She's having her lawyer in this afternoon. I don't know who she's going to sue because she fell downstairs in her own house." He enfolded me again. "Anyway, she didn't break a hip or her neck, thank God, so she'll be home in a day or so and find out I haven't gambled the farm away behind her back."

"Where were you when she fell?"

"I'd been walking all over the farm for a couple of hours, ever since I left you. I couldn't settle down, so I took Jason and went out again." He sat on the arm of the sofa and balanced me on his knee. "I kept wishing you were with us. We saw a fox, raccoons, one skunk, one of our barn cats—Tom Tiddler—and over in the east woodlot there were five deer. And I heard wild geese going over."

"Oh, Rory, I have never in my *life* heard them! Just in movies or on TV. Oh, why did I have to miss that?" I wasn't acting out acute disappointment; I felt almost as if I'd missed Rubinstein.

"Darling, you'll hear wild geese, I promise you." Solemnly he kissed my forehead, nose, and chin, as if conferring a blessing. "You look about ten years old. Look, maybe we'll hear a wildcat scream or a fox barking. Deer make sounds too. They——"

"Rory, love," I said wryly, "how will you be able to stand it in New York?"

"Music is a whole different world," he said in gentle astonishment at my having to question. "This one's like my heredity. I'm part of it wherever I go. I can't lose it."

He had to go back and put in an afternoon's work, and I told him I didn't expect him that evening, since he'd been up all night. Rain started in late afternoon, and around seven I was seriously considering going to bed with a book when the jeep came noisily down the lane, defying potential mud. There wasn't just Rory, but Faye and the two hired men.

"Everybody's half out on their feet," Rory told me, "but we need a little fun."

"I keep hearing that crash," Faye told me, "and seeing her like that. Even if she's all right, I know I'll dream about it."

Ruel astonished me by singing as loud as the rest of them around the piano, and later he brought out a harmonica and played it while Leni, Faye, and Rory taught me a Finnish dance in 6/8 time. I think I was as happy that evening as I'd ever been in my life.

# chapter 24

Rory was to bring his mother home the next afternoon. I wanted to show some special sign of interest besides going in to see her and making the usual inquiries. I had seen a fishbowl tucked away on the top shelf in the bedroom closet. I got it down and washed the dust away, and then went out to gather material for a terrarium. I had loved to do this when I was a kid.

In a world of verdure and gray-dappled skies I collected mosses, lichens, a clump of tiny white violets in bud, miniature ferns still tightly curled, highland cranberry plants, an infant spruce tree. Brook-washed pebbles, and a transparent yellow land-snail shell. The results delighted me.

In the later afternoon I went to the house. Faye sent me to the living room, where Kitty was settled in a wing chair before the fire, wearing a peacock-blue caftan. There was a small dressing on her forehead. Being Kitty, she'd missed getting a black eye, and she wore her lipstick and earrings, and her hair was lustrously in order. There was a tall vase of mixed spring flowers on the stand beside her.

She made me take it away and put the fishbowl there, and exclaimed over the terrarium as if she'd never seen one before. I sat opposite her, beaming idiotically.

"And did you make this just for me?" she demanded.

I nodded.

"It was sweet of you, Miriam, it really was. Anyone can call a florist." She nodded with a wry little smile toward the flowers. "But you did this yourself. Thank you, dear."

I was almost blissful at that "dear." Surely we weren't in for such an awful time after all. Kitty Barstow had considerable charm when she chose, and I was ready to confide in her at once about my claim to the Glidden place. I think I had even begun to say *Mrs. Barstow* when she said, "Just wait until the others see it." She raised her voice. "Eunice, you can't guess what Miriam made for me!"

Eunice came in, carrying a tray. She'd had warning; her face was all ready, not frozen even for a second. I had to admire the seeming spontaneity of her greeting.

"Oh, *hello*, Miriam! Just in time for a cup of tea. I must have been psychic, I put an extra cup on the tray." She set it down on the low table before the fireplace and went to admire the terrarium. Rory came in carrying a heavier tray, and the voices receded halfway to infinity as we looked at each other; it was a good thing the other two were examining and discussing my work, because that look would have given everything away with no reservations.

Jason, who had followed him in, came over to me, and Rory moved again and set the tray down beside the other.

"I see you have a new butler, Mrs. Barstow," I said.

She laughed. "Oh, yes. I thought his looks were wasted on outside work. Rory, come see what Miriam's done. Would you ever think she was a city girl?"

"No, because she isn't. She's got her roots in good farm soil like the rest of us." He didn't even glance at me.

"Eunice drove down with Rory to bring me home," Kitty said to me. "Wasn't it nice of her, with all she has to do?"

"It certainly was," I said inanely.

"Eunice, you pour the tea. My right shoulder's so lame. In fact I'm lame almost everywhere you could mention."

"Good heavens," I said, "I forgot to ask how you were."

"I'm so black and blue all over I look like the Tattooed Lady." She was very jolly about it. I wondered if it was her idea or Eunice's for the girl to drive with him to the hospital.

Eunice poured tea with her mother's grace. I couldn't tell whether hers was a gallant smile or a triumphant one. When she started to pass a cup to Rory to give to me, I got up quickly and took it from her; I wasn't going to watch Rory hand around the teacups like something the two women had tamed between them. And in a kind of shattering vision I saw Eunice as a young Kitty.

I tried to give Faye's orange bread the proper attention while Kitty explained to me gayly what she was doing on the stairs at four in the morning. I hadn't asked, but she told me anyway. "I woke up early, and began thinking about this new bill due to come up before the legislature—I won't try to explain it, Miriam, it's too complicated for anyone but us farmers." She laughed lightly to show this was a joke. "I just had to get up and go down to the office to read it again and see if I had it straight." More laughter. For someone who was all black and blue and almost too lame to move, she was merrier than I'd ever seen her. But that could be reaction and relief after the terror of the fall. "If I'd gone down the front stairs at least the carpet would have softened the fall, but on the other hand the turn kept me from going the whole way and landing on my head."

"Well, you were very lucky, and we're all very thankful," I said. I carried my cup back to the table. "I won't stay any longer, but I'll drop in tomorrow."

"I was going to ask you to, anyway, for a particular reason. Would you make it about ten in the morning?"

"Yes, of course." This chilly fingertip of suspicion trailing down my backbone was getting tiresome. There was something inexorable about all the good humor around here. Rory stood apart from us, his face turned away toward the windows and the day of tourmaline and pearl.

"Good-bye for now, everyone," I said. As I crossed the threshold into the hall Rory's voice followed me, and it was like his hand taking hold of the back of my neck.

"Your mail's on the table, Miriam."

"Thank you!" I called back sunnily. I went to the table and looked at the scattering of mail there. It meant nothing, I couldn't even recognize my own name. *I must get out of here*, I thought. Then a movement in the mirror attracted me, and I looked in it and saw Rory coming toward me from the living room doorway.

The oval glass was like a painting of one of those Dutch interiors, all sunless luminosity, and I was the girl who saw her lover's face in a mirror and didn't know if it was himself or his ghost. Rory certainly looked as if he had been face to face with something deadly, and for the first time I really hated those two with their smiles and talk and genteel play with the teacups.

He said very clearly, "Did you find it all right?"

"Yes," I answered, for my voice to carry. "I've just been admiring the carving on this mirror."

"It's not very old."

"That doesn't matter, it's still nice." He had reached me. We gazed at each other by way of the glass. We could still see the living room doorway but no person. They were talking in there.

"She called me this morning and told me to bring Eunice when I went for her," he murmured.

"Is that what's bothering you?"

His hands were braced against the edge of the table and I touched the back of the nearest one.

"Don't let it.... Didn't you sleep last night, after all that singing and dancing?" There was a dark smudging under his eyes, and short, new lines at either corner of his mouth.

"I'll be down tonight," he said.

"Rory!" his mother called as if on cue. "Will you get the copy of that bill from the office?"

We turned away from the mirror then and toward each other with slight despairing smiles, and I scooped up my handful of mail and went out fast.

By mid-evening he hadn't come. I had worked until I felt I wasn't fit to do justice to the job. I put it away and washed my face in cold water to rouse myself. Then I sat down at the piano and crashed vigorously and carelessly into Mendelssohn's *Spring Song*, and sang at the top of my lungs the sentimental words we'd sung in Chorus at high school. Louder and louder and worse and worse it got, but I knew all the time it was a substitute for throwing things, for screaming and fighting.

Then out of the corner of my eye I caught movement at the end of the piano. I stopped in mid-yell, whipping around, and saw Jason. He was looking up at me with his ears laid back in polite protest against the noise, but his tail waving steadily. Rory stood against the door.

We didn't say anything. We flew together and hung on with the mindless clutch of capsized boaters hanging to a branch that might break at any minute and let them go over Niagara Falls.

He was saying something unintelligible. I kept asking him what, but we were smothering our words against each other. Finally we loosened up and looked at each other. My heart rattled as if I'd been running uphill.

"What is happening?" I asked, taking his hand and holding it to my face. The knuckles were cold against my cheek. "Rory, you frighten me," I said faintly, because fear does things to my throat. "Are you sick?"

I hoped he was: that I could cope with. Then he seemed to come back to his face, at least a recognizable Rory appeared in his eyes. He said violently, "To hell with them. To hell with them both." I realized he must have been saying it all along.

"What have they been doing?"

"What have they been doing?" he repeated in that savage voice. "They've been *existing*. Just for that I could kill them. I look from one to the other and there's no difference. You know that, there's no bloody goddamn difference. I went out after you left, back to work. Eunice followed me. Whatever I did, she was always there, right at the edge, off in the distance, somewhere in the picture. She stayed to supper. I said I had a headache and went to bed. Kitty sent her up with a tray."

Strong color blushed into his face. "So she was in my room.

She offered to rub my shoulders and my neck. Christ, I felt like kicking her in the teeth, but I was sorry for her."

"We're both sorry for her," I said. I pulled him over to the sofa and down beside me, and we wrapped up snugly in each other's arms. "And we're both on edge because we're lying, or just the same as. I wanted to tell your mother something this afternoon, about the Glidden place, at least. Only Eunice was there.... And we're so damned civilized we keep waiting for the right moment, and then afterward we know there never was a right moment. We should have just gone ahead and done it anyway."

I suppose the sound he made was intended for a laugh. "I did," he said. "I went ahead and did it anyway." Before I got the sense of the words he was going on. "I told her I didn't want my shoulders rubbed, I didn't want the heating pad, I wanted to sleep; get Faye or Leni to drive her home. I turned my back on her. But she insisted on putting another blanket on me. God, she was so damned *adoring* it made me feel like a fool and worse. A scoundrel, a lowlife. So I sat up and I told her it was no good, it never would be any good, and forget it. And if I *had* kicked her in the teeth she couldn't have looked any more—any more——"

"I know," I said. "I know. But it had to be done and now it *is* done. Did she go to your mother with it then?"

"My mother was knocked out with something the doctor gave her for pain. But Eunice had some pride left, and she stood up straight and told me she'd been with Kitty a couple of days ago and told her I had somebody else, and it was no use."

He sat with his elbows on his knees, looking at the hearth rug between his feet.

I said, "Did she tell your mother who it was?"

"No." He turned his head and gave me a sardonic smile. "You want to know why Kitty was up at that hour? Not to get something out of the office to read over again. She was trying to catch *me*. I wasn't in my room so she was going to be ready for me when I came in the door."

"That's why she wasn't speaking to you when she went to the hospital."

"Yes. She was so damned mad. But she never gives up. She thinks I'm sleeping around with some tramp, so of course ol' buddy ol' playmate Eunice still has a good chance if she just hangs in there . . . and ol' buddy ol' playmate wants to believe it too—even if she knows its you—so they really went to work on me. I had the damnedest feeling when she came to my room she didn't care what happened; in fact she'd start things going if she had to. Kitty was asleep by then. Faye and the men went to the Grange meeting."

"You could have raped her, but of course for her it wouldn't have been rape. Look, your mother and Eunice adore you in their separate ways, but in the same way they've been loading you down ever since you can remember. And if you were really a scoundrel you'd get a lot of sadistic pleasure out of seeing two women tear themselves to pieces over you."

"I love you," he said, taking me into his arms again, but this time gently. "And I'm not going back there tonight. You can't drive me."

"Is she still there?"

"No, she took Kitty's car. I told her to call when she got back to Windhover, I didn't want her driving off a bridge somewhere."

I had to smile. "You see, you're no scoundrel. Did she call?"

"Yes. Good old Eunice."

"If you'd married her out of pity it would have been a worse cruelty than what you did tonight. She doesn't have to settle for pity."

"I tried to tell her that. Did you hear what I said? You can't drive me away tonight. I brought Jason so he won't be prowling around at the crack of dawn." He was very quiet. "You said afterward we know there never was a right moment. But I think this one is."

We sat outwardly calm looking at each other, the firelight on our faces. I considered everything, including my own origins, and then I said, "Yes."

# chapter 25

At two in the morning we were in the kitchen. Rory was making French toast. "My treatment of this is really superb," he said. "I'll give you my secret since we've got no others between us now." He moved toward me and I said, "Stay with your skillet."

He was so beautiful. He had said *I* was; he had whispered it in a way that put tears in my eyes. He had said, "You're all mine now," but I couldn't say it back for fear that in the next instant he would be struck away from me.

"What are you thinking about?" he asked.

I couldn't have begun to explain; he was so outrageously happy, and I was afraid to be. It was as simple as that.

"I was thinking about how experienced you are," I said severely.

"And a good thing too," he said. "It put me in charge."

"Where did you get all your experience?"

"Oh, here and there. Sit down and eat, you need food. Eunice was neither here nor there, if that's what you suspect." He put me in my chair, and leaned over and kissed me. "Excuse me. We weren't going to mention her. There's nobody on this spaceship but us and my brother Jason here."

"It's an island, not a spaceship," I said dreamily. When we were touching, even as lightly as this, it seemed that nothing could ever happen to us, we were joined in a magic circle and as long as we didn't step out of it we'd be all right.

"Why *shouldn't* we live happily forever after?" I asked defiantly.

Rory burst out laughing. "I love you," he said. "Oh God,

Miriam, how I love you. I never knew what the word meant until now."

"Neither did I," I said.

We went back to bed, to sleep this time, wrapped comfortably around each other. I had set my little alarm clock, but I woke before it went off. Rory was still sleeping, half his weight and his arm across me pinning me down, his face against my shoulder. I moved my head until my cheek lay against his hair. The scent and texture of it was as familiar as if we had been waking this way for a long time. I thought how in a night all of him had become known to me; a night was really a year.

He woke in a few minutes, at once as fully conscious of me as I had been of him, and we talked, watching for the warning of daylight around the shades. Jason breathed deeply in sleep on the rug beside the bed.

"Your mother wants me to come up this morning," I said. "I don't know why. Maybe somebody's coming in for coffee. I want to tell her about the place, Rory, so I'll get there before ten and make a point of it. Or do you want us to be together to talk to her, and tell her the whole thing? Maybe tonight? We'll get it over with."

"No." He was tranquilly decisive. "I don't want her to know *anything* until I'm ready to walk off the farm. And if that sounds heartless—if it's wrecking your ideas of honor— you've never heard Kitty in full cry."

"Isn't she going to be wild anyway when she finds out how you've treated Eunice?"

"Yes, but it'll be just that," he said. "*You* won't be her target, and that's what I'm worried about. Look, in three days the doctor will be back, so I can make sure I'm leaving her in good health, not dying bravely on her feet. And in that time I'll have somebody lined up to help out here, because I can't leave Leni and Ruel with all the extra work. Young Tip'll do all right for some things, but I think I can get back the man she fired last fall. He's damn good with the stock. . . . His wife was sick, he thought she was dying, and he wasn't thinking straight that day he left the gate open and Apollo got out."

A nervous little snicker got away from me, and he squeezed me and said, "What's that for?"

"The bull. He's inescapable. He keeps coming in when you least expect him."

He chuckled. "When he got into the Leadbetters' barn they didn't expect him either. First we knew he was loose, one of the kids called up and said Apollo had his father up in the haymow, and his big brother was loading his rifle. Leni and I went over with a truck and brought him home. Kitty fired Tom while we were gone. She said he'd almost cost her eight thousand dollars. I wasn't consulted; I'm not an actual partner in Fourleaf, no matter what she says."

"But would your mother have him back, even if he's willing to come?"

"She should be. He's a good man, and they're hard to find, as the song goes. He won't be worrying about his wife now, and leaving gates open."

"Oh, she recovered then."

"No. She died that day. —Kitty's a practical woman, and she'll take him, and he'll take the job because he's fed up with cutting pulpwood and because I did everything I could to make up to him for what she did." He ran his hand over me under the bedclothes. "I love your belly."

"That's the nicest thing that was ever said to me. It's like the Song of Solomon."

"If I don't get out of here now I never will." He threw back the covers and got up.

"You're brown all over," I said, drowsily appreciative as he dressed. "I like brown rabbits better than white ones. Brown eggs better than white. Brown——"

He leaned over and kissed me. "Go back to sleep." He tucked the blankets around me and went out. Jason's nails clicked and his tags jingled as he followed. I surprised myself by falling asleep again. When I woke up the sun was shining and a purple finch was singing from my rooftop. I felt not in the least sinful or lost, but positive that we had already turned the corner into our own new world.

Still in my robe, I took my coffee out onto the front doorstep and hunched there in the strengthening sun, watching the brook slide shining by, listening to its many voices, now as familiar to me as the parts of a musical composition. *Like the melodie that's sweetly play'd in tune*, as our song went. Our song. I giggled at the phrase, as I'd giggled cruelly at any chum of mine who'd gone cow-eyed with love and could be depended upon to clutch a damp Kleenex at the mere mention of *our song*, which I always thought of collectively as *You Are My Sunshine*.

I bathed and dressed and walked up to the house about twenty before ten, with some idea of wandering out toward the barns, apparently aimlessly in case anyone was watching. I might get a glimpse of Rory and see if he looked as good as I felt. I supposed it was as banal as *our song* to see last night as a miracle, but that's what it was. I whistled as I walked in the spring morning and thought I had discovered at least one lost April.

The egg truck was just leaving. Jason lay sleeping in hedonistic luxury in the crocus bed beneath the end windows, a golden blossom crushed under his hairy chin. I walked around to the back door, looking toward the outbuildings for a sign of human life, but before I could turn that way Faye came out from the entry.

"*Good* morning!" she called. "Kitty's in the dining room and she saw you coming. She says come in right away." She began hanging up dishtowels.

"What's going on?" I asked. "Anybody else in there?"

"I dunno, to one question, and not yet to the other. You look real happy and springlike this morning."

"Who wouldn't, on a day like this? It's a time for someone to say, 'Rise up, my love, my fair one, and come away. For, lo, the winter is over and gone; the flowers appear on the earth; the time of the singing of birds is come——' "

She applauded. "My lands, if Leni came in and quoted that

at me I'd fall right over where I was and he could have his will of me. I'd never lift a finger to defend myself."

"Maybe somebody should tell him."

"Listen, he doesn't need any more ideas than he has already!"

No sign of Rory. I went into the house and through to the dining room. Mrs. Barstow sat at the table, with papers and notebooks spread before her.

"How are you today?" I asked.

"Oh, so much better than yesterday that I'm surprised. And *you* look very nice today, Miriam. My word, when you go home somebody's going to take a deep breath at sight of you." She became a little arch. "There *is* somebody, isn't there? There has to be."

"Several somebodies," I said, smiling back with the horrid suspicion that I was being just as arch. "The trouble is to choose one. I hoped a month away would help me make up my mind. I still don't know, and I've got only about a fourth of my month left."

"It doesn't seem possible. Where does the time go? And we'll miss you, Miriam, we really will."

"Thank you," I said demurely.

"Well, sit down, sit down!" she said. "I'll tell you what I wanted you for. My lawyer is coming this morning, bringing my new will, and I'd like you to witness it. He's bringing his secretary for the other witness."

"Oh," I said. The moment was anticlimactic, to say the least.

She put on her glasses and began looking over the papers. "You may wonder why I'm fussing around with a will now. I should have all that behind me. Well, I did have it attended to, long ago when Rory was small. But now I've changed it." Her voice had become dry of either tone or color. "I made up my mind to that the night I fell downstairs. I had Ralph Bannister come to see me in the hospital, and I told him what changes I had in mind."

She took off her glasses and gave me her full attention. "Remember what I told you about Eunice? Well, she came to see me the other day, and she told me that there was absolutely no chance for her, that she was giving up and wished I would. Rory is seeing some other girl. Doing more than that, I presume," she added grimly. "Sleeping with her is more likely. Girls nowadays have no shame. Not that it's anything new, there were plenty of them around when I was a girl. But there's a lot more of it now—as you no doubt know —with the Pill or without it. I may be treading on your toes, but facts are facts."

I pretended the sun made me squint and hoped this strained expression hid everything else. I was hot—not with shame but with wondering if Kitty knew who the girl was, and was trying to get a reaction from me.

"If Rory wasn't such a stupid and conceited boy, he'd be thanking God for Eunice's devotion," she said. "I was going to tell him so that night, but he didn't come in before I went to bed. He wasn't back at three-thirty the next morning, so I was going to be waiting in the kitchen when he did come sneaking in ... well. I *didn't* break my neck, worse luck for him."

"Oh, don't talk like that," I protested. "I know you're disturbed and worried about him, but——"

"Yes, I'm disturbed and worried!" she snapped. "I've been expecting her to turn up here any time to tell me she's pregnant by him. I know the type. They've always been around, the kind who would lie down for anyone who had a decent family and some property behind him. And I know just how to take care of *this* one. She'll drop my son fast enough when she finds out that Rory Barstow *is* nothing and *has* nothing."

I must have been staring fixedly at her because she nodded at me with her most charming smile. "Yes. I've changed my will. Unless Rory marries Eunice, he gets nothing—but one dollar. Fourleaf Farm will go to her. And she can't give it back to him, unless they get married. I've fixed that. It's to go to *her* children."

I was glad I was sitting down. Sweat was running down my back. "Does Rory know?" I asked.

"He doesn't need to know until later. To find out that it's already legal should make him think. Eunice doesn't have to know either. She'd have put up a big fuss."

Jason began to bark outside and Mrs. Barstow said, "That must be Ralph now. Will you let him in, dear? And then go back and talk with Faye, or across the hall and play the piano while he tries to argue me out of this again. He disapproves." She caricatured legal disapproval, then laughed. "We'll call you when we need you."

I was too stunned to resent her tone, and was glad to get out of the room. I opened the front door to a good-looking gray-haired man, and a girl with a gamin haircut and a tartan pantsuit. I pointed the way to Mrs. Barstow and tried not to obviously run for the kitchen.

"Have a cup of coffee?" asked Faye.

"Not yet, thanks. Where's Rory? Not out in the northwest forty, I hope."

"The *what?* If Kitty wants him, she should know where he is. Didn't she tell you?"

I went on outdoors. Faye called something after me, but I didn't stop. If he wasn't somewhere within reach, I would have to delay signing somehow, even if I were forced to refuse pointblank.

Oh yes, I could defy her, and the prospect was savagely satisfactory. I could blow everything in one glorious explosion, except that I had no right to make war behind Rory's back. Unilaterally, as they called it these days.

Rory was coming through the barnyard gate. He laughed when he saw me. "Timed it just right, didn't I?" He took me by the arms and said in a low voice, "All I could think of was that I would see you at ten. How are you, sweetheart? Any regrets? Because for me it was the most—well, I guess I don't have the words."

"Neither do I," I said. "No regrets, Rory. I know it's happened to billions of people, yet it's as if it never happened to anyone before; we're the first discoverers." I was a little weak even now, transported suddenly from the path between garden and clotheslines back to the night.

"In a minute," he said, rather shakily, "I'll be sweeping you off to the hayloft."

"I'd love it," I said, "but I'd better tell you what your mother wanted me for."

"Hey, she hasn't by any chance found out you're a Glidden——"

"No. She's changed her will, and she wants me to be a witness. But she made the mistake of telling me about the changes. Unless"—something new—"she *wanted* me to know, for a special reason. She didn't sound as if she suspected me, but she could."

He shook me gently, smiling. "Stop meandering and come to the point."

"You're disinherited, Rory, unless you marry Eunice Parmenter. Otherwise when your mother dies the farm goes to Eunice, and there's no way she can give it back to you outside of marriage. It's to go eventually to Eunice's children. You see?"

The truth came hoarsely from a dry mouth while I watched shock replace his amused and tender curiosity. His hands loosened on my shoulders. He looked past me at the house, squinting his eyes as if in a too glaring light. "My father must have willed the farm to her," he said, slack with amazement. "She always let me think he died without a will." *Just as she let you think she had cancer*, I thought, but it was no time to say it aloud. "It was supposed to be cut and dried. One-third hers, two-thirds mine. And I was willing to sign off my share to her when I left." His laugh was sudden and uproarious. "My God, at least I'm saved from making *that* big gesture. Do you know what this means? *Do* you?" He shook me again. "It means I'm free! She'll do the dirty work. She's casting *me* off. She'll save her pride, you see, and she doesn't even know she's doing it!"

"But these are your ancestral acres, not hers!" I was having a hard time trying to smile. "Barstow land, and you're a Barstow. Even if you went away, they should still be yours to come back to."

"We'll have *your* ancestral acres. Now go back in there and sign the thing, and brighten up, honeybunch. It's the emancipation proclamation, don't you see? It's setting me free." He said more quietly, almost to himself, "When I think of all the years and all this rot about being a partner, and no part of it was mine. It's like you finding out your name wasn't really your name, and coming here sure you'd find your father but finding nothing——"

"I found my ancestral acres," I said. "I found *you*. And that's everything."

He didn't answer. He was looking around, off past the cattle barn and silo toward the orderly rows of apple trees beginning to show green clouds of tight new leaves, and I saw his eyes lift and follow the rise of land toward the sky. A family of crows rose up from the pine woods, small at this distance but as black and distinct as spatters of ink flung at pale blue paper.

He said in a quiet voice, "It's not as if I never loved it. I still do. It can't be turned off like a faucet. I would always love it, wherever I went." The small cries of lambs came to us, and a calf was bawling. Rory smiled fondly. "That's Apollo Junior. I know his voice. He'll take over for the old man one day."

"Listen," I said, "my earthy inheritance is making my blood boil. I think it's unforgivable for her to use the farm as a weapon, but I can still see her side of it. It's her life and she can't stand thinking it's endangered. She doesn't know what you're up to, so why shouldn't she be afraid you're in the hands of some mysterious tramp who's trying to latch onto a good thing? Let's tell her, *now*."

"Then you'll become the mysterious tramp who's trying to latch onto a good thing. You're not Eunice Parmenter, so you're next thing to a whore. No, we'll do it my way. Come out with the truth now, and inside of five minutes you'll be swearing to yourself that if you get away with a whole hide you'll never, never tell the truth again."

He kissed me hard, turned me around, and pointed me at the house. "Go on in and do it. I'm going back to work. I'll be down to see you as soon as I can. You don't have a bottle of champagne stashed away, do you?"

He went back through the gate, whistling. I wanted to believe his relief was genuine, and not subject to backlash when the shock wore off. My own powers of instant recovery were weaker.

When I went into the kitchen Faye was preparing salad vegetables at the sink. "They want you back in there, Miriam," she said over her shoulder. I realized the sink window looked out over the area where we had been, but Faye needn't have seen. What did it matter now, anyway? She turned around and said in a low voice, "Listen, Miriam, I don't know what's going on, but I'm for you kids, whatever it is, so don't forget it."

It was almost disastrous. My cheeks burned and my nose began to prickle with incipient tears. "Thanks, Faye," I said rapidly.

Entering the living room was like coming on stage; I felt like the ingenue in a drawing-room comedy, unless the secretary was the ingenue and I was the woman who was having an affair or was the victim of one. Did they know, or was I hiding the truth skillfully or gallantly? (Depending on my role?)

"I'm sorry to keep you waiting," I said charmingly, with what sounded to me like theatrical precision and clarity. "I went out to see the lambs."

"Oh, we didn't mind," said Mr. Bannister with smiling gallantry.

Everything was ready to be signed, folded over so I saw nothing but the indicated place. The secretary signed after me, and we both signed two more copies. Then Kitty dismissed me, graciously and with many thanks. Mr. Bannister and the girl were staying for lunch, but I wasn't invited. I wondered apprehensively if Rory were expected to join them and how he could sit at the same table with his mother, with other people present, and not struggle to keep from saying, *I know what you've just done.*

# chapter 26

Who'd have believed that my search for my name would have led me into such a complexity of battering, bruising relationships? My life before Parmenter, when my only problem had been the question of my identity, now appeared as a safe little green island which I'd left to row across to Europe in a dory. But when I returned to the cottage, it still held last night intact, on a safe little green island of our own making, and all the rest fell away. I sat on the edge of the bed and shut my eyes and allowed myself for the first time that day to remember how it had all been, from the beginning.

After this, I could have shouted like Alice at all the rest, "You're nothing but a pack of cards!" and seen them flap and flutter and collapse into nonexistence.

I got back to Andric's manuscript, and with its hero Ivo I was hiding out in a mountain cave with a wolf during a skull-shattering thunderstorm, when Rory came. It was about three in the afternoon. He walked in, picked me up from my chair at the table, and wrapped his arms around me and put his face in my neck. He smelled of the tub and a fresh shave, and was dressed in good clothes.

"Well!" I said in delight. "*Well!*" I had to tickle him around the ribs to make him let go, and then I kissed him. He gave me a ferocious leer and dropped me on the sofa.

"Now you're in my power. It won't do you any good to scream."

"Who's screaming?" I said.

"Damn, you've spoiled it. I like my women to yell. That's why I go through the village, raping left and right." We separated and sat up, flushed and slightly rumpled, looked at each other and burst out laughing. Then he said, "How soon can you be packed?"

"What?"

"Yes. We're getting out of here. We'll take your car. There's a motel outside of Camden where we can stay till everything's squared away, but I'm leaving Fourleaf Farm now."

"Did your mother——"

"No." He sliced that off with his hand. "I haven't seen her to speak to. I stayed out of sight till I knew they were eating, so she'd think I was working somewhere a good distance from the house. Then I went upstairs and cleaned up, put my tooth-brush and razor in my pocket, and came away without anything else, in case I met her. I can get anything I need in Camden, and I'll be back to pack up my gear later anyway. When I talk to her."

He was not speaking out of rage or recklessness, but thoughtfully. He looked much older to me now than he had the first time I saw him. "I can't stay on the farm another night. I need to get away, to see things in proportion, get hold of them. It'll be easier to handle her if I've already left. Can you see that?"

"Yes. All right." I began to get the manuscript together. I was much more nervous than he was, and yet beginning to lighten with relief.

"I called Tip from the kitchen, and offered him twenty-five dollars for an afternoon's work over here. He's saving for a motorcycle, so he grabbed. Faye thinks I'm taking off for the afternoon and evening and just didn't want to tangle with Kitty about it, so she won't say anything."

I carried the box of manuscript into the bedroom and he followed me and talked while I packed. "We can stop at Tom's on the way out of town, about his taking on my job here. Tip's willing, but he's unreliable. Once he gets his mo-torcycle he'll be thinking of that all the time. Tom's got kids to think of."

"When do you plan to talk to your mother?"

"As soon as I talk with Pierce, so I'll know whether she's dying gallantly on her feet or not. If she is, I'll see her through, but not under false pretenses. If she's all right, then I clear out. Either way, she gets the truth: who you are, and what we're going to do. If she wants to accept it gracefully, there needn't be a permanent split. I'd like to be on good terms with her."

"So would I," I said. "I liked her so much when I first came."

"By good terms I mean equal terms," he said. "But it'll be all up to her."

There was a fearful racket outside, as if a truck were plunging down the lane at high speed. It turned out to be the jeep, with Leni driving. He pulled to a rocking pause behind my car, then bucked around in a wild circle until he was heading up the lane again, parked, and was out over the side and across the lawn faster than I'd ever seen him move.

"Hey, Rory!" he was yelling. "You in there?"

We both made for the front door. I don't know what I expected, only that it had to be something terrible.

"The bull's out!" Leni shouted. "He's over at Quimby's Corner!"

"What in hell is he doing over there?" Rory jumped over the railing.

"He musta got out that gate on the woodroad, where we used to take 'em across to the Tinker Field." They were running for the jeep. "The nomads are out in this weather like worms after a rain. No tellin' who's been foolin' around that woodroad, and not knowin' enough to stay away from the gates."

I ran after them. "I'm going with you. I won't get in the way." I climbed into the back and crouched among the conglomeration of articles that clanked or rolled or bounced. One thing was a chain saw, I remember.

With Rory driving, the jeep bounced in the ruts like a boat caught in a tide rip, and we fairly exploded out into the sunny open and shot past the main house. Leni's voice suddenly came out clear and loud. I'd never heard him talk so much.

"I saw a bunch down t'the common yesterday, knapsacks and bikes and all, come from Massachusetts. City kids, you could tell. They coulda camped up the woodroad last night. Wouldn't be the first ones to do it." He chuckled. "Probably they was chasing each other around in the mornin' dew among the cow pats, and never knew there was a bull within five miles of them."

He and Rory both laughed. We went around the righthand post on two wheels, along the road about five hundred yards, and took a sharp curve to the left. Ahead of us, in a stationary line, were three cars, a pick-up, and a school bus crowded with children. The woodroad opened off to the right just beyond the first car. Across the black road from it Apollo was delicately nibbling at fresh green grass. He looked twice as big as when he was fenced in. Beyond him and facing our way was a line consisting of a station wagon, another pick-up, and a loaded pulpwood truck.

It was very quiet, except for the birds. Rory edged slowly along beside the parked vehicles on our right. He stopped abreast of the pick-up, whose driver gave us a wordless salute. Rory stepped out in a fluid, soundless movement. Even from the school bus there was not a suspicion of excitement; these were farm children.

Leni handed Rory a package of cigarettes and Rory walked along the middle of the road without hurry. He was taking a cigarette from the package as he went. The stillness grew oppressive. I ached from the way I was crouching, but I was afraid to move for fear something would make a sound. My eyes ached also from watching Rory's back and his dark head as he kept going away from me. The suspense was very nearly another physical agony. I wanted reassurance from Leni, but I couldn't scrape up a whisper, and he too seemed spellbound into mute immobility.

Apollo kept munching, moving along. Almost up to him, Rory whistled, and the big head came up and turned toward the man. Rory held out the cigarette, almost close enough to touch the broad nose. I could see that he was talking, but of course I couldn't hear what he was saying, it was all so low-keyed and gentle.

After an hour-long moment of deliberation, Apollo took the cigarette and ate it, and stretched his head toward the pack in Rory's hand. Rory turned and started across the macadam to the woodroad, and Apollo followed him. Rory was still talking, and he would look back and hold out the package and then go on again. Apollo speeded up a bit, not enough to dissipate the impression of enormous dignity.

Once they were in the wood road, the watchers were still quiet because any sudden sound could still ruin the whole performance. Leni's shoulders slumped, and I saw people reaching for cigarettes, or turning to speak to their companions. But no car doors opened and no engines started. The children were still hushed. Leni and I kept watching the place where the woodroad disappeared into the trees.

"Do you think——" I didn't get any further.

"Should get him to the gate all right," Leni said tersely.

It seemed like a long time that we waited. Suddenly Rory appeared, and horns began to blow. Someone yelled, "Hey, champ!" A girl shouted from the station wagon, "*Olé!*" The schoolchildren cheered and applauded.

Leni looked around at me with a grin. "Godfrey, ain't he something? I think he could stand up on Bonfire Hill and tame a thunderstorm."

Rory was stopped by several people, but finally traffic was beginning to move again and everybody went off with a holiday air. Rory came back to the jeep and swung himself in behind the wheel.

"They're going to have to put springs and locks on all the gates," he said. "This is getting to the foolish stage. Suppose I'm not here to round him up sometime. I don't know what can happen to him, or to somebody else."

"Couldn't anyone coax him with cigarettes?" I asked. "Doesn't he know Leni?"

"Thanks," Leni said dryly. "Sure, we know each other. With a DMZ between us. I could make of him when he was a calf, but I wouldn't try it now."

"No, there's something between him and me," Rory said seriously, "because I raised him." He turned the jeep into the woodroad, then backed around until we were facing the way we had come. "But every time I go to get him I wonder if this is the time when it ends. When suddenly I'm no longer his foster mother or his chum, but just something in his way."

It was oddly sad, all the more so because it came after a moment of great suspense, beauty, and exhilaration. I said, "I have a feeling Apollo will live a long life and leave hundreds of sons and daughters."

"Well, he's already got a good start on us at producing descendants."

"Ayuh," said Leni seriously. "Makes a man think, don't it?"

"You'd better get busy, Leni," Rory said.

"That Faye, she's some set on keeping fallow." They laughed uproariously, the way I'd heard them in the kitchen sometimes.

# chapter 27

We drove straight down to the cottage. Kitty's car was parked beside mine. It was so unexpected I couldn't even begin to conjecture. Rory stopped the jeep and we three sat there in silence, gazing toward the cottage as if we expected it to tell us something. Beyond the lawn the brook cast off a glittering haze.

Then Rory said, "Well—"

"She must have felt good enough to move around and get outdoors," I said. "So she drove down to see me, that's all. Why don't you just drop me, and——"

Rory jumped out. "Leni, see that Tip doesn't act like a Hell's Angel on that tractor, huh? Tell him I can go back on my deal."

"Sure."

I climbed out, and Rory took my hand and pulled my arm through his. "So long," Leni said, and backed the jeep around. As it went up the hill we crossed the lawn arm in arm. We said nonsensical things I don't even remember any more, and laughed; this was for her, if she was watching, to tell her quickly how it was with us.

When we went in, Mrs. Barstow stood on the hearth rug waiting. We couldn't tell, of course, if she'd been watching us cross the lawn, but she must have seen our hands unlace as we entered—only because the door was too narrow for us to come in side by side.

"Hello!" I said. "This is a surprise! You must be feeling a lot better. Sit down, and I'll go put the tea kettle on——"

"*Don't.*"

The word stopped me like a portcullis dropped before me.

She said pleasantly, "I don't know how I could have been so stupid as to miss what's been going on under my nose. It didn't hit me until they wanted you to round up the bull, Rory, and Faye sent Leni down here after you. I just *happened* to be lying down in the office." The smile moved from one to the other of us. "I could look out and see Faye. The instant she said it, she looked in at me, and she turned purple. I'll have something to say to her later."

"You can leave Faye out of this, Mother," Rory said. "She's not my keeper, just because she happened to know where I was today."

"And does she know why you're all dressed up, and called Tip in?"

Rory didn't answer. He moved closer to me and put his arm snugly around my waist. Mrs. Barstow nodded her head toward the open bedroom door.

"You're packing, Miriam. Were you leaving without telling me?"

"I was going to tell you." We were all underplaying it. "I hadn't had time yet. Apollo interrupted."

"And a good thing too." She moved to a chair; she must have been tired, but she managed not to look as if she were driven to it. "Otherwise I might not have found out until you were ready to tell me. . . . Rory, I suppose that while we were waiting for Miriam this morning she was telling you about my will."

"She came to tell me she couldn't be the reason for my losing Fourleaf Farm," he said. "I told her I'd rather lose the farm than her. Since I never had it anyway." Her smiling poise was jarred for an instant, I thought she was going to exclaim or protest, but Rory went on. "We decided to leave. We were coming back tomorrow to talk to you. We'll be married eventually, and when we do we'd like to have you at the wedding."

His courtesy was impeccable, and it restored me. "Yes, please think about it, Mrs. Barstow," I said.

"My dear, ignorant girl," she said. "*You* think. You'll be marrying a man who's worked as a hired hand all his life; a man with nothing of his own but what he's managed to save from his earnings. I'm sure you *have* thought about it, very hard since you heard the truth this morning. . . . Do the two of you really think you'll win me over, and that I'll change my will next week?"

"Mother, I was leaving the farm anyway," Rory said. "What you did today was make it a whole lot easier, that's all. It took away any guilt I felt. It set me loose; I feel like a helium balloon." He smiled at her. "I've got somebody to take over my work, and you're not the type to cut off your nose to spite your face, so you'll keep him on. As soon as I get a report on your health——"

"My *health?*" She looked startled at last.

For someone who hated even to think the word, he did well. "The trouble you had. Cancer." His fingers pressing into my side jumped when he said it.

"Oh, that," she said with a sardonic curl to her mouth. "I'm surprised that you ever kept it in mind, you've apparently been so taken up with your own frustrations."

"I've never forgotten it, Mother," he said very softly. "It's always scared the hell out of me. And it kept me from doing what I wanted to do more than anything else in the world."

"You mean the ridiculous nonsense that woman pumped into your head?" She wasn't hiding the old rage very well; it raised flags on her cheekbones. "Haven't you grown up *yet?* Don't you realize now she was just amusing herself with you? Maybe she didn't take you to bed, but she might just as well as. If I hadn't——" She stopped, put her fingers against her lips, and started again. "I was terrified by what they found in me, but I was glad of it too, because if it hadn't been for that God knows where you'd be now and what would have become of you in her hands."

Rory's fingers were beating a steady and painful tattoo on my ribs. But I'd gone beyond the shaky, sick reaction to bullying. "Mrs. Barstow, there's nothing ridiculous about Rory's voice, and he has a right to find out just how good it is and what he can do with it."

"And Maggie Dundas is going to mastermind the project, I suppose."

"We don't know. I think we can do it on our own, but Rory's going to let her know he's finally made his decision."

"*His* decision! Hah! *Yours* is more like it. You come in here as she did, meddling, unscrupulous—I'll never rent this cottage again, I swear it."

"I'm neither a child nor a puppet, Mother," Rory said. "I guess maybe that's what you think I am, or wish I were. I've never forgotten what I want to do, any more than you can stop thinking about cancer. But I wouldn't go if you were sick——"

"Thank you," she said with such contempt I felt like kicking her. "And when the thing falls through, and you haven't a cent left, is Miriam going to keep you on her pay?" She laughed. "What a life for a Barstow! A kept man, not a puppet or a child!"

"We can always come back to the land. I'm still part farmer and always will be." He wasn't arguing; he was stating. I wished that we'd had time to talk in those few minutes before we met her in the cottage, or that I'd known then what I knew now, that I didn't want to say anything about myself. I wanted only for us to go away with it all left unsaid. But it was like watching a great wave rear over us in an arch of green water, or a fire racing through dry timber; Rory was under way.

"Miriam has a farm. It needs a hell of a lot of work to put it back, but we're young and we can do it. I'll earn my partnership, it won't be dangled in front of me like something you hang on a baby's crib to keep him entertained, and take away when you feel like it." With a smile very like hers, he added, "And Miriam can keep the books. She'd never have let me lose Fourleaf, Mother. She's too bright, and she has too much respect for the land. She *came* from land."

"Where is this farm of yours, Miriam? Two acres in Connecticut?"

"Two hundred and fifty acres in Parmenter, Mother," Rory said. "The Glidden place."

Kitty Barstow's mouth opened as if someone had punched her in the belly and she was trying to suck in air; color fled her face and then rushed back to suffuse it darkly. I took a step toward her but Rory held me. "Rory, listen," I began in a panicky protest.

"She asked for it," he said. "In all ways." No, he was neither child nor puppet.

She recovered quickly, but she must have hated us for seeing that lapse into shock, if she hadn't hated us already. "So you're the heir," she said coolly. "Whose secret are *you?*"

"My mother's. She was Helen Glidden."

"Can you prove it?"

"I have a boxful of proof in there." I nodded at the bedroom. "The selectmen have other proofs as well."

"So you're Helen Glidden's daughter," Mrs. Barstow said meditatively. "If I'd known who you were, you wouldn't ever have rented this cottage. You wouldn't have gotten into Parmenter."

"Unfortunately you don't own everybody in Parmenter, yet," Rory said. She ignored that. She contemplated me as if I were a calf to be saved for breeding or killed for veal. *It's veal*, I thought with a shaky impulse to maniacal laughter.

"Yes," she said as if to herself, "I see the likeness. Funny how it comes out all at once."

"To my *mother?*" I was honestly startled. "But I don't look a bit like her."

"I hated your mother," she said. "I still do."

"Why? And how can you go on hating someone who's dead? If they didn't want to die but they were killed, isn't that enough for you? Whatever your reason was?"

Rory said, "Honeybunch, go in and finish packing." He tried to start me toward the bedroom. I was willing, but she spoke again.

"How can you go on loving someone who's dead? I've never stopped, even if I've never forgiven him, either."

"Whatever it's all about, it's over and done with, Mother," Rory said. "We're all young, you too. Let's forget it and start off brand new today." He was kind. "You know what they like to say: 'Today is the first day of the rest of your life.'" He took my hand and squeezed the fingers. "Go and pack."

I returned and yet resisted the pressure, not able to look away from her. "You knew my father," I said huskily.

"You should never have been born," she said. "You and your mother wrecked my life."

"Why don't you stop right there?" said Rory. He took me by the shoulders and forced me around and through the bedroom door. "We've got it all said, and now we'll go."

I wanted to go, all right. I wanted to run, because I didn't want her telling me who my father was. I didn't want her poisoning the pure romance that had sustained me for so many years. It had been bad enough, almost intolerable, to hear her say my mother's name the way she did. Rory shoved me into the bedroom and came with me, and was just about to shut the door when she said lazily, "I hope you two have kept your heads. Incest is an ugly word."

It was so ridiculous, so incredible, it didn't register at first. Not until we met each other's eyes and both turned to look back at her. She nodded as benignly as if she had just given us her blessing.

"Yes, you share the same father. She played the piano for your father to sing, Rory, and that's how she got him. Through *music*." She spat the word. "That carroty redhead. All through high school she played for him, and she wanted him, and finally she got him, after he was married to me, because he was as foolish about music as you are." She flipped that at him with a sneer that reached even through my silent shouting *Shut up shut up shut up*. Rory was white, and I don't know how I looked. I reached out for him and clasped a rigid arm.

"But he couldn't marry her," his mother said carelessly, "if he'd wanted to, which I doubt. Oh, she could play the piano. I'll give her that. Otherwise she was no better than a whore."

At that word I thought my head was going to explode. But I wouldn't satisfy her either by attacking or collapsing. "Rory," I said, surprised that it came out audible.

He glanced around, nodded, and went over to my cases. "What else goes in here?" he asked. In a deadly calm we finished packing. He fastened the bags, and I took my topcoat over my arm, and we went out into the living room where she still sat. I avoided the sight of her as if she were something indecent.

"Any of these books yours?" Rory asked.

"Just some of the music, and there's my tape recorder." He closed that up while I gathered my music. Because she was watching me, I could keep my hands from shaking. Finally, still without a glance in her direction, we went out the door.

"Don't think you can hide the truth," she called after us, "just because I've been too proud all these years to tell it. I'm not too proud now. It'll follow you wherever you go."

Rory kept on going as if he didn't hear. I turned back into the cottage. "Mrs. Barstow, I don't think you've ever told the truth in your life," I said. "You've been lying to Rory all these years about the farm. And did you really have cancer that time, or was it just something you invented to keep Rory chained to you?"

Her eyelids quivered as if from the force of a blow. "You're insolent. You're your mother all over again even if not in looks. You're the vicious kind who wouldn't mind seducing her own brother." I turned away, and she called, "And I can prove he *is*. I never dreamed I'd have to use the proof, but I've got it under lock and key."

"She's mad, Rory," I said, "don't listen."

"Who's listening?" His eyes looked almost black.

"I hope you're already pregnant by your own brother!" She came shouting after us. "Because he can't marry you and everybody'll know why! I'll see to that!"

We ran to the car, loaded the luggage into the back, and I

gave Rory the keys. We drove up the hill without looking back, and without speaking. When we were passing the house Jason trotted across the lawn under the maples. Rory stopped, and I opened the back door on my side. Jason climbed in, all happy panting. I didn't wonder what we'd do with him at the motel; at the moment it seemed perfectly natural to take him in. The three of us had been together so much.

# chapter 28

When a little later we swung off the black road and down the lane to the Glidden place, that seemed entirely natural too. We stopped in the dooryard and sat there without moving. Then Jason breathed hard and imploringly in my ear, and I let him out. For what seemed a long time we sat watching the dog explore around the trees and the cellar holes, his tail waving in excitement. The birds kept singing, and more daffodils shone in the grass. I had a new concept of hell; instead of being plunged in eternal fire, you were surrounded forever by beauty which you could neither touch nor smell, nor your sight delight in.

Still we hadn't spoken, and suddenly we turned to each other at the same instant. "Rory, she was just——"

"How about staying here tonight? I don't think I can stand being under a roof. It's warm, and I can drive into Fremont and pick up a couple of sleeping bags and some grub."

He sounded in complete charge of himself and me, and I thought with relief *He believes as I do, that she was just throwing in anything she could think of to shock and stop us.*

"All right," I said. "I'd love it. Hey, don't forget something to cook in, and to get water in."

He took me by the shoulders as he was always doing and gave me a little shake, smiling. "I won't forget." I ducked my head to put my cheek against his hand, and Kitty's obscene word exploded in my head. It was just a weapon, a handful of filth, and it dirtied her more than us. I took his face in my hands and kissed him. His forehead was wet, but why not, after such a scene with his own mother? I wasn't sure how my legs would feel when I got out of the car.

"I'll go with you," I decided.

"You afraid I won't come back?" His grin was fairly natural. He took my hands from his face and held them against his chest. "I'll be back. You could start gathering some stuff for a fire."

"All right." I got out reluctantly and watched him turn around. Then he waved at me and drove off up the lane. In the silence I could hear him all the way to the black road, and then I was almost sure I could tell he'd turned toward Fremont and not back toward Fourleaf. The stillness began to fill the clearing again like water running in. The sun was warm and the breeze fragrant, and I stood on land that was my own, two hundred and fifty acres, more or less. But even itemizing the fact couldn't demolish my new perception of hell as a place in which you were numb to everything but the anguish of being numb.

It will be better when we talk, I thought, and in time to come the worst of it will fade away. Who knows, she might make a gesture herself, when she comes to her senses. . . . Jason came to me, wearing a collie smile of pleasure. I picked up a few armfuls of wood around the barn cellar, and an old stove grate, and carried it all down to the lake shore. I wandered around in the sunny pine-scented isolation gathering more wood. The ice was all gone now. A kingfisher's rattling cry sounded in the quiet, the sun shone on the loons' white breasts. I heard, without seeing them, a soft conversation of ducks. Across the lake, too far to be seen, someone was trying out an outboard motor. Jason sniffed ecstatically at tracks and treetrunks. I knelt to repair the crude fireplace we'd found there earlier.

Jason heard the car in the lane—I didn't—and made it clear by going to the path and then returning to me, ardently urging. Finally I went with him up through the pines. He gamboled like a pup, rushing back to me with his ears laid flat and his tail going in mad circles.

Rory took me in his arms, and the word came again but not so explosively. He had two sleeping bags, foam rubber pads, a box of groceries, a plastic container of water, some basic cooking utensils, two enamel mugs, plastic plates and cutlery, plus a couple cans of dogfood and a small ax. We loaded ourselves up and carried the gear down to the lake. The activity began to have a calming effect on me. No one knew where we were; Kitty probably fancied we were on our way out of the state. I wondered if she were desperate enough to forget all her pride and set the state police on us with fake charges. But I couldn't see her making that much of a fool of herself; she must already be curling up like a burning leaf in the fires of mortification.

I wanted to talk with Rory, but he kept so busy with finding just the right place for our beds, getting them ready, then repairing my already-repaired fireplace, that I couldn't find a place for breaking in. I longed for the brashness to say, "Hey, knock it off a minute and let's get this out in the open," but I couldn't make it. Despairingly I saw constraint between us like a heavy glass shield, or rather around him; he was too industrious, too painstaking, too elaborately and artificially absorbed in what he was doing. When he spoke to me briefly about what he was doing or had just done, his eyes were as bright as the lake and as impersonal.

Finally, when he started to open up the food, I exclaimed, "*Rory!*"

He looked up at me with mild surprise. "Bee bite ye?"

"Rory, before we eat, let's sit down and talk. Come here." I patted the sand beside me. It was nightmare to watch him hesitate, cast around for reasons not to come. I got up and went to him and grabbed his shoulders. "Rory, you're acting as if you *believe* her! Can't you see she was just striking out? She couldn't use cancer again, so she chose the one thing she thought would stop us, that's all."

"Do you know if you're pregnant?"

"No. And I doubt it. But if I was, I'd be proud."

"Even if——"

I didn't let him finish. "That is not so, Rory." For a moment I wildly considered telling him I'd been lying all along and knew who my father was; but it wouldn't work. I repeated, "That is not so."

His smile was as quick as a reflex. "All right, honeybunch. Let's eat. I never got any lunch this noon, remember." Food was the last thing I wanted, but the important thing was to keep communication open.

"I'm starved myself. What did you get?"

"Steaks, what else? And a loaf of French bread, and a bottle of wine—we're just missing the book of verse."

"I always thought 'And thou beside me in the wilderness' was a beautiful line, and here I am and thou art." We both laughed as if I'd said something wonderfully witty. Jason was pleased, either with us or the sight and smell of steak. He had been fed first, but watched us with limpid eyes and we both treated him lavishly. I think he got more than we did, but at least the steaks disappeared. In the shadow of the pines we sat by our fire drinking coffee and watching the afterglow dye the lake rose and apricot. An owl passed silently over our heads. When the little flames shot up enough to light Rory's face it seemed peaceful enough. So I didn't try to force conversation then. He could be thinking his own way through.

We burned our trash in the fire, drowned it, and then took a walk around the shore in the dusk. Jason came sedately behind us. Now the lake faded away into the dark so that we could have been on the shore of a silent sea. We passed a few cottages, but they were shuttered and dark, boats still hauled up and overturned by the doorsteps. This only enhanced the aura of isolation. The place was given over to the owls and the night prowlers. When we came back to our fireplace, a couple of raccoons were investigating and Jason made a token dash, but didn't follow them.

Our bed was on a little flat rise among the pines, the foam pads laid over time's cushion of old needles. I unzipped the two bags and made them into one big one. We took off our shoes and went to bed in our clothes, rolling at once into each other's arms. Jason pressed his back against our feet, sighed loudly, and slept. In my arms Rory also sighed, his warm breath on my throat through the open neck of my shirt. I stroked the back of his neck and kneaded the big muscles going from neck to shoulders.

"You know it's all right, don't you?" I murmured. "You can see it now, can't you? *Feel* how crazy it was, how impossible? She's probably horrified herself by now."

"But why should she say she has proof, under lock and key? Why *that*, unless—oh, my God, Miriam," he said. "No pictures of him anywhere in the house. And the farm left to *her*—his son left out entirely—she could have managed that, working on his guilt. Oh my God," he repeated with the softness of infinite despair. "*Miriam!*" He started to push me away, but I hung on and clamped a hand over his mouth. "*No.* You ask her for that proof, Rory. You make her produce it, and tell her we won't accept anything forged. If it's a written document it'll go to the best handwriting expert I can find, along with samples of her writing and his. No, *I'll* tell her, because I'm going with you."

He pulled my hand away. "But she wouldn't lie about something so damned final, so damned killing. It would make her a monster, and she's not that. She's proud, she's self-centered, she's arrogant, but she's no monster."

"She's lied to you about the farm all these years." I remembered something else. "And listen, Rory, she lied about you to me almost at the first. She said you'd never taken your voice seriously, never wanted to do anything with it. But that was the one big, real thing you wanted to do, that you fought with her about!"

"That wasn't a matter of life and death," he said unwillingly.

"Wasn't it? —And you don't know yet if there was a cancer operation. I mentioned it to Faye and she looked at me as if I'd flipped. She was with your mother then, wasn't she?"

"She's been with us since she was in high school. But Kitty's so scared of something like that, it's almost as indecent to her as syphilis. It's one way she isn't hard. She swore me to secrecy."

"It can't ever be discussed with her, because she can't stand the mere mention of the word. So you can go on struggling under the weight of it for the rest of your life. You know something, Rory? At this rate she'll outlive you. You've got to escape to survive."

"Do you see her as a monster, then?" She was his mother, after all; he must have some good memories.

"No, but something's helped to make her like this, and I don't think it was my mother seducing your father."

"But to lie about that!" He pushed me away and sat up, running his hands through his hair. "I just can't see anybody slamming that at us if she didn't believe it herself! It's worse than rotten, it's deadly."

"She wanted to be deadly." I sat up with him and put my arms around him. He was like cold marble. "She had to be, to keep you. Listen, darling, we'll go to her tomorrow for the proof, show her we're not afraid, and who knows, maybe she'll give in so she won't lose you altogether."

"What if we can't break the proof?"

"I refuse to admit that."

"You've got to face it." He took hold of me then. "Listen to me, Miriam. It could be. Stranger things have happened. *It could be.*"

"No, no!" I wanted to fall apart then, in howls and torrents of protest. "No matter what, we aren't brother and sister! We came together as strangers! Neither knew the other existed!"

Now he was doing the stroking and calming, the whispering. "There. There . . . But don't you see, we'd know. No matter how we felt, we'd know. We could go somewhere where she'd never find us, but we'd know. And it would corrupt everything. Eat it away like leprosy. As long as we didn't know, it was beautiful. That's when we were innocent."

"*Is* beautiful," I said. "*Are* innocent."

"But no more," he said. "No more." The words were like a lament. I caught him and pulled him down with me. For the first time I raged against my mother for not telling me my father's name. Because Rory was right, for all my protests; I knew it as we held onto each other under the pine trees like the last two people on earth, waiting for death. If his mother produced proof that nothing could shake, then we could never embrace again without knowing. *How fair is thy love, my sister, my spouse* . . .

"I can't give you up," Rory said in my neck.

"I can't give *you* up."

"Where can we go?"

"We've got the world," I said valiantly.

# chapter 29

*I* remember not wanting to leave Rory awake and alone, and I remember knowing by the dead heaviness of him that he had fallen asleep. Then I slept, too exhausted to be aware of the night world around us except to feel extraordinarily safe in it. I dreamed that I was lying awake, and a moose came wading out of the lake and walked up to our bed and looked down on us with a regally beneficent gaze. Nonexistent moonlight outlined his antlers and sparked in his eyes. Jason didn't even wake up. In the dream I was enchanted by the happening.

When I woke up it was as if the moose's footfall on the pine needles had roused me, and his breathing as his amiable curiosity drew him close to us. My pleasure was still there. Instantly I remembered why we were here, but without anxiety. The dawn was mild and the bird chorus was gathering new members every instant. I lay with my eyes shut listening to the lake sounds and the delicate sibilance of the breeze in the pines, and trying to sort out the scents and fragrances, wondering with amusement if a moose had really come by and Jason was just too tired, or too sensible, to care.

I also wondered what kind of night Kitty had had, and if she would be relieved to see us today. I was exquisitely happy to be waking outdoors like this, with Rory within touch. I turned over to see him for myself, not to wake him. But he wasn't there. Jason slept in the rumpled folds, his head where Rory's had been. He opened one eye at me and sighed into sleep again.

I wasn't alarmed. We'd put all the food up in the car last night to foil the raccoons, so he'd gone up to get it. The least I could do would be to start the breakfast fire, if I could bring myself to crawl out of my warm nest. I'd shed outer clothes after a while last night but had prudently kept them in with me, and we'd used my topcoat and his sports jacket for pillows, so nothing felt damp. I dressed under cover, and combed my hair with my fingers, my toilet articles being in my luggage in the car. I washed my face and hands in the lake—very cold—and dried them on the square kerchief I'd found crammed in my coat pocket. Jason wandered around checking on the night's traffic.

When I had the fire going, Rory still hadn't come back, so I thought he was walking around the shore, expecting that I wouldn't wake for a long time yet. I couldn't go up to the car myself and get the food, because the car keys were with him; he'd put them in his pocket when we came back from stowing the food away last night.

Because I awoke as an optimist, I was convinced that he had too. Sleep does wonderful things sometimes about restoring perspective. I put water on to boil. At least we hadn't taken the coffee to the car.

Behind the hill of pines the sun was rising. It shone on the tips of the woods across the lake, and the sky turned blue over head, flecked with pink feathery clouds. I made instant coffee in a mug and sipped carefully; nothing was ever hotter. Jason came looking for toast or doughnuts.

"It's all in the car," I said to him. "Where's Rory anyway?" His ears pricked and he looked around. "Where did Rory go? Find Rory."

With enthusiasm he picked out the track up through the pines to the house. He'd already started that way several times, but had come back. Rory must have told him to stay with me.

"All right, let's go," I said. "He's probably cleaning up around the cellar holes and planning out a new house, and he's lost all track of time. Know what, Jason?" Jason looked intelligently questioning. "We may not have to sell the place. We may be able to get a mortgage on it. It's valuable real estate. Land is gold nowadays, so that makes me a wealthy woman. Hey, how do you like *that?*"

Jason gave me his collie smile.

There was no car; Rory had gone without me to his mother. I was a little flattened, but not completely. If he could work it out with her alone, so much the better. It was going to be hellish enough for her to give in, without my being there to see. Yesterday I had felt like killing her, but this morning I had no wish to humiliate her, if she would only accept gracefully Rory's decision.

I went back to the shore to drown my fire, and then returned and began piling up the old brick from the chimneys for us to use again sometime.

I had spent an hour before I knew it, and I was hungry, and also suddenly conscious of suspense like a stab in the belly. He'd been gone for a long time, even if it was from just before I woke up. Wait until I told him I thought his touch on my face came from a moose. I tried to laugh, but found myself incapable of it. I rounded up Jason—I couldn't whistle, my mouth was too dry—and went back to the campsite. I separated and rolled up the sleeping bags and pads, and took them halfway up the track, then went back and got the water container and the carton with the coffee, mugs, and saucepan. I put everything inside the little chicken house I'd found on the first day, buried in shrubbery and vines a good distance from the house.

Then Jason and I set out. Anxiety was keeping step with me now; I couldn't outwalk it. I kept looking back for an approaching car to pick me up, but no one had come along by the time I reached Seven Chimneys.

The children were riding their tricycles again on the drive. They saw me coming along the road and pedaled madly, shouting, "Hi! Hi!" I waved limply, slogging ever on, until I saw the German shepherd coming at a dead run.

I have never felt so hopeless, so completely exposed, as I was then. Jason went forward with his ears pricked and his hair rising along his backbone, growling softly. He would fight, but an amiable collie was no match for what was coming.

"*Frankie!*" shouted one of the tots with truly awesome volume, and the shepherd came to a skidding stop. The youngster rode up beside him and took him by his collar. "Mama!" the other child shrieked, and through a haze of enervating relief I saw a young woman appear in the doorway of the ell.

"Frankie, come back here," she called. The dog trotted back and followed her to the end of the ell, where she fastened him to a chain on a wire run between the house and a sturdy post. Then she waved to me cheerfully and started back to the house. I waved back and leaned weakly on the mailbox. Maybe something would come by eventually. The fright had been the last straw, and I could have been facing a thousand-mile hike instead of five miles or so.

The children came up to me, lifting bright, curious faces. "What's his name?" they asked, patting Jason. "What's your name? Where do you live?"

"He's Jason. I'm Miriam. Listen, kids, will you ask your mother if I can use the telephone?"

"I'll do it," the boy said importantly and spun his tricycle around and started for the house. The little girl patted Jason and said, "They wouldn't fight. Frankie's a girl. Frankie's short for Frances."

"Is that so?" I said.

"Yes. She's named after Aunt Frankie."

The boy came pedaling back with all his might, yelling, "She says come in!"

Mrs. Rollins was a chubby, apple-cheeked young woman, breezily friendly, wearing tight jeans decently veiled by her shirt tails. She was setting bread to rise, and the kitchen smelled of yeast and coffee. Jason took a long drink and flopped with a groan.

I explained with inspired ease that I'd gone out for a long sunrise hike this morning, but it was too much for Jason, even if I didn't mind plodding the distance home. So I'd like to telephone the farm and see if someone would come and get us.

She'd been working while she listened, her short square hands fast and competent, but when I said the dog's name her hands went suddenly still and she looked around at me with something like awe.

"Is that the Barstows' dog? I recognize him now. When he was younger he used to win all the local sheepdog trials."

"I'll bet he did," I said brightly. "But he's retired now."

"You must be the lady editor renting the cottage." It wasn't awe. It was more like apprehension, unless she'd heard some fantastic fable about me. I nodded. "May I use the telephone?"

"Then you don't know about the fire."

"What fire?" I was reaching for the book hanging below the wall telephone.

"At Fourleaf Farm, this morning. The men are still there, my husband and my father-in-law—they're on the volunteer fire department, and more engines came from Fremont, and . . ."

I heard her words echoing cavernously in my head. It took a while to get out the aspirate. "H-h-how bad?"

"I don't know. The men folks got the call and tore out of here. Don't you want to sit down?" She sounded alarmed.

"No, I'm fine now," I said. "It's just that I have this awful thing about fire. I'd like to get back there now, there must be something I can do."

"Well, look, I can drive you over," she said eagerly. She spread a clean dishtowel over the outsized mixing bowl and set it on the sunny counter. "Where Hank's a fireman, he gets real mad at sightseers, but this way I'll have a legitimate reason. Come on. I'll round up the kids."

It was a short drive in her station wagon in fact, but I thought we'd never get there, and when we approached there were enough cars lined up along the main road to justify Hank Rollins's disapproval of sightseers. Inching around the bend, I couldn't see the house past the alder swamp where my brook finally came out, but we could smell damped-down smoldering wood, and my coffee boiled up nastily in my throat.

And then we were around the bend and could look up across the field and see the gleaming scarlet apparatus, and a blackened obscenity behind the maples. "Mama, can we go real close and see?" the boy cried. "Look at all those fire engines!"

"You hush up, Bobby Rollins," she said fiercely. "It's no circus, it's nothing good, it's just plain awful."

There was a state trooper by the mailbox, waving the cars on. We slowed down, and she called importantly, "This girl lives here."

"You sure?"

"Of course I'm sure. My husband's one of the firemen, and if you think I'm lying——"

"Can you walk up?" he said to me. "There's no room for her to turn around up there."

"I can walk."

The children moaned with disappointment.

"Thanks," I said to the girl. "I'm very grateful."

"I was glad to help. I just hope nobody was hurt."

"Me too."

Jason and I stood at the side of the road while she drove reluctantly away. The trooper looked as if he had something more to say, and I wanted to ask him if anybody *had* been hurt, but a man hailed him from one of the cars he was waving on. "Hey, how'd it start anyhow?"

"I don't know, sir," he answered civilly, so I supposed I'd have gotten the same, with "miss" on the end. I started up the drive with the dog. It was like the tortuous treadmill pace of bad dreams, so finally I began to run. I had to stop part way to throw up, and when I straightened up, wiping my face, and my strained and watering eyes cleared, Apollo was regarding me from across the fence.

Everyone has seen the ruins of a newly burned house: the chimneys still standing, a stairway sagging in space, fragments of walls wearing scorched wallpaper, shattered windows, maimed furniture, fabrics still burning, and over all the stench of the house's death. The pumper was sucking up water from the farm pond so the hose could still play over the smoking, fallen beams. The sooty-faced men in their firefighting gear, and all the extra apparatus, gave the house the importance of a corpse, a murder victim obliviously surrounded by the panoply of justice.

I stood on the drive staring at where the fanlight door had been. The brick doorstep remained, and a gleam of clear butter-yellow under a blackened timber was a crocus. Jason leaned against me, trembling, and I stroked his head with a hard firm motion, for my own comfort as well as his. Nobody saw me. I could see through to the kitchen and beyond. The farm buildings were untouched, though some cows were bawling. I thought, *That's where they all are, Kitty, Faye, Leni, Ruel ... Rory.*

I went well out around the western end of the house, past a Fremont fire truck driven up on the lawn, and out to the back. There were troopers here as well as firemen. There was also an ambulance in the drive. Holding Jason's collar I walked slowly toward it. A trooper stopped me, heavy-chested, heavy-voiced with irritation.

"What do you want, ma'am? How'd you get up here?"

"I rent the cottage here," I said with a vague gesture over my shoulder. "I was away overnight, I just got back. I want to know if—" My tongue began falling over itself. "Will you please tell me—"

The way he eased up was a warning. "I'm afraid—" he began, then Faye shouted my name. She came running from the farm yard, and Leni was coming behind her. Ruel shut the gate after them and leaned on it. Sagged, rather. He kept shaking his head. Queer how I noticed the way he kept doing that, while Faye kept screaming my name.

She was in pajamas and bathrobe, a raincoat over that, boots on her feet. Her hair was wild, her face purple-blotched and swollen. She was as unlike Faye as the mutilated skeleton of the house was unlike Fourleaf. She stumbled toward me with a wail, holding out her arms, and we embraced. What she was saying made no sense to me at first, and then it became most freezingly lucid.

"He woke me up and the men, and he called the fire department, and he went back for his mother. *No!*" she wildly corrected herself. "We all came out, but she wasn't there. He kept saying, 'I got her up, where is she?' So he went back in. And he never came out. Neither of them came."

We held each other, she weeping and myself slowly turning to stone. Leni came up to us, muttering, "Now, now," and taking hold of her. His red-rimmed eyes in a grimy face met mine and slid away. "I'm sorry," he mumbled. "Sorry as hell."

# chapter 30

One fastens on insignificant details as if to lifelines. I saw how the dog looked worriedly after the sobbing Faye, and I called sharply to him and told him to come with me. When I walked down the hill to the cottage, the wind blowing in my face nullified the stink of burning with a verdant freshness, like the scent of all my days here until this one.

Faye had been mistaken, of course. They just hadn't seen him come out. He would be waiting at the cottage. Sick at not being able to save his mother, needing me more than ever, but *there*. Not a *something* to be groped for in the sodden char as soon as it was cool enough. No, he was waiting for me.

The car was in the turnaround, everything still in it, my luggage and the food. I took the carton in. I was talking to myself, shaping the words without uttering them aloud, as I crossed the lawn and went up the steps. The *weirdest thing happened, I dreamed the house burned down and they thought you were in it*. No, that wasn't right, because it *had* burned down. *Rory*, my lips vivaciously formed the name, *you'll just have to go up and let them see for themselves*.

I opened the screen door and went in, Jason pushed by me, and we confronted a sunny vacancy in which not even a clock ticked, and the door closing behind me shut off the brook; I could have gone suddenly deaf, but not dumb.

I heard in my startled ears my long howl of protest. "Oh, no, no, *no!*"

I was in the kitchen putting the food away. I didn't know why, it just seemed the thing to do. Jason lay watching me. I could hear his elbows trembling against the floor. Someone came up on the porch and opened the door and stood there in the opening. I could recognize Eunice against the brilliant outside by the aureole of light around her head, though her face was in shadow.

She said in a very shallow voice, as if she hadn't the breath to be louder, "I called to you up there, but you didn't hear me. Will you drive me home? My uncle isn't ready yet."

I cleared my throat and said, "Why not?" We didn't say anything else. I didn't want to drive by the house, but I realized with a great relief that I didn't have to look. In fact, I didn't even have to *think* about it. That long wail might have been uttered by somebody else.

Ruel was waiting for us at the top of the lane to take Jason, and the dog went to him gratefully. Ruel was like some old glacial boulder that's always been in a certain pasture, the storms of the centuries bouncing off him. He and Leni were going to camp in the bunkhouse built for the apple pickers who came from out of state. Faye's brother had come and got her, he told us.

We didn't speak all the way to Windhover. I don't believe Eunice moved her head or turned off that blind stare through the windshield. But when we were almost at Windhover she said suddenly, "Your luggage is in the back seat."

"Yes. I was ready to leave today."

She said nothing more. We turned in between the gateposts. I drove around to where we had parked on that other day, and when I stopped the car one horse whinnied imperiously in the silence and then another. I saw them clustered at a white gate off beyond their barn.

"I'll go speak to them," she said. "Go on in."

"I was leaving."

"Don't be foolish," she said. "You're in no condition. You look ghastly." She left me, with one of the dogs loping behind her.

*I don't know what I'm doing here*, I thought, *but then I don't know what I'm doing anywhere*. I walked through the summer kitchen, where the lamb rose up with tiny bleats. The screen door was open into the main kitchen, and Mrs. Parmenter was trimming raw piecrust off a pie. She looked around and exclaimed softly, "Why, it's Miriam! How are you, dear? It's so terrible I can't take it in. Where's Eunice, poor child?"

"Gone to speak to the horses."

"Well," she said dubiously, "she'll take some comfort from them, I suppose."

A huge exhausting *nothing* took hold of me. I stood in the middle of the kitchen, neither willing nor able to take a step in any direction. *Something* required me to face it, but I would not accept its existence.

There was a stifled explosion of wonder. "*That's* the resemblance. It's been bothering me ever since you were here. . . . Don't move, dear. It's the turn of your head, and the way the light falls, it brings out the line from ear to chin. And there's something you do with your mouth." She stared at me, marveling. "Uncanny! For a stranger to walk into this house, and——"

"Do you think I could lie down?" I asked, exacerbated by the gentle babbling.

"Oh, of course you can! It's been hard for you too, hasn't it?" She led the way upstairs through the silent house, showed me a room, pointed out the bathroom. "Would you like me to bring you a cup of tea? Or hot chocolate?"

I shook my head. She folded back the coverlet on the bed. "There's an electric blanket, dear, so if you begin to feel cold, turn it on. Chills almost always follow shock."

She left and I sat on the bed with my head in my hands, idly picking out the colors in the hit-or-miss rug under my feet. The whole scene was insane; my being here was a hallucinatory experience. One ought to escape, but where? How did one wake up, and to what?

Two taps on the door. The thumb latch lifted and Eunice looked in. "I brought up your dressing case, you might want something from it."

"Oh. Thanks." We looked bleakly at one another. Her eyes

reminded me of amber beads. She withdrew and shut the door.

So I was here, and the thing for me to do was to carry my bag downstairs again and drive away. I knew that. Instead I took off my shoes like a well-brought-up girl and lay down on the bed and looked up at the ceiling. Reflections of light from the pond danced over it, crossed by the swift shadows of swallows. Yesterday I had seen swallows around the pond at Fourleaf while I talked with Rory by the barnyard gate, and today Rory was nowhere.

How could it *be?* I hadn't caught up with it yet. It was still yesterday for me, last night at the latest. My mind wandered around in a kind of limbo, neither past nor present, and there was no future. Presently I became aware of pain. If Rory was nowhere, and I was nowhere, why couldn't we have been consigned to the same vacuum?

The house was silent. A man called out by the barn. Farther away a power saw buzzed and droned like a furious bumblebee. The light on the ceiling was hypnotic. Time passed. I may have slept, for after a while the light had changed in the room, the luminous pattern had left the ceiling.

"Are you asleep, dear?" Mrs. Parmenter whispered. I hadn't heard her come in.

"No." I turned my head on the pillow to look at her, politely questioning.

"*There*," she whispered. "The way you lift your eyebrow. Now that I've pinned it down, I can't escape it. Which is a funny way to put it, because why should I want to escape it?"

This whispering woman was a part of the general insanity. She pulled up a chair and sat down beside the bed. "I'm just surprised that Kitty missed it," she said in a kind of innocent wonder. "It caught me the very first time I saw you, but I couldn't place it. So it nagged at me. Kitty hasn't the patience to be nagged. *Hadn't*, I mean. . . . And then she wouldn't have kept Harry in mind as I have. Why should she? She must have gotten over it. Cleveland Barstow was a very attractive man."

"What are you saying?" Limbo was dissolving and I tried to hold onto the protective murk.

"That you're Harry's daughter, of course," she said. "You came back to claim the Glidden place, didn't you? It's been wonderful of you not to make a big thing of it, because Eunice doesn't know about her father."

"Neither did I." I sat up and hauled up my knees, clasped them with trembling hands. "I never thought of Harry Parmenter. But you knew," I said. She nodded.

"Harry had you and your mother on his conscience. He told me about it before he went overseas. It"—she looked away from me with an ironic little smile—"it made it a—a peculiar parting, to say the least. He was going to do something about you when he came back. I was carrying Eunice then. You were already born."

"How did it all happen?" I asked. "Here, or somewhere else? And how? And why? Mrs. Parmenter, this must be awful for you, but it's what I came here to find out."

"It's not awful for me any more, dear, and you're as innocent in it as Eunice is." She rocked gently, her hands in her lap. "Eunice is out in the pasture, with the horses. That's where she always goes for comfort. She doesn't have to know about this."

"No. But I have to."

"You must understand that I'm not a native here, I grew up in Rhode Island, and we met when Harry was stationed at Newport. So what I know about his growing up here is what he told me, and Sam's filled in some gaps, and other people have, because everybody liked Harry and they still like to talk about him. A few adored him. One was Kitty Adams, and she worked hard to get him. Your mother was another, but she wasn't aggressive. And that attracted Harry—because she wasn't obvious. She was such a quiet, dreamy girl, he said, who seemed to care only about music. It made her mysterious to him. A challenge."

"So he had to win," I said bitterly.

She shook her head at me in gentle reproof. "It was a kind

of idyll, the way Harry remembered it. They kept it quiet, and that made it all the more romantic. I don't think anybody knew about it except her grandparents, because he used to go out to the Glidden place to see her, and they walked and talked for hours. It was all pure and idealistic. A lot of other girls were willing to make themselves available in back seats after dances and movies, and Kitty was one." She put her hand on my arm for a moment. "I'm not blackening her, dear. She was a passionately determined young girl, she was used to getting or winning almost anything she wanted—honors, prizes, championships—so why not Harry Parmenter? The Adamses were always poor; the father was an honest man but that was about all you could say for him, and it made her very anxious and ambitious. And Harry Parmenter, in addition to having a good deal of charm, was—well, a Parmenter of Parmenter. That mattered very much to Kitty."

Her name kept her before my eyes, not the girl whom Dora Parmenter described, but the woman who only yesterday had destroyed us. I couldn't think of her as anything else but arrogantly and hatingly alive, over there in her office at Fourleaf waiting for her son to come creeping home like a dog who'd been out all night. That's what she must have thought when——

"Harry didn't take Helen to the graduation ball," Mrs. Parmenter's voice flowed gently like *Sweet Afton;* the boy and girl, hands clasped, moved gawkily and intensely to the music in my head. "Helen didn't know how to dance. But she wasn't a jealous girl, and they both wanted to keep this precious thing secret between them until they could marry. So he took another girl to the dance. I don't remember her name, but I know it wasn't Kitty." She paused. "Did your mother ever tell you about that night, *after* the ball?"

"She never told me anything." I was so cold my teeth were chattering. She switched on the blanket and I got under it.

"He went out to the Glidden place," she said, "and they rowed on the lake in the starlight for hours, and cooked their breakfast at dawn on the shore. I don't think the grandparents ever knew she was out, and his people thought he was with his gang somewhere. The rest of the class thought he was with the girl he'd brought to the dance, and *she* never let on that he'd taken her home when the dance ended. He let her think he was coming down with something. There'd been some sort of virus going around.

"Anyway, they had their summer, with Harry living one life in the open and another in secret. Because they were able to do so, they were sure it was meant to be, they were as positive about their future together as they were about the sun coming up."

"He told you all this?" I asked incredulously. "It must have been horrible for you. How could he?"

"Don't blame him, dear. By the time he told me he couldn't help himself. It was like blood spurting from an artery.... In the fall he went to Bowdoin and she went to study in Portland. They saw each other when they could, but it wasn't often. Still, they were sure of each other, and they were looking forward to meeting at home in Parmenter at Thanksgiving. He never knew how Kitty found out about them."

I made an involuntary movement, and she nodded as if in sympathy.

"He thinks—he thought she might have caught a glimpse of them in Portland. He'd spent a few Sundays there with Helen. Anyway, she wrote Helen a letter telling her that Harry had taken her, Kitty, out on his last weekend home, and had confided in her about Helen, saying that he was tired of the whole thing and was only letting it drag on because he didn't know how to break it off. Because Kitty somehow had gained a reputation for uncompromising honesty, Helen wrote him a stiff little letter releasing him, and transferred to Boston. When he came home the first weekend after getting her letter, feeling pretty sick, he intended to go to the grandparents and find out where she was. But Kitty got to him first, playing the good-hearted, concerned third party, telling what Helen had confided in *her*——"

"And wanted to break off but she didn't know how," I said.

"Yes. For the sake of another music student, who was her reason for going to Boston. —If they'd only faced each other! But they were children, really, and so terribly hurt . . . and Kitty——"

"And Kitty never lied," I said. "Oh yes. I've heard that." *Yesterday she killed us with a lie.* "Did she succeed in anything else? I mean, did he go out with her?"

"No," she said with unusual emphasis, for her. "She must have realized after a while that nobody loves the bearer of bad news. The role of the good-hearted third party doesn't get much applause." And Kitty Barstow had called this woman a nonentity. She had evoked my parents into both sweet and bitter life, such strong life that while they moved before me they dimmed the morning's horrors.

Harry slacked off in his studies and finally left Bowdoin and enlisted in the Navy, before Pearl Harbor happened. After basic training he was sent to Newport, where he met Dora. He was homesick, still bruised about Helen, and Dora's gentle charm must have been soothing. He didn't tell her about Helen. They became engaged, then married, and he took her back to Parmenter. Harry was then sent to the Navy Yard at Charlestown.

Two weeks after their arrival at Windhover Farm, Kitty Adams married Cleve Barstow. He was classified 4-F because of a heart murmur, but nobody took that seriously. "My, how she *preened,*" Mrs. Parmenter said.

By pure accident Harry met Helen again, crossing the Public Garden in Boston. "Not that they called it accident," Mrs. Parmenter said wryly. "It was Fate. They talked and talked, and of course they found out what had been done to them. . . . I've never blamed them for what happened," she said courageously. "Harry didn't tell me everything, only what he had to—after you were born. But I've filled in the gaps for myself. To think of what they had lost—well, it threw them together in such a passionate way, you see. Whereas, if they'd been left alone in the first place, the boy-and-girl affair might have just faded out in the most natural way. . . . And with a war there's something so violent and frightening in the air. A desperation to seize what you think you will never have."

"And so—*me*."

"Yes, you . . . To finish quickly, your father was killed in the North Atlantic before Eunice was born, and you were a year old."

I curled up tight under the blanket, head down to my knees.

"I'm so sorry about your mother," she said. "You must have been very close."

"We were." But not close enough. *Oh, Mother, why didn't you tell me?* But no such anguished questions could reach the world of the unapparent dead.

"Eunice doesn't know anything about this," Mrs. Parmenter said. "If her father had come back, I don't know what might have happened. But he didn't, so——"

"I'll never say anything," I said into my knees. One thing that struck me at that moment was the realization that I hadn't been literally conceived in Parmenter, but in another sense I had been.

"Wouldn't you come down to the kitchen and have something to eat?" she asked, rather wistfully. "I can't do a thing for Eunice, even feed her."

"All right," I said. "But in a little while."

"I understand." She went away with only the faintest click of the thumb latch.

I was left alone with my parents. I could have used a picture of Harry right now, but this guest room was probably the only room, except for the two kitchens and the bathrooms, where there was no picture of Harry.

There were no pictures of Cleve Barstow in his house, except in his son's room, because his wife had married him only to show that if she couldn't get a Parmenter she'd get the next best thing.

And she saw the resemblance too, I thought. Finally. If she'd caught anything earlier, it hadn't registered, but when she found that I was Helen Glidden's daughter it all fell into place, along with the scalding recollection that Helen was studying in Boston at the same time Harry was stationed at the Navy Yard.

So it was Harry Parmenter whom she couldn't forgive because Cleve became the father of her son, not Harry. But to marry her son to Harry's daughter meant they would be united through possession of land and shared grandchildren. A ghoulish marriage which reminded me of the Faulkner classic, *A Rose for Miss Emily*.

I was Harry's daughter too, but by the wrong woman.

Maybe I was wrong in my piecing together. But, stalked by what I couldn't ignore out of existence, and exhausted by catastrophe, I had reached a point of clear seeing so exquisitely detailed that *clairvoyance* would have been the perfect name for it.

There was no point that night in imagining over and over the gruesome explorations in the cooled embers for what had once been two passionately alive human beings. There was no point, but neither was there any escape. Neither was there any comradeship, even mute, in knowing that Eunice was going through the same thing, locked into it as if in a grave.

At daylight I took my bag downstairs into the kitchen. I was going to leave a note on the blackboard I'd noticed yesterday. But Sam Parmenter was already there, drinking coffee from a tremendous cup. Events had aged him since the first time I'd seen him.

"I didn't think anybody was up," I said. "I'm leaving."

"What about your place?" he asked gruffly. "Barney told me yesterday about it. He wouldn't have, but he was shook up."

"It's all right." I wondered how much else he knew.

I wrote my address on the grocery pad he shoved at me. "They can send the tax bill here. Then maybe I'll make a present of the place to the town. They can sell it for what they can get."

"Good Godfrey, girl, don't be so numb! Think of your kids. If you don't figger on having any, look out for yourself! If you don't want to live here, *you* sell it. Put the money away for your old age, or a trip around the world or your own airplane, or some other foolishness. These gifts to the town cause a damn sight more trouble than they're worth. Start more feuds over what to do with them then they ever had in the Blue Ridge Mountains."

"Thank you, sir, for your gracious advice," I said, and his mouth twitched.

"Have some grub before you light out. How far are you going?"

"To Augusta to take the next plane for New York."

He grunted something. We drank coffee and ate doughnuts in silence. I wrote a note of thanks to Mrs. Parmenter and Eunice. Unexpectedly he went out to the car with me. We shook hands, and he held onto mine afterward. "Went deep with you, didn't it?"

I nodded. For the first time tears came to my eyes. "I suspected," he said. "Boy got so happy all at once ... It was a god-awful thing to happen. I don't know when Kitty last had the wiring all gone over. These old places are tinder-dry, and one short could send a house up like a pine torch." He let go of my hand. "I knew your mother. Always liked her. Don't be in a hurry to get rid of the place. Glidden blood and sweat's in it."

*And tears too*, I thought, remembering my own and surmising my mother's when she came home to sign off her claim to the place. If I'd been with her then, I was undetected by everyone else. If I was already born, she'd left me with someone for those few lacerating days of good-bye. Still, perhaps she'd been hopeful then too, as well as sad, expecting Harry to come back to her and not to Dora.

I had that much to go on when I drove out of town, and I kept it within limits, rather like taking care never to see beyond that fifth crow.

I remembered the stuff hidden away in the chicken house

under the apple trees, but I didn't go back there on my way. There was nothing I wanted. Besides, I'd have had to go by Fourleaf Farm. Neither did I want a last look at the Honor Roll and my father's name.

At a roadside dealer's outside Augusta, I sold the car, with a qualm of affection and betrayal, and something more piercing. Rory's fingerprints must still be on the wheel, under mine; how strange that something so intimate could be there when the fingers themselves were gone.

I flew back to New York and worked on the manuscript at home until my month was up, and then went back to work. I was under no illusion that I looked vibrant with health, and told everybody I'd had a bad virus attack. After that I used migraines.

Looking back now on the past three years I don't know how I did it; how I could ever have held out, and up, and on. Perhaps the spring floods each April were the safety measures taken by my overburdened system.

# chapter 31

By writing in the early mornings and every evening, Miriam had her manuscript finished toward the end of April. The paring away of scar tissue without anesthetic had been so excruciating at times that she'd had to leave it, swearing she'd never go back to it again, she'd burn it first. But the next morning or the next night she would doggedly return. At least it was conscious pain, and the by-product was that she no longer woke herself with her own harsh weeping.

Mike took the completed manuscript home with him early one night. Now she felt both depleted and directionless. She took a long soak and went to bed, thinking, *Well, at least I've gotten through another April.* She was too drained even to wonder if Mike had started yet to read. The vacuum was restful; yet when she awoke to it the next morning it occurred to her that she might have lost or given away some essential part of herself, that her secret might have been all that gave her any dimension in her own eyes. *I'm a paper doll*, she thought with sour humor. *Anybody could keep me in an envelope in a drawer and never miss me. I wouldn't even miss me.*

Mike met her after work and took her to dinner at a small place they liked, and then they went back to the flat. She thought afterward she wouldn't even have mentioned the manuscript, but he did, the instant they were through the door.

"I read it all last night."

"What do you think?" It seemed required of her.

"Needs work," he said. "And of course you realize it'll never sell to the movies. As a paperback, I don't know. There's no scene we can use for the cover. You know, the castle with one lighted window in the tower, and the girl fleeing in her nightgown."

"You *nut!*" She was shaking with suppressed convulsions of laughter that threatened to turn into something else. "All right. I've told you what you wanted to know, and that was the idea, wasn't it? Now it's over with. Drink?"

"And I was there too," Mike said. "All unbeknownst to me. That gives me a damn peculiar feeling, you know that? And what a job of editing you did, and under what circumstances!" He kept looking at her as if he were really awestruck. "So I came to New York just to meet this genius of an editor who made me a better writer than I thought I was."

"And God knows you were conceited enough already."

He pulled her down beside him. "Tell me how *you* think the fire started."

"Do we have to?"

"We have to. Don't tell me you wrote all this down without surmising or suspecting, even fleetingly."

"It was probably the wiring, as Sam Parmenter said. Don't you want that drink?"

"Up there do they automatically check for arson even if it's not suspected? Don't they have to try to discover the reason for fire?"

"I don't know! I suppose so!" She was antagonistic. "What are you getting at? Why must we—" The very reek of that day was suddenly so strong in the room that she looked wildly around for its source. "Mike, did you ever lose anyone by fire? Seen an ambulance waiting to take whatever was left?"

"I've lost them by other ways. How about torture, and murder from ambush? Death in a concentration camp? Come on, tell me what you think."

"If there was any investigation, I don't know anything about it. I wrote to Faye after I'd been back a while, and told her I'd enjoyed knowing her and Leni and Ruel, and Jason of course, but I never mentioned the fire. She wrote in the summer that she and Leni were married, and she didn't mention the fire either. The next Christmas we sent cards, and we've done that ever since. And I get a tax bill each year for the Glidden place, and I pay it. That's the sum total of my communication with Parmenter." She tried to get free of him. "That's it. *The End*. Period. If you don't want a drink, I do."

He was amicably relentless. "But you thought *something*, girl! You knew the state he was in when he left you."

She sighed. "What I think," she said slowly, "is that he woke up very early and went home to make his mother produce her proof." She was not yet free to say his name. "He found the fire already under way. She was back in her own room on the second floor and he woke her, then roused the others, and when they all got outside he found his mother wasn't there. So he went back to get her, and a—" She thought she was going to gag. "A ceiling fell on him or a beam. Maybe the stairs collapsed. They *did*, because I saw them, or what was left of one flight. The other just wasn't there." She would retch in a moment. Her eyes begged him to release her.

"Why do you think she didn't get out with the others?"

She swallowed and went painfully on. "Maybe she didn't think the fire was moving that fast, and she was trying to gather up something to take with her. She might even have gotten as far as the office and was trying to save the books. He could have run upstairs again looking for her, and been trapped. The same thing could have happened to her. Being trapped, I mean. The fire went so fast. Like a pine torch, Sam Parmenter said."

"Well, it'll serve," Mike said. "And it probably has."

"What are you getting at?" she demanded. "Are you trying to say that he killed his mother and then burned the house down over them?"

"No," he said reasonably, "but you've seen the possibility, haven't you? Even if you wouldn't admit it? He was absolutely sunk, wasn't he? Horrified, despairing, because he couldn't believe that she'd lie to him. If he'd found out that morning that she did lie, he'd have been reborn, in a manner of speaking. But supposing he couldn't break her down, and she just kept hammering *incest* at him over and over." Mike took her cold and twisting hands and wrapped them in his. "She was a wicked woman, Miriam. She'd been thwarted. Nothing else mattered to her but revenge, even her own child didn't matter. All it comes down to, in the end, no matter how or what happened, is that she murdered *him* when she told him he was your brother."

"No." She wrenched her hands away from him and got up. "I did it when I went there. That's what you've made me discover by your rotten vivisection. Eunice told me that I would destroy everything, and I did."

"The woman carried within her the seeds of her own ruin and his. She was dangerously obsessed. If you hadn't come, would he have ever made the move to get away?" Mike shook his head. "If he did, what kind of move? Self-destructive eventually, I'm positive. Maybe you could have saved him, Miriam."

"I *know* it!"

"All right then." His voice tried to gentle her. "Stick to your theory of the accidental fire. You lost him by an accident that was waiting to happen."

"But don't you see, except for me, he wouldn't have gone back to the house and been caught in it!"

"My dear girl, if you hadn't been there he might have been burned to death in his own bed that particular morning. No, it all comes back to Kitty Barstow."

She stood staring down at the night street through tears. He came up behind her and put his arms around her. "We'll go to Parmenter next weekend."

"We will not!"

He was maddeningly matter-of-fact. "You still own your land there."

"Yes, because I haven't faced facts long enough to put it up for sale. Christmas cards with Faye each year is enough contact."

"You're facing facts now. You're paying taxes which have probably increased a hundred percent or close to it. You ought to decide what you're going to do with that land. End this section of your life once and for all, and begin the new part with no encumbrances from the past."

She flinched, and he said, "Listen, I'm not heartless. I could have bawled for that boy. I've had the tape all this time, I've played it several times, and last night when I finished reading I played it again. What I felt was something like what you said about the fingerprints on the wheel. Remember? And I knew that when he was singing that song he'd probably never been happier in his life, and you'd given him that." He hugged her close to him, whispering, "It's the right thing to go back. You'll see."

They flew to Rockland on Friday night, took rooms at a motel overlooking the harbor, and Saturday morning they rented a car and drove to Parmenter. A cold wet April was giving way to warm premonitions of May.

"Beautiful country," Mike exulted. Miriam kept silent. The road from Rockland was unfamiliar to her, she had never traveled it, but any moment now she would see something familiar, and she refused to be taken unawares. But the ambush almost succeeded; Mike commented on some horses running across a hillside, and around the next bend she saw the Windhover gates and sign. Something new had been added, the painting of a hawk hovering over the words. The Windhover. Mike needed no explanation. He slowed at the drive and said, "Want to turn in here?"

"No. Not yet, anyway," she qualified it, surprising herself. "I'd like to see Mrs. Parmenter. But later. Let's go straight to the Glidden place. We have to pass Fourleaf to get there from here, so let's get it over with."

On a spring Saturday morning the village was busy. The new leaves of the elms lightly moving caused the sunlight to shimmer like water over the common. Mike was enchanted. "It looks just like the old *Saturday Evening Post* covers! Hey, I think they've repainted the Honor Roll. The gold on the eagle looks fresh. . . . Stop here?"

"Later," she said again. She saw O'Brien and son putting cartons of groceries in the trunk of a woman's car; she thought the woman was the young tax collector, but she wasn't sure. Chuckie O'Brien was three years taller and thinner, but his father didn't look discernibly different. Selma Hitchcock was coming out of the post office, detouring around the same Labrador, who was gray-muzzled now. She found herself looking specifically for Barney Knox. Other faces were familiar even though she had never known the names; someone made her think of Sandy, and she was aware of a knife of disappointment when it turned out not to be. But of course Sandy might not have stayed on afterward. She wished now that she had written to him and said something—anything.

The signs were still there at the Fourleaf drive, and the maple avenue losing its red bloom to leaves. Crows took off across a delicately fleecy sky, but no bull watched traffic from behind the wall, though a herd of Holsteins grazed in the middle distance.

"Either Apollo's been sold, or passed on to the Eternal Pasture in the Sky," said Mike piously.

"Or he's at Windhover," Miriam was able to say quite casually. "Eunice inherited, remember." She was able to look up across the field at the house now, and found the familiar transmuted into the foreign. A low Cape Cod house had been built over the cellar, and she was conscious of a great relief at the difference.

"L. Waisenen," Mike read off the mailbox.

"Leni and Faye manage the farm for Eunice."

"You know," he said, "you almost lit up then."

"If you knew Faye and Leni, you'd light up too." But the brief flare was over. He let her sink back into silence, and was busy noticing everything they passed. When they came to Seven Chimneys, the bikes were two-wheelers, and the girl was learning to ride hers, wobbling around the driveway while the boy criticized. They waved, distractedly.

"Do you suppose that's Frankie digging up the lawn?" Mike asked.

"It looks like her. —I'm glad I wrote everything out in detail. It saves explaining." There was a disturbance in her insides that had nothing to do with her recent breakfast. "I hope we can get down the lane. It may be full of blowdowns and alders."

"We can walk, then."

But it had been kept passable. "Natch," said Mike. "Your average Parmenter-type lover wouldn't want to lose such a good place to park."

The open ground around the cellar holes hadn't grown up as thickly as Miriam had expected. One chimney had fallen down. Two crows sat on the other one, shouting warnings of intruders. *One for sorrow, two for mirth*, she thought, *and let's stop while we're ahead.*

"Listen to the robins," Mike said, a sentimental mountain bandit, swarthy face lifted to the sun, black eyes searching for the singers.

"One's a catbird," she teased him. "Another's a warbling vireo."

"They're all robins to me."

She left him and went down to the chicken house under the apple trees, huddled deeper into the bushes now, slowly slanting and sinking into the soil. The door stood ajar, and jammed, so she had to squeeze herself around it. The sleeping bags and dishes had been taken, and she was glad of it. She went outside. In the hothouse atmosphere of this hollow a few apple blossom buds were appearing like tight pink-and-white nosegays on thick black twigs.

She went back slowly toward the granite doorstep. Mike was sitting there and he greeted her with a happy shout. "I've found your mother's iris!"

"It sounds so normal and nice when you say it like that. The last time I grubbed around them Rory was already dead and I didn't know it." She heard herself say the name.

"This year you'll see them in bloom," he said.

"We're going to talk about selling it, remember?"

He shook his head. "Not yet. Don't do it yet. You've got

your roots here and don't knock that fact. My father was chased out of land that had been Andric territory since before the Flood."

"But you said——"

"That was before I'd been here. Now Old Earthman Andric says a Parmenter can't cut Parmenter out of her heart any more than she could cut out her heart. Same goes for a Glidden. And think of your kids."

"That's what Rory said."

"And Sam Parmenter too, remember. And before you call me Old Male Chauvinist Andric, show me the lake."

On the way back he turned into the Fourleaf drive without consulting her, and stopped at the front door. They heard the lambs. Jason lay sleeping in a flowering border, a Red Emperor tulip by his ear. For the first time today she felt like crying, and saw the old dog through tears as he lifted his head to Mike's whistle.

"Jason," she said. He got up stiffly and she went down on her knees and took his head in her hands. His ears pricked and the tail began to move. His eyes went liquid with pleasure. "Oh darling, I hope you remember me," she said thickly, half-laughing. "It's hard to tell, you're so friendly anyway."

From the front door Faye shrieked, "Is that you, Miriam Guild?"

After the weeping and the hugging and well-I-never's were over with, Faye said they would all eat together. She'd accept no refusals. Leni and the men would be back at noon for dinner.

"We'll be here," Mike told her. "But we'd like to go to the cottage first. All right, or is there someone there?"

"No, she's never rented it. I'll get the key."

While they waited Miriam kept fondling the dog and thinking, *I don't want to go to the cottage I don't want to—* She was about to break out with it when Faye came back, tossing the keys to Mike as if they'd already formed an *entente*. "*He's gorgeous*," she mouthed shamelessly at Miriam.

"So are you, Faye," Mike said, and her delighted laughter seemed to spiral up to the skies.

They walked down, and the scents were the same on the hillside, damp earth and green growth, but with May the alder catkins hung in gilt and perfumed tassels, and the first violets were growing along the side of the road. The brook was lower, its voice lesser in volume, but not at all subdued in its endless gayety. The red-winged blackbirds whistled in the swamp below. The lawn hadn't been mowed for a long time.

When they went in, she wanted to come right out again. She kept the door open and stood there, half on the porch, while Mike walked into the other rooms and then all around the big living room, examining everything, stopping to read titles of books until she felt like yelling at him or running away and leaving him there. When his leisurely progress took him to the piano, she said, "Don't." But it must have been too faint for him to hear, if she actually did say it.

He opened the piano and amateurishly played a scale. It was out of tune, badly enough to stab a musician to the heart.

"They've never had it tuned!" she blurted out.

"Why should they? Why should it matter to them? To Eunice in particular?" he asked reasonably.

She went into the room. "Yes, it wouldn't matter to her. If she thought of it at all, she'd be glad to let it die. A beautiful instrument like that. It's not to blame for anything." She touched a key more tentatively than Mike had done. Mike put his arm around her waist and they stood looking at the piano for a moment without speaking.

"Maybe we could buy it for our place," he said finally.

"Oh, *Mike!*" she said in anger and dismay.

"You wouldn't want to keep a piano that Margaret Dundas played?" he asked. "A piano that's been a precious part of your life? You owe him something better than that."

"Just let's get out of here," she said. When he was locking the door she was forced to turn away so as not to see, and possibly make some inarticulate, meaningless cry of protest. She went toward the brook and in a moment he joined her. They watched a red-winged blackbird spread scarlet epaulettes and, apparently offhand, Mike said, "Did you ever let Margaret Dundas know?"

"No. He'd never got the letter written and mailed, so she didn't know what he was planning, and to write to her myself and tell her what happened— Mike, I couldn't leave that picture with her even if I could have described it."

Somberly he said, "No. Let her remember the boy as he was when she knew him."

"Maybe she should know which way he chose," Miriam pondered. "She would be pleased. But . . ." Tears thickened her voice.

"Maybe some day," Mike said. He put his arm around her and kissed her under the ear. "Let's go now, and see if Apollo's still around. Hey, are Faye's dimples real?"

"They certainly are!"

They walked slowly up the hill. The lambs' voices came on the wind and a rooster kept crowing as if he were infatuated with his own talent. Jason was coming to meet them, stiff but genial.

"What will we call our place, Miriam?" Mike asked.

"You're taking a lot for granted."

"Come on," he teased her. "Supposing we did build there, and clear it for farming again. What would we call it?"

"Don't you have some rich-sounding Montenegrin name?"

"Not for the gentle hills of Parmenter. Hello, Jason." He hunkered down to look into the dog's eyes. "And it's your place to name," he added.

"Five-Crow Farm," she said without even thinking first.

## About the Author

Elisabeth Ogilvie is celebrating her second year in a home of her own in Maine—close, as usual, to her favorite setting for a novel. Fur and feathered friends continue to be friendly companions, though she mourns the death of one of her Australian terriers—Sherman—who succumbed to a heart attack last fall. Despite some undercurrents of soap opera among selected citizens in her town, matters continue relatively tranquil in Knox County. Miss Ogilvie got a call for jury duty not long ago. When she turned up at the courthouse on the appointed Wednesday, she was told the case up for trial was off the docket because of a guilty plea. "Nothing much happening in the crime line," the clerk told her. "Why don't you go on back home and come around again, say, Tuesday?"